LOVE IN THE LOOKING GLASS

LUCINDA RACE

MC TWO PRESS

Cover art by Meet Cute Creative
ISBN 978-0-9986647-0-5
ISBN Paperback 978-0-9986647-1-2

Published by MC Two Press

Thank you for purchasing Love in the Looking Glass. I hope you enjoy reading Ellie and Pad's story. I love writing characters who deserve a chance at happiness. So, turn the page and fall in love in with the McKenna Family.

If you'd like to stay in touch, consider joining my Newsletter. I release it twice per month with tidbits, recipes and an occasional a special gift just for my readers.

https://lucindarace.com/newsletter/ and there is a free book when you join! Happy reading…

This book is dedicated to my GF and her MF

They're an inspiration that love conquers all.

"The Looking Glass." The words rolled off Ellie's tongue. Her fingers traced the gold lettering on the dark, wooden sign. "Amazing, don't you think, Ray? This represents the culmination of a year's hard work. I wonder if Mom felt the same way when she opened What's Perkin'." She glanced at her stepfather, Ray Davis. "Were you there for the grand opening?"

"Your mom wasn't there when I installed the sign. It wasn't until later she saw it, and she was as excited then as you are today. You've worked hard, Ellie. We're very proud of you."

Ellie did a little jig. "Thanks, Ray. I couldn't have done this without the family's help, especially yours. The way everyone pitched in painting, building shelves, refinishing floors, there was so much I needed to do before I opened, and now, tomorrow is the big day."

Ray tweaked her nose. "Kiddo, now the real work begins. You'll need to discover new artists, build a customer base, and promote the heck out of the gallery."

"I have a couple of people stopping by this afternoon

to drop off pottery, jewelry, and a few small sculptures. Then before the weekend, a photographer is coming through town and wants to show me his photos. If it fits with the theme, I'll display his work too. I'm thrilled my dream of artisan's work in any medium will be on display for everyone to see. This gallery will be immersion of the senses, if you will, just like my favorite book, Alice in Wonderland. Remember when she falls through the looking glass and discovers a dazzling world? Well, I hope that's how people feel when they enter."

"I'm sure everyone will be enchanted when they discover this place." Ray placed the rest of his tools in the back of the truck. "What time do you need us tomorrow night? Mom said she was coming over in the afternoon to set up the buffet tables. Do you need some muscles?"

"No, I've got it covered, but thanks. If you could come around six thirty that will keep me busy so I don't wind up a buddle of nerves. The official invitations are for seven. You and Mom should enjoy yourselves at the open house."

"All right then, I'm taking off unless you need something else."

"Nope, all set." Ellie threw her arms around Ray's midsection and squeezed tightly. "Thanks for believing in me. I couldn't have done any of this without you."

Ray shrugged his shoulders. "Don't give me too much credit. All I did was follow your lead and swing a hammer." He dropped a fatherly kiss on the top of Ellie's head and mumbled something about needing coffee.

"Say hi to Mom and tell her coffee is on me."

Ray hopped in the truck and waved goodbye as his truck disappeared down the street.

Ellie skipped up the wide front steps and bent to deadhead a deep purple petunia. She straightened and noticed a dark car creeping past, and then it sped down the street. Shrugging, Ellie pulled an old-fashioned hanky from her pocket and polished the antique, brass door knocker, pausing on the threshold to admire the interior space.

Ellie had arranged to rent her sister-in-law, Abby's, childhood home, transforming it into an art gallery with a spacious floor plan. Large, cherry columns supported the structure, and the grand staircase opened to the second floor, leading the way to Ellie's apartment. During the day, there would be an old-fashioned, amethyst velvet rope to close off the stairs from shoppers. Former small rooms were now alcoves featuring art.

Ellie hummed as she crossed the main room to the back of the house where the kitchen was located, adjusting a few items as she passed. She hadn't wanted to install a kitchen upstairs since it was just her, so keeping this part of the original house made sense. Besides, at some point, if she relocated her business, Abby could turn this back into a family home with very little effort.

Ellie turned on the burner under the teakettle, chose a raspberry blend, and readied the infuser with loose tea. The front door chimed, interrupting her mid-pour. Ellie peeked around the corner, not realizing until that moment how quiet the house had become.

"Hello, may I help you?" Ellie greeted an older woman. She was average height with warm brown eyes, dressed in a brightly colored, long, flowing tunic over slim black leggings and a matching floral print scarf covering her hair. On her arm she carried an oversized woven bag.

"Good morning. I'm looking for Ms. McKenna." The woman's eyes roamed, an ever so slight smile played on her mouth, taking in each minute detail. "Would you be so

3

kind as to inform her that Winifred Simpson would like a moment of her time?"

Ellie masked her nerves by quickly extending her hand. "I'm Eleanor McKenna. It is a pleasure to meet you, Mrs. Simpson."

Winifred Simpson was well-known in the art world. Her contemporary paintings commanded high commissions, and she had a loyal following, like Thomas Kinkade. Although, Mrs. Simpson had never mass marketed her work.

"Really? Well, frankly I'm surprised. You are terribly young to have opened this establishment." Without waiting for a response, the older woman began to thoroughly inspect each alcove without interacting with the young woman who trailed after her. After several long minutes, Mrs. Simpson spoke. "I'll take this space. The light will be favorable for my work."

Ellie did a double take. "You want wall space, in my gallery?"

"Why else would I be here? Frankly, Ms. McKenna, I thought you would be thrilled."

"I'm sorry," she stuttered. "I don't mean to sound disrespectful, Mrs. Simpson. You've had major exhibits around the world. What exposure could The Looking Glass give you that you don't already have?"

A small smile hovered on the older woman's lips. "It is quite simple. I love the name of your shop. I live nearby and supporting a new female-owned business that has the creative spirit I embody spoke to me, so…" her arms opened and she twirled in place, "here I am."

"I'm speechless," Ellie said.

"I have that effect on people. In time, you'll find it easier to be around me. Now, if you would be so kind as to help me, I have four paintings in the car that I would like to hang. I know it is too late for printed invitations but feel free to post an announcement on social media that I will be here tomorrow night, for your grand opening."

"Of course, Mrs. Simpson. I'm thrilled you'll join us." She followed the artist to the front door. Ellie almost bumped into her when she stopped short.

"Eleanor, you don't mind if I call you by your first name, do you?"

Ellie shook her head.

"Excellent. You may call me Winnie."

"Certainly Mrs....uh, Winnie."

With that settled, the pair walked outside to Winnie's van parked in the middle of the driveway. Ellie rushed around to open the back doors as Winnie clicked the key fob. The side doors slid open revealing one large canvas, and three smaller sizes standing on end, each one protected with layers of bubble wrap.

Winnie stood to one side. "Now do be careful, Eleanor. We need to move one at a time." Winnie fussed about like a mother hen with her baby chicks, making a clucking sound each time Ellie picked up a new painting, and followed as it was carried inside. After the final trip, Winnie pushed the button to close the doors, and with a spring in her step, led the way inside.

"This is fun, don't you think? The thrill of hanging a painting on a wall in all its splendor? It always gives me a thrill."

"They'll look beautiful once we get them positioned just the way you want, Winnie." Ellie deferred to the artist. She was still in awe that someone of Winifred Simpson's caliber wanted to display work in her modest establishment.

The two women worked in tandem placing the larger painting first and adding the smaller canvases on an adjacent wall. Once Ellie moved the final painting a fraction of an inch, Winnie stepped back to scrutinize the results.

Ellie slowly exhaled. "Is this what you had in mind?"

"You certainly have a flair for bringing out the best in the artwork. I don't think there is anything else we can do at this time." Winnie graced Ellie with a cheek-splitting grin. "I'll bet this was a surprise for you?"

"Oh gosh, yes. I didn't expect to have these here. I'm curious why you chose today and didn't wait until after the opening to see if it was successful."

"After my dear friend mentioned your gallery, I did some checking and then I remembered I saw you in what's her name's gallery, Karlene Johnson? I love that you're young, energetic, and have a wonderful concept."

"Well, thank you, but I had no idea you lived close by."

"Do you know the old Moore estate?"

Ellie nodded, awestruck.

"That was my late husband's family home, and I inherited it when he passed away. I seriously took up painting as a hobby to fill the long, lonely hours, and here we are today." She glanced at Ellie, whose eyes were filled with unshed tears. "My dear child, what's wrong?"

"As kids, we thought that house was haunted. We used to stand at the gates and wait for the ghost to appear. One time we saw a lady, dressed in a flowing white robe in the window, and we were so scared we never went back. I never thought she might have been real and well, lonely."

Winnie chuckled. "I knew the stories about the lady in white and in full disclosure, that was me. I used to wear a white smock over my clothes so I didn't get covered in paint. It was easier to replace the smock than constantly shop for clothes. The lady in white was born. My dear husband, Howard, loved my sense of humor, even if it was a bit twisted. I encouraged the ghost stories so I could concentrate on painting. When I needed human companionship, I went into the world. My self-imposed isolation allowed me to become the dabbler of paints I am today."

Ellie sensed the depth of Winnie's loneliness. Her comment seemed to have touched Winnie if her endearing smile was any indication.

Ellie leaned forward and flashed her trademark grin. "I think the time you spent dabbling, if I can use your word, paid off. I've been a fan since my mom and I went to a gallery in Boston. Your paintings spoke to me on a deep level." Impulsively, Ellie gave the older woman a fierce hug. "I'm so glad you're coming tomorrow night. The party starts at seven and feel free to bring a guest. If no one else shows up, my family will be here so it will be a party either way."

"I just might do that. I'll have to see if he's in town yet." Seemingly pleased with the impromptu meeting, Winnie gathered her bag and then kissed Ellie on both cheeks. "See you tomorrow evening, my dear. This has been a lovely day."

Ellie watched as Mrs. Winifred Simpson left with the same flare as when she entered. Talking out loud, she said, "I wonder who recommended The Looking Glass. I certainly owe them a big thanks."

The phone rang and Ellie tackled a problem with the newspaper advertisement. Such is the life of a business owner, she thought.

Distracted by a loud thump on the front steps, she went to investigate. She opened the front door, unsure what to expect. Ellie discovered a delivery girl carrying two large, glass vases up the front step. She rushed to help, sidestepping a large balloon bouquet and two tall planters.

"What's going on? You must have the wrong address. I didn't order flowers."

The girl glanced at her notebook. "This is The Looking Glass, and you're Ellie McKenna?"

"This is, and I am."

"Then it's your delivery. Must be people wanting to congratulate you on the grand opening." She pointed to a banner on the balloons. Until that second, Ellie hadn't noticed the banner.

"Let me help you."

Ellie propped the door open as the girl gasped and stepped in. She nodded and gave a low whistle. "Your place is really cool. When I get some time, I'll stop back to poke around."

"I'm having a party tomorrow night at seven. Feel free to stop. I'm serving light refreshments, and some of the artists will be here to talk about their work. It'll be fun." Ellie beamed as her words came out in a rush.

"I might just do that. I'm going to get the last of the flowers, and then I need to hit the road."

Ellie lingered on the steps and noticed the same dark car slowly cruising by again. A vase started to slip from the girl's hands, and all thoughts of the car vanished.

Ellie grabbed the vase in the nick of time.

"Jeez, good thing I have cat-like reflexes."

2

---

*E*llie smoothed the front of her simply tailored, deep purple dress, turning on high stiletto heels to check each angle in the three-way mirror. She secured a stray lock of hair into her chignon. "Well this is it. I don't have time to change again."

The sound of slamming car doors caught her attention, and Ellie peered out the bedroom window. She pushed up the sash and called to her parents, "Ray, Mom, I'll be right down." Taking one final glance in the mirror, she dabbed on deep pink lipstick. "Showtime."

Ellie hurried down the wide staircase, securing the rope when she got to the bottom. She held the door open as Ray and her mom made several trips from the car with additional trays of appetizers. On cue, the wait staff Ellie hired arrived, parking their vehicle out of the way for guests. Ellie sailed into the kitchen amid the bustle of the new arrivals. After a short conversation with the head waiter about where to set up the bar, Ellie went back into the main room. If all continued to go smoothly, tonight would be a huge success. She adjusted a few frames, moved one sculpture a fraction of an inch, and was satisfied all exhibits were showcasing each spectacular item to its best advantage. Ellie wasn't expecting any sales tonight but lived by the adage, You never get a second chance to make a great first impression. Ellie wanted each guest to end the evening with plans to come back and shop.

Voices hummed on the front porch. Ellie stepped out to greet the first guests and cried, "Kate!"

Ellie grabbed her sister and her rather large tummy, holding her tightly. "I can't believe you came. This is amazing."

"Did you really think Don and I would miss your big night?" Kate flashed a sweet smile at her adoring husband who gently supported his wife's arm. "Wild horses couldn't keep us away."

Ellie was completely the opposite of her sister. Kate was tall, brunette, and had emerald eyes, and looked a great deal like their mother. Ellie was petite, blonde, with deep sapphire eyes and resembled their late father, Benjamin McKenna.

Don planted a kiss on his sister-in-law's cheek. "It looks like you're ready for business. You've done a great job with the house, but can we get your sister inside?"

Ellie ushered them in. "I hope you brought your credit card. There's a couple things that would be perfect for your cottage."

Ellie surveyed the room. "If you'll excuse me, I need to greet some more guests. Look around and please get something to eat and drink. Also, there are plenty of chairs when the expectant mommy needs to sit."

"I never thought I'd enjoy sitting down so much. These last couple of weeks have been tiring and baby Price is wearing me down." Kate rubbed her tummy and sank into an overstuffed chair where she could witness the action.

Ellie greeted each new arrival personally. Her brother and his wife, Shane and Abby, were next accompanied by Jake and Sara, her step-brother and his wife. Her grandparents, Dave and Susan Riley, strolled up the walk hand in hand. Ellie ran down the steps to greet them. "Gram, Gramps, this is unexpected." Ellie's words tumbled out. "Mom didn't tell me you were coming. Kate and Don surprised me too. They're inside. Wait till you see Kate, she's as big as a house."

"We wouldn't miss your big night, Pixie." Gram lapsed into Ellie's childhood nickname that Kate bestowed on her. When Ellie was born, Kate announced since Ellie was tiny like Tinker Bell that should be her name.

Gram grasped her youngest granddaughter's hand. "Tell me all about Mrs. Winifred Simpson. Your mom said she has paintings on display. What's she like?"

"I'll introduce you and you can decide for yourself." Ellie pulled her grandmother toward the house. "Come on, she just arrived."

"Oh no, Honey, I don't think a famous artist wants to meet your grandmother." Susan flushed several shades of pink.

"Gram, she's not like what you think. She's super nice and down to earth. You'll see." Ellie pulled firmly on her grandmother's hand, steering her through the maze of people until she found Winnie talking with Kate and Don.

At a lull in the conversation, Ellie interjected, "Mrs. Winifred Simpson, I would like to introduce my grandparents, David and Susan Riley."

Ellie saw her grandmother hesitate and gently nudged her forward.

Susan extended her hand. "It's a pleasure to meet you, Mrs. Simpson. I've been a fan of your work for a long time."

"Thank you, Mrs. Riley, and please, call me Winnie." She winked at Ellie. "It is a pleasure to meet more of Eleanor's family. She is a lovely girl."

Susan beamed. "Please. I'm Susan and my husband, Dave, and yes, Ellie is amazingly talented."

Blushing, Ellie murmured she needed to attend to a few things and withdrew from the conversation. She wove through the crowd, pleased so many people from Loudon and the surrounding towns had come to the opening. Her former boss Karlene was even wandering through the gallery.

Ellie stood next to Karlene.

"Ellie, you have to tell me how on earth you got Winifred Simpson?" Karlene gave her a sharp look. "I've tried for years to get her to agree to a show to no avail. She is very particular."

Ellie's eyes sparkled. "I still am not sure how it happened. She came in and said that it felt right."

Karlene kissed Ellie's cheeks and slipped away. "Enjoy your evening, my protégé."

Ellie glowed as she wandered amongst the guests, pleased to hear people ooh and ah over pottery and small paintings. Ray was at the cash register handling a transaction when Ellie rushed over. "Don, I was teasing before, you don't have to buy something."

"Your sister pointed out an amber necklace so I picked it up for her as a gift from our baby." Don grinned and tucked the box in his jacket pocket. "I think I've succeeded in being sneaky, and I plan on holding out until after the little one makes his or her appearance before giving it to her."

Ellie placed a hand on his arm. "Someday I hope to find a guy, just like you."

Don chuckled. "The right guy will find you when it's time, El." Don looked over the top of her head to where Kate was resting with her feet up. "Please excuse me. I need to get back to my bride."

Conversation buzzed, causing Ellie to turn around. What was causing the stir? Winnie stood on the bottom stair, waiting patiently. A hush fell over the crowd. Unsure what was about to happen, Ellie walked over to stand next to the famous artist.

"Winnie?"

The older woman smiled graciously. "Good evening, everyone. I hope you will indulge me for a few moments. I wanted to thank you all for coming to the grand opening of The Looking Glass, a charming intimate gallery. As you may have noticed, I have a few oils hanging, and I've heard some talk about why I would allow a brand new establishment to have my most well-known canvas on loan. Well a couple of weeks ago my nephew stopped in for a visit and happened to mention when he was driving through our quaint little town of Loudon he noticed a new gallery opening. He discovered the name and was enchanted and suggested I check it out for myself. I've always wanted to support entrepreneurs in the art business, such as this. What you might not know is I had a very difficult time breaking into the art world. I understand how much opposition we can encounter. So I've been skulking around a bit, driving by, asking questions about Miss McKenna's personal integrity."

Winnie glanced at Ellie. "Don't worry, Eleanor, people spoke very highly of you."

Clasping her hands together, she continued. "After meeting Eleanor personally, I felt it was the right opportunity for both of us. Eleanor, to have a boost from my modest success," a smattering of laughter ran over the group, "and I have the benefit of a local presence where I can have different types of art on display, maybe water colors or charcoals or whatever might strike me as fun. So please come back often to see the ever-changing inventory and, tell everyone you know to visit this little slice of artistic heaven."

When Winnie was finished speaking, she pecked Ellie's cheeks and attempted to fade into the partygoers. Ellie laid a hand on her shoulder. "Winnie, I don't know how to thank you for such a wonderful endorsement. If nothing else people will come out of curiosity on the off chance they might run into you."

"My dear, in no time at all you are going to have many major artists displaying their work within these walls. I'm predicting you will be a rousing success. It will be due to your hard work. All I've done is open the door."

"I hope someday to meet your nephew and personally thank him."

"You'll meet him in all due time, I'm sure of that. He actually is quite fascinating, with a dark past and a bright future." Winnie gave a conspirator wink. "I'm going to slip out and let you bask in what remains of the evening. Good night, Eleanor."

Ellie accompanied the artist to her van and waited until Winnie drove down the street. The cool evening air caused her to shiver slightly, and she wrapped her arms around herself for warmth. Ellie turned to go back inside, but not before she took one last look around. She had the distinct feeling of being watched. Shaking off the fanciful notion, she decided it was nothing more than exhaustion. Ellie had been on the fast track to open for months and tonight was the culmination of planning and hard work. It was time to savor the achievement and then of course clean up after the party.

🥂

*E*llie rolled over, legs tangled in the sheets. She glanced at the clock on the nightstand and chose five more minutes of sleep. She lay back, reveling in the memory of last night. The gallery opening had been a huge success with many people attending and even a few sales other than family members. Don and Kate were stopping over with the family for breakfast before going back to Crescent Lake. Luke and Dani, her mom's right and left hands at What's Perkin' were going to open so her parents could join in the fun.

Ellie's phone buzzed. She glanced at caller id and said, "Hey, Mom."

"Good morning, Ellie. I wanted to let you know Ray and I are on our way with quiche and muffins. Sara's bringing a fruit salad and Abby cooked bacon and sausage, so you might want to brew a large pot of coffee, maybe two." Her mom's enthusiasm was evident in her voice. "See you shortly."

Ellie rolled out of bed and dashed through the shower. It wouldn't be long before her house was rocking. She did a little jig as she bopped down the stairs. Life can't get any better than this.

Breakfast was in full swing, with four children under

the age of five running in the back yard, and the adults enjoying hot coffee and a bright sunny day. Abby kept a watchful eye on Devin as she scooped up some fruit. "Ellie, do you think you'll be busy today?"

"I have a photographer coming in, Padraic Stone. I'll start prepping for a couple of events featuring a few artisans, but I don't know what to expect as this is the first normal day of business. Truthfully, I can't wait. The anticipation of opening is behind me, and now I can find a new rhythm for my day. It's going to be so much fun."

Ellie was obviously in her element. Sara said, "Padraic Stone, that's an unusual name."

"It's an old-fashioned Irish name. You know me I had to look it up." Ellie giggled. "But I wasn't able to find a picture of him. I guess the photographer's camera shy."

Sara laughed. "You'll have to let me know if he's some old, weathered guy. How did you hear about him, anyway?"

"He called me a few days ago and then emailed me a link to his website. He has a great eye for landscapes and candid images. He does black and white too, like Ansel Adams. It should be an interesting meeting. If all goes well, they should be a nice addition to my gallery."

Shane listened to the conversation. "I haven't heard of this guy. Do you want me to swing by? Sis, I don't like the idea of you hanging out with some stranger."

"Shane," Ellie said. "Stop being an overprotective big brother. I'll be fine. I'm scheduled to meet with him later this morning. If you're that tied up in knots, call me after lunch, and I'll tell you all about it. This won't be the last time I have a meeting with someone, by myself. It is part of my business. People will come and go all the time."

Kate watched the exchange and caught her twin's eye.

Ellie saw her brother and sister share a knowing wink. "Kate, I'm sure Shane will call and give you a full report."

Just as quickly as the family descended, they were packing up to leave. Ellie walked Kate and Don to the street, fiercely hugging her sister. "Call as soon as you feel the first twinge of labor, and Mom and I'll hit the road." She rubbed her sister's belly. "I can't wait to meet this baby!"

Kate laughed. "Not to worry, you'll be at the top of the call list, but I'm sure there will be plenty of time for you to get to Crescent Lake. The doctor says first babies take their own sweet time."

Don held the door for his wife as the sisters gave each other one last lingering hug.

"Love you, Sis, and you too, Don. Drive carefully and call me when you get home." Ellie sounded like an old mother hen and certainly not like the baby of the family. The couple pulled away from the curb with a sharp toot.

Jake and Sara packed their triplets in the minivan, and Abby secured Devin into her SUV before everyone waved their goodbyes with a promise to see each other soon. Her mom and Ray watched the bulk of their family head in different directions before turning to Ellie.

"Thanks for hosting breakfast. Everything's all cleaned up and the leftovers are in the fridge," Mom said. "Is there anything else you need before we go to work?"

"Nope, I'm all set." Ellie grinned, hugging her mom and stepfather. "Now go. I want to change into something a little more business-like before Mr. Stone arrives." She glanced at her watch. "Oh shoot, he'll be here in less than a half hour." With hands waving, she shooed her parents to the car. "I'll call you later. Love you, Mom."

She dashed into the house and up the stairs. She flung

open the doors to her massive closet in hopes of finding the perfect outfit on the first try.

Ellie looked at the clock for the third time in ten minutes. She was banging on the computer keys when the small bell on the door chimed. Ellie froze, unable to breathe. The man who walked in couldn't possibly be a photographer. He looked like he belonged in front of a camera lens.

The man was tall and his biceps strained the fabric of his black, short sleeve button-down shirt. He wore form-fitting, black jeans and well-worn black cowboy boots. Amber eyes were framed by chestnut brown hair, which curled at the collar. Deep dimples appeared as he smiled.

Grasping Ellie's hand with a firm, cool grip, he said, "Hello, I'm Padraic Stone."

His deep baritone voice caused her insides to quake.

"You must be Eleanor McKenna?"

Stunned by the pure physical reaction to this man, Ellie nodded mutely. Taking his outstretched hand, she was taken aback by the electricity that surged through her as their skin touched. She looked down. Turning her hand over, she expected to see it red, evidence of the burning sensation.

"Yes, I'm Eleanor McKenna," she continued. "But everyone calls me Ellie."

"Since our relationship has become instantly casual, please, call me Pad." He cocked his head. "Did I come at a bad time? You seem to be preoccupied."

"Oh no, not at all. I was just," she pointed to the screen, "you know, working. Always paperwork to do in business and this one is no exception. You're probably not aware, but my grand opening was last night, and I was checking the sales. Surprisingly we did a brisk business. My stepdad was in charge of the cash register so I had no idea..." Ellie stopped mid-sentence, realizing she was babbling.

"Well enough about all of that. Let's talk about your work and if we're a good fit for each other." Ellie blushed crimson, wishing she could retract that last statement. "I mean if my gallery would be suitable for your photos."

Ellie felt Pad's eyes study her as she rambled on. Her hand touched the back of her hair, secured in a chignon. A few tendrils had escaped curling around her face.

Pad said, "Did you have an opportunity to check my website? I left several prints in the car. If you'd like I'll go get them. You can choose what you'd like to display, if any."

Ellie stepped from behind the counter. She was used to men giving their eyes free rein at her expense. She stood tall, straightened her shoulders, and said, "I would like to see your photos. Shall I come with you?"

"No, I'll bring them in."

"Then let's go into the kitchen. You can lay the prints on the table. It will be easier to get the full effect without all the distractions in the main room." Ellie led the way and gestured to the carafe. "Coffee?"

Padraic poured himself a cup while Ellie studied each photo. She could hear his fingers tapping on the edge of the cup. She tried to ignore him as she immersed herself in each image before moving to the next.

"These are incredible. The way you've captured shadows and light is unique. Where were they taken?"

"The White Mountains in New Hampshire. I like to wander and stop whenever the mood strikes. Typically, I don't have a destination in mind when I pack up and hit the road, just a vague direction, north, south, east or west."

"What did you do before photography?" Ellie placed the last framed photo on the table and picked up her cup. "Did you go to art school?"

"I don't have formal training. I was in public service. After a few tough years of seeing too many unspeakable things, I packed it in and picked up a camera."

Ellie sensed he didn't want to talk about his past and respected his privacy. "I must admit I can't wait to get these hung and make the announcement that Padraic Stone originals are available. That is, if you would like me to take your work on consignment?"

"I would. Your place has a good feel, and I think we will work well together." Padraic gathered up the prints. "I'll hang them for you."

"You'll need to sign some paperwork before you leave."

Padraic glanced at his phone. "I have another appointment in the area. Can I swing back either later today or first thing tomorrow?"

"That works too." Ellie walked past Winnie's paintings and noticed Pad smile. "Do you know Mrs. Simpson's work?"

"I've been a fan for a long time." Without elaborating, Padraic set about hanging the photos while Ellie directed how she thought they should be arranged.

Stepping back, Pad slipped his hands in his pockets.

"Perfect." She smiled at Padraic

"I'm assuming you're talking about my work," he teased.

Flustered, she smoothed the front of her blouse and crossed the room to take refuge behind the counter. "The photos are breath taking." Ellie hit a couple of keys in an attempt to steady her hammering heart. "Stop back at your convenience. I'm open today until four and tomorrow ten 'til four as well."

Padraic gave a mock salute. "I'll be seeing you."

Ellie sank down onto the stool and waited until the rushing in her veins subsided. What's come over me? It's like I've never seen a handsome man before today." She crossed to the window and peeked out from behind the curtain, watching Mr. Padraic Stone drive away. Ellie stood there long after his car was out of sight before returning to her paperwork.

3

*S*hane had checked in as expected and now shadows filled the room. Ellie rolled her shoulders. Hearing a board creek on the front porch, she stepped away from the desk and peered into the darkness. The sky was dark with just a few stars making an appearance, the moon a mere slice of light. It was eerily quiet. Just as she pushed the door closed to lock it, she hit the floor. She struggled to gain her footing, instincts screaming, run. Before she could flee, blinding pain and then darkness enveloped her.

"Ellie, you need to open your eyes. Come on, sweetheart I know you can hear me."

Ellie struggled to sit up, gingerly touching the back of her throbbing head. Something felt wet and sticky. "Well that can't be good," she whispered.

"Ellie?"

Holding back a scream, she croaked, "Who's there?"

"Don't be scared little one, it's Daddy?"

"Am I dead?"

"No, honey, you're very much alive, but unfortunately

you have a nasty bump on the back of your head. I'm not able to help you."

Ellie sat quietly, contemplating why she could hear her father's voice after all these years.

"Daddy?" Her voice trembled. It's really you? Well if I'm not dead I must be dreaming, unless…" She stared into the darkness. "You've never come to me before, why now?"

"Always my logical little girl. I've never been far from you, but Pixie, you've never needed me, until tonight. I've been watching over you all these years and you've grown from a little girl I held in my arms, into a remarkable woman. Your mother has done a wonderful job with you, and your sister, and brother."

"You remember my nickname."

"Of course, I was there when Kate announced your name should be Pixie Dust, and we had a devil of a time convincing her your official name was Eleanor. She was so cute cradling you in her arms saying you looked just like Tinker Bell."

Ellie's head stopped swirling as her father talked in a soft, gentle voice. It reminded Ellie of when she was a child waking from a bad dream. "I remember when I was little you used to sit on my bed and talk to me, just like now. All soft and slow, so I must be dreaming."

"You're not."

"Where am I? I don't remember anything except I was working." She whimpered, "Do you know what happened?"

"I don't. I was pulled here when you were surrounded by darkness. You called to me."

"I did? I can't remember." Ellie tried to stand and promptly bumped her head. "Ouch, that hurts." Tears filled her eyes, and she sank to the cold floor. Several minutes passed as she waited for the throbbing to subside. She got on her hands and knees and began to carefully crawl around the space, sweat soaking her blouse. She moved backward and hit a wall, put both arms to the side and found another wall, and then carefully moved in the opposite direction and found an outline of a door. Reaching up, she found the handle and twisted, but it wouldn't budge. Ellie leaned into it with her shoulder —nothing.

"Ellie, don't move!" Her dad hissed.

Instinctively, she trusted the voice she hadn't heard in years. She froze, not daring to make a sound. On the other side of the door, something scraped across the floor. She could hear things crashing. What was going on out there? If someone wanted cash, the register was empty. They didn't need to destroy the place too. Ellie struggled to remain silent while her dream was being shattered. All she could do was wait.

Then silence. Minutes dragged. It dawned on Ellie no one would be coming by tonight; she was very much alone. Silent tears coursed down her cheeks.

She felt a comforting embrace and discovered the not quite solid image of her father holding her.

"Hush now you're safe," he murmured. Ellie sat in the circle of his arms with her eyes closed, imagining how it would feel if her dad were real.

Ellie's head continued to throb, and her butt cheeks were asleep. "You know nobody's going to miss me tonight. I talked to Shane and told him I was going to bed early. Mom doesn't expect me to call until tomorrow. So best case Mom or Ray will swing by in the morning when I don't answer my phone."

"Patience, little one." Her dad looked toward the door and put his finger to Ellie's lips. "Someone's outside."

Ellie strained to hear. Was the intruder coming back for round two or worse to cover his tracks and set the place on fire? Fear strangled her heart. A door banged and Ellie shrank against the back wall.

It sounded like someone was kicking things aside and walking around the shop, searching for something. A low whistle was barely audible. This waiting was killing Ellie. She longed to call out for help. She couldn't take that chance.

※

"*E*leanor McKenna are you here?" Pad demanded. Silence.

"Ellie, if you can hear me, answer. It's Padraic Stone. I drove by and saw the lights."

Ellie cried, "I'm here."

"Where?"

"In a closet, I think."

The door flung open and Padraic crouched down and found Ellie crouched against the back wall and clutching an old umbrella. "See it's me. I won't hurt you."

She held out her hand. "Can you help me? I'm a little woozy."

Padraic crawled part way into the closet and pulled her into his arms, holding her tightly. He felt hot tears dampen his shirt.

"Can. You. Put. Me. Down?" Each word was separated by a hiccup.

Pad held on to her arm while she tried to stand. Just as he suspected, she began to pass out. Scooping her up, he cradled her in his arms, and then he took the stairs two at a time. He went from door to door until he found her bedroom. Laying her on the bed, he could see her face was deathly pale. Not wasting a moment, he dialed 911.

Pad knelt by the bed. Rubbing her cold hand, he urged, "Ellie. The EMTs are on their way. Please open your eyes."

The strobe of red and blue lights flashed through the window. Pad hesitated, torn between leaving her and getting help. "I'll be right back, I promise." Padraic dashed down the stairs and flung open the door.

Two EMTs stepped onto the porch, laden with gear.

"Follow me."

Leading the way upstairs, Pad stepped aside. "She's in here."

"Sir, can you tell me what happened?"

"I suspect Ellie was knocked out by an intruder. When I arrived, she was locked in the closet. I'm not sure how long or if she lost consciousness. I helped her out and within a minute, she fainted. I carried her upstairs and called you."

"Are you bleeding, sir?"

Padraic shook his head. "No, I'm fine."

One EMT pointed to his arm. "You have blood on your shirt."

"I carried Ellie, she must be injured."

The other EMT pointed. "There's a large gash on the back of her head with some dried blood. It looks as though it happened some time ago."

Padraic needed to focus. Who could have struck her and thrown her in the closet? She could have died. Padraic failed to notice two police officers had joined them until someone touched his arm.

"Sir, let's step outside and give the EMTs room to work. We need to ask you a few questions."

Padraic followed the female officer with the male officer trailing him. They stopped in the main room of The Looking Glass. The officers surveyed the damage and made some notes before addressing Padraic.

"Can you tell me what happened here tonight, Mister…?"

Padraic looked at both officers, "Padraic Stone. Yes, Officer…?"

The man spoke, "I'm Greene and this is my partner Officer Bell. Can you tell us what happened here tonight?"

"Earlier today I had a business meeting with Ms. McKenna. I'm a photographer, and we had agreed she was going to display some of my work. Anyway, Ms. McKenna asked me to stop by either tonight or tomorrow and sign a contract. About a half hour ago, I was driving through town and decided to swing by. If she was still open, I was going to sign the contract. I saw the OPEN flag out front and the lights were on. Thinking she might be still working, I parked in the driveway, and as I walked up I glanced in the window and saw the destruction. The door was ajar. I walked in and looked around to see if the perp was still on the premises. At that point, I surmised the gallery was vacant. I called out for Ellie." Pad corrected himself. "Ms. McKenna."

Officer Bell took notes, nodding to encourage Pad to continue.

"It took several minutes before she answered. The closet door was barricaded with a broom handle jammed under the knob. Upon opening the door, I discovered her trying to stand. I helped her up, and then she collapsed. That's when I called it in."

Officer Greene made additional notes while Bell studied Padraic carefully. Bell said, "Did you notice anyone loitering when you left today?"

"No. I didn't see anyone out front or any cars parked in the street."

Officer Greene paused in his note taking. "Where did you say you went after your meeting with Ms. McKenna?"

"I went to visit my aunt. You can call to verify my whereabouts."

Greene nodded, adding to his note pad. An EMT came down the stairs and went out to the porch, quickly returning with a gurney.

Pad grabbed the other side. "Let me help you."

Setting the portable bed down, Pad looked at Ellie. She was awake and trying to speak. Pad leaned down.

She whispered, "I need my mom."

"I'll call her. Do you remember where you left your phone?"

"On the desk."

The EMT had Padraic step aside and prepared their patient for transport. "Tell her parents we're taking her to the emergency room."

Padraic jogged downstairs in search of Ellie's phone.

"Mr. Stone, we will contact the victim's family," Bell stated.

Understanding this was customary, Pad took charge anyway. "I told Ms. McKenna I would call her mother and I will. If you'd like to call her as well feel free but we're wasting time."

Padraic turned his back, cutting off any additional conversation, and picked up Ellie's cell phone. He frowned when he discovered it wasn't protected with a password. That would be a topic for conversation in a couple of days.

He scrolled through the contacts and found "MOM." Hitting the auto dial button, Padraic waited.

On the third ring, a woman answered, "Hi, Pixie, I'm surprised to hear from you this late. Shane said you were going to bed early."

"Mrs. McKenna? This is Padraic Stone."

"Uh, actually, it's Mrs. Davis. Why are you using my daughter's phone?"

"Ma'am, I'm sorry to inform you but someone broke into your daughter's place tonight, hit her over the head, and ransacked the place. I found her about a half hour ago. The EMTs are on the scene, and they're transporting Eleanor to the emergency room. I thought you might want to meet the ambulance."

"Oh, my stars, yes!" Pad could hear Mrs. Davis shout before the line went dead, "Ray we have to go to the hospital, it's Ellie."

Padraic slipped the phone into his back pocket and waited at the bottom of the stairs. The EMTs carried the gurney with Ellie securely tucked in. Pad looked deep into her blue eyes. "I've called your parents, and they'll meet you at the hospital. I'll stay here with the police and then I'll lock up."

Ellie gave a little smile before closing her eyes.

Padraic held the door and waited while Ellie was loaded into the back of the ambulance. An EMT slammed the doors tight. With lights flashing, the ambulance wove around parked cars and flew down the street. Padraic went inside to see what he could learn from the police officers.

Time dragged. He strode into the darkness and studied the area. "Don't they know how to do their job?" he muttered.

Officer Bell stood in the doorway. "Mr. Stone, would you come inside, please? Officer Greene and I have a few more questions." She held the screen door open, waiting.

He demanded, "What have you learned?"

Ignoring the question, Officer Bell reviewed her notes.

Pad took a deep breath. Understanding he had better change tactics with both cops. "I'm sorry, Officer Bell. I'd like to get to the hospital and check on Ms. McKenna."

Judy Bell spoke softly. "Let's go over your story one more time. You say you drove by, saw the OPEN flag, and that caused you stop." She paused and glanced at Pad. "Finding the shop in shambles, you called out for Ms. McKenna." She glanced down at her notes. "Did I miss anything?"

"So far you are correct. A noise drew my attention to the closet door. When I saw it was jammed shut, I opened it. Ellie was struggling to get up and then she collapsed. I carried her upstairs and called 911. You showed up and know the rest."

"What is your relationship with Ms. McKenna?"

"Today she agreed to represent my photography in her gallery."

"Had you met or been in this shop before today?"

"No. We'd never met but I knew her by reputation from her previous employer."

"Can someone verify where you were tonight?"

Frustrated, Padraic nodded his head. "Of course. As I stated, I'll give you my aunt's name and phone number. Feel free to give her a call." Padraic was furious. He had never fallen under suspicion of a crime before tonight. "Am I free to go? I'd like to check on Ms. McKenna."

"Where can we reach you? In case we have more questions."

Padraic took a business card from the counter and scrawled his cell and aunt's information on the back. "Here's how you can reach me, and don't worry I won't leave town without contacting you first."

Without waiting, Padraic leapt from the porch and took off at a dead run. Whoever did this was still out there, and Padraic was sure no one knew if Ellie got a look at him, including the guy who did this.

Padraic looked over the emergency room parking lot for anything out of the ordinary. The automatic doors whooshed open, giving him access to a brightly lit hallway. He looked around and saw a large group of people sitting in the waiting room. Recognizing the dark-haired, green-eyed woman from a picture in Ellie's bedroom, Padraic approached.

"Mrs. Davis? We spoke on the phone. I'm Padraic Stone."

Two very tall men rose, flanking each side and towering over her, one about Pad's age, the other, maybe Ellie's father.

The older of the two stared Padraic directly in the eyes and demanded, "Do you know who did this?"

Padraic thrust out his hand. "You are?"

"Ray Davis, Ellie's stepfather." He pointed to the other man. "This is Shane McKenna. Ellie's brother and of course my wife, Cari Davis."

"Padraic Stone," he said and firmly shook both outstretched hands.

Cari's face was ashen. "Can you tell us what happened tonight?"

Padraic relayed the story exactly as he had told the police without interruptions from the family. Upon finishing he asked, "Does anyone remember seeing

31

anyone loitering around the gallery over the last few weeks?"

Shane paced the small sterile room. "If we had, do you think we'd have left my sister alone? When I called today she was going to finish up and go to bed early."

"What time was that?" Padraic inquired.

Shane stopped mid-step. "Just before five I think."

Padraic glanced at his watch. "I got there around nine-thirty. That means in the span of a few hours, someone forced their way in, hit Ellie on the head, and trashed the shop." Pad fell silent, mentally reviewing the scene.

Cari stood and addressed the man wearing green scrubs. "Dr. Black, how's my daughter?"

Another giant of a man came bursting through the door. Ray waved him over. "Jake, glad you're here. We're just getting a report from the doctor."

Surrounded by four powerfully built men, the doctor paused and looked at Cari. "Your daughter is very lucky. She took a blow to the head that will require a few staples. She was unconscious, but I can't say for sure how long, and she'll have a nasty headache for a few days. I want to keep her overnight for observation but she should be able to go home tomorrow barring any complications."

"Can I see her?" Tears choked Cari's voice.

"We're going to move her upstairs but I'm sure she'd feel better seeing her family first."

Cari, Ray, and the boys started toward the exam room when she paused mid-step. "Do you want to come in Mr. Stone?"

"No, go ahead. But if you don't mind, I'll wait until you come out, just to make sure she's going to be okay before I leave."

"Of course." Cari pushed through the swinging door.

Settling in a hard, plastic chair, Padraic once again let the events churn. Why would someone break in and toss the place? What were they looking for, and the bigger question, did they find it? Once Ellie was feeling better, Padraic planned on asking her a few questions.

Putting all thoughts of the attack aside, Pad mulled over how he felt to have the petite beauty in his arms carrying her up the stairs. Her pert nose and those deep blue eyes were enough to make any man's protective streak come out, or at least it should. This was a first for him. Pad had always wanted to protect people, but this feeling was very different, and one he would wait to examine another day.

4

*E*llie had rested even with the nurses waking her every hour. The events of the previous night were fuzzy. However, she had complete clarity of the man with intense amber eyes holding her in his strong arms.

Ellie sat up in bed, holding her aching head, and cried out, "Daddy." The dam broke, tears falling freely.

Cari walked and found Ellie sobbing. "Sweetheart, do you need the doctor?"

"Oh, Mommy," she wailed. "I saw Daddy last night, when I was locked in the closet. He talked to me but then he disappeared."

Ellie sank into her mother's arms and wept until she was spent. Her mom tucked a lock of blonde hair behind Ellie's ear, cupped her chin, and looked into red-rimmed eyes. "Are you sure he left?"

Ellie sniffled and hiccuped. "One minute he was talking to me and then next he was gone."

"El, it never worked that way with me. When someone was coming within hearing range, he would usually stop talking so people wouldn't think I had lost my mind. You were injured. He wouldn't leave until help arrived. Mr. Stone rescued you, but rest assured your dad will be back. He's drawn to you now and he won't leave until you're ready to let go."

Ellie used the tissue her mother offered. "Do you really think I'll see Daddy again? I have so many questions and things I want to tell him."

"Trust me. When you need him, he'll be there."

Ellie's hand trembled as she took a cup of water her mother handed her. Slowly her hiccups lessened. "How's the gallery? I don't remember much, but I am assuming if someone broke in and made a lot of noise, they left a huge mess. At least that's what happens in the movies."

"What do you remember?" Her mom asked gently. "I'm sure the police will want to talk with you today, and it might be better if you talk about what happened."

Before Ellie could answer, someone rapped on the metal doorjamb.

"Good morning, Ms. McKenna. I'm Officer Paul Greene and this is my partner, Judy Bell. If you're up to it, of course, may we ask you a few questions?"

Ellie straightened the blanket on her bed. "Come in. This is my mother, Cari Davis."

Officer Greene gave a curt nod, and Officer Bell said, "A pleasure to meet you, Ma'am."

They waited patiently for Ellie to begin. "I was working on the computer, you know writing a press release, advertising, and I must have lost track of time. I noticed it was getting dark."

"Do you know what time that was?" Officer Bell interrupted.

Ellie shook her head and cringed. She pressed her fingers against her temples.

"Okay, go on," Bell encouraged.

"The front door was open part way, and I wanted to lock it. I was going to grab something to eat and take it upstairs. It had been a long day. I was shutting the door and remember flying through the air and hitting the floor. Everything went dark until I woke up locked in the closet and my head was bleeding."

"How did you know you were bleeding if you were locked in a dark closet?" Officer Greene paused.

"My head hurt really bad, and when I touched the back of it, it was warm, wet and sticky." Horrified, Ellie put her hand up and touched the bandage. "Did they shave my head?"

"Honey, relax," her mom reassured her. "What they shaved was a very tiny area, no one will ever see the scar, and you'll be able to arrange your hair to cover the staples short term."

"How many stitches do I have?"

"You have seven staples. The wound was fairly deep."

"Oh, no wonder it hurts wicked bad." Ellie reached up and gently touched the bandage. "Do you know why someone broke in?" She looked at both police officers, noticing for the first time Paul Greene was tall and lanky with dirty blond hair, while Judy Bell was short with red hair secured in a bun on her head.

"As far as we can tell, nothing is missing but there is a fair bit of vandalism. We'll need you to take a look and confirm if anything is missing. At this time, we're treating this as a random act of violence."

Ellie stared out the window. "I've seen a dark car parked across the street a couple of times, and the windows were dark like they have down south. Maybe it's the same person?

Her mom's eyes widened. "Ellie, why didn't you tell us that someone was watching you?"

"The gallery doesn't have any cash, and I didn't have anything of value until the art work and jewelry started being delivered, so I didn't think it was that big of a deal."

"Ms. McKenna, do you have surveillance cameras installed?"

"They're activated by some computer software, and I have four angles covering the showroom. I can give you access."

Officer Bell said, "That would be helpful. Can you describe the car in more detail?"

"It was a black, two door, kind of sporty looking but definitely like a guy's muscle car. I never saw the license plate. One time when I started to walk out to the sidewalk, whoever it was took off. I've seen it a couple of more times you know, just driving by, really slow."

"Is there anything else you can think of at this time?" Officer Greene quizzed.

Ellie started to shake her head and grimaced. "I'm sorry but I can't think of anything.

Officer Bell handed her a card. "If you think of something no matter how small, please call us. When you've been released, give us a call and we can take a look at the footage."

Ellie took the card and laid it on the bed. "Thank you."

"Mrs. Davis, could we speak to you, please?"

Her mom touched the blanket. "I'll be right back." She followed the officers into the hallway.

🍸

*C*ari looked from one police officer to the other. "What didn't you want to say in front of my daughter?"

"We don't think this was random. Based on the methodical search of the building, whoever this was is a professional and wanted something very specific. We would recommend that for now, your daughter doesn't stay there or at least not by herself until we can get more information."

"I appreciate your concern and trust me, Ellie will not be staying there alone. My husband and I will stay with her, unless I can convince her to temporarily move in with us."

"Please call when she has been released. We must walk through the crime scene with her before it has been cleaned up."

"Ellie should be released later today. We will be in touch tomorrow."

Cari watched the officers get on the elevator and then walked back into Ellie's room.

"So, what didn't they want me to know?" Ellie demanded.

Cari debated whether to tell the truth. Making a fast decision, she said, "The police don't think this was random, and the intruder didn't find what they were looking for. They suggested you stay with us for a few days."

"Like that will happen! It will take more than some vandal to keep me away from my home and business." Ellie's mouth was set in a thin hard line, and Cari knew from past experience there was not going to be a discussion. "All right, Ray and I will be sleeping in your guest room."

Ellie glared at her mother. Both women were strong-willed and they knew when to give in on a small point.

"Fine. Now when can I go home?" Ellie spoke softly. "I want to see how bad my beautiful gallery was trashed."

"We have to wait for the doctor. If you're okay by yourself, I'm going to run to What's Perkin', pick up a few things at the house, and of course, call Ray."

"Sure, I'm fine. I'll watch TV." Ellie grabbed the remote and flipped on the morning news. "Hey, Mom?"

Cari took Ellie's hand. "What is it, honey?"

"Thanks for staying with me tonight. It'll be good to have some company."

"We'll have a nice dinner and relax, with all the lights blazing." Cari grinned. "Thank goodness I don't have to pay the electric bill." She kissed Ellie's cheek. "See you in a bit."

❦

*E*llie adjusted the bed and sank into the pillows, gently readjusting her head to keep pressure off the bandage. She closed her eyes, drifting back to the conversation with her father. As horrifying as it was to be locked in the closet, her father was there to comfort her. A soft knock on the door interrupted her thoughts.

"Ellie, are you awake?"

Padraic Stone stood in the doorway.

She blinked several times, "Yes."

Pad pulled up a chair and settled in. "How's the head?"

"It could be worse. I have a blazing headache, and

Mom told me they shaved part of my hair. I'm hoping I'll be able to cover it once I get home with a scarf or hat."

Padraic grinned. "Just tell people to take a look at the other guy."

Ellie laughed. "Will do."

"Have the police stopped by?"

"They left just a few minutes ago. Did you know they don't think this was random?"

"I suspected as much. The vandalism was almost an afterthought rather than the objective. At least that is my observation." Padraic fell silent for a moment. "Did anyone tell you about the Simpson painting?"

"Which one? We hung several." Ellie pushed upright, her stomach lurched.

"The painting of the waterfalls, it was slashed, from a top corner to the opposite bottom corner. It's beyond repair."

Ellie gasped. "Has anyone called Winnie?"

Padraic held up a hand. "No, she doesn't know yet. There is enough time to tell her when you're feeling better."

Ellie turned toward the window, her hands clenching and unclenching as the wall clock's minute hand crept forward. "I want to find out who did this, and they should be made to pay restitution or whatever it's called. Destroying artwork is unconscionable. It's a thing of beauty!"

Ellie's eyes were cold and hard.

"Anger is good for recovery," Pad said. "I promise you, we will find who did this and why."

Ellie looked hard at this virtual stranger. "Why do you want to help me? You don't really know me, and I'd certainly understand if you don't want to proceed with our arrangement. If I were in your shoes, I'd think twice."

"It will take more than a petty criminal to make me change my mind. I don't scare easily and things can be replaced."

"Well thank you, Padraic."

Silence filled the room.

Ellie piped up. "May I ask you a question?"

"I think you just did." Padraic grinned. "And you can ask me another one if something else is on your mind."

"Ah, I like it when people have a sense of humor. Life is too short to be so serious. But I digress. What kind of name is Padraic? Is it a family name?"

"Yes, I'm the fifth generation of Padraics. It's an old Irish form of Patrick, who as you may know was the patron saint of Ireland, and legend has it he drove out the snakes. My mother said it was the perfect name for me as I tend to be a bit solitary and a deep thinker. I'm good at looking at situations and figuring things out. But my friends call me Pad. It's less formal, and only my mother ever called me Padraic."

"Pad." Ellie smiled and settled back on the bed, drifting to sleep with his name hovering on her lips.

❧

*P*ad liked how she said his name. He leaned back in the chair, keeping watch and mulling over some ideas about the break in. He wanted to get back into Ellie's gallery but didn't get the chance to ask her if it was okay. He pulled a small notebook from his leather jacket and jotted down notes.

41

Ellie was sleeping peacefully when Mrs. Davis walked into the room.

"Oh, I didn't expect to see you here," she exclaimed.

Padraic stood up and crossed the room. "Hello, Mrs. Davis. I stopped to see how Ellie was feeling, and she drifted off to sleep. I thought I would sit with her for a while in case she needed something. Hospitals are notorious for lack of attention unless you're in ICU."

"Please call me Cari." She touched his jacket. "I wanted to thank you for last night. I shudder to think that Ellie might have been locked in that closet all night, bleeding. Who knows what would have happened to her."

"No need to thank me, ma'am."

"How is she doing?"

"Other than a nasty headache she seems fine, but I have to warn you a little while ago she was spitting fire. She's decided whoever did this will pay for damages. I didn't have the heart to tell her she should settle for him living behind bars for a long time."

"I agree, but that's my Ellie, wanting to right every wrong, justice for all." Cari wrapped her arms tightly around herself. "She's always been that way, ever since she was a little girl." She shuddered. "Can I ask you something?" Cari chewed her bottom lip. "What if he comes back? The police were here, and they don't feel he found whatever it was he wanted, as nothing seems to be missing. Oh, and did you hear they're hoping they got the person on video?"

Pad didn't want to burst her bubble. "Cari if this person was a pro they may have found their way around the system or worn a disguise."

Cari looked at the floor. "I hadn't thought of that possibility."

"Would it be okay for me to run over and look around outside, see if there is something the police overlooked?"

Cari looked at him. "Don't you think we should leave the investigation to the professionals?"

"If I tell you something can you keep it on the down low?"

Her eyes narrowed. "Maybe. It depends if my family would be hurt by me keeping quiet."

Pad straightened. "I give you my word this will not harm a single member of your family. In fact, it might help put your mind at ease."

Waiting for Cari to agree, Pad confessed, "In my former profession, I took an oath to 'protect and serve.' I promise you I will do my best to find out what happened to Ellie. I have time to devote to this case where the police have many to juggle. It would make it easier if everyone didn't know what I was doing. You'd be amazed how many times, when word gets around, information is withheld that can help change the course of an investigation. I'd like your permission to do a little undercover work, so to speak."

"Do the police know you were in law enforcement?"

"They may suspect something by some of the questions I asked last night."

"Under one condition. Hank Booth is the chief of police in Loudon. If you agree to talk with him and let him do a background check on you, I'll agree."

"Consider it done. I'll go down to the station when I leave here and ask Chief Booth to give you a call after they run my credentials."

Pad reached out to seal their bargain.

"Padraic, don't make me regret this or I will let my husband and sons know about this conversation, and we have many friends on the police force. Your visit to Loudon will be cut short."

"Understood. Rest assured I am exactly who I say. I give you my word as my mother's son." Pad quietly left the room.

5

*T*o Padraic, all police stations looked and smelled exactly the same: drab white walls and old, burnt coffee lingering in the air. He sauntered up to the counter which was surrounded with bulletproof glass. He tapped his foot and waited for the desk officer to get off the phone.

"Can I help you?" The officer spoke through a metal grate hole.

Speaking loud and clear, he stated, "My name is Padraic Stone. I'd like to talk with your chief. I'm a friend of Cari Davis." Pad handed the officer his driver's license and credentials.

The officer gestured to a hard plastic chair. "Have a seat. I'll see if Chief Booth is available."

Pad stepped aside. It wouldn't be uncommon for this to take a while.

Moments later the desk sergeant returned. "Mr. Stone, follow me." He held open the door to the inner sanctum. "Please empty your pockets and walk through the metal detector."

Pad did as requested. Pleased the small-town force followed standard protocols, he said, "You can never be too careful these days."

The sergeant nodded. "A lot has changed in a short time. Just a few years ago, people would never have thought of strutting into the station armed. Heck, everyone's wearing body armor now too. You just never can tell."

"I hear ya." Pad retrieved his loose change and wallet and followed the officer down a long, narrow hallway until they reached the last doorway on the right.

"Chief Booth, this is Padraic Stone." The desk officer left them in private.

Pad partially closed the door.

Chief Booth was a large, powerfully built man with deep lines around his eyes, more than likely from years in the sun.

He stuck out his hand. "Nice to meet you. Have a seat."

"Thank you for seeing me. I'm sure you're very busy." Padraic eased back in the only available chair.

"Rob mentioned you know Cari Davis. Do you mind if I ask what this is about?"

"I'm sure you're aware of the break in last night at Ellie McKenna's gallery, The Looking Glass."

"Yeah. I heard it come over the radio, and I checked with my officers. They assured me she was going to be fine. But it's terrible stuff. On her first official day and all."

Pad liked the chief's style—laid back but keeping a sharp eye on the newcomer. "I was first on the scene."

"So, I hear. Now how did that come about?" Hank leaned back in his chair, arms folded across his chest.

"I'm a photographer and I'm going to have a display

at Ellie's. I have a fairly good following, but I want to reach a new audience, and this gallery's style fits my needs. As I mentioned in the report, I met with Ellie earlier in the day and planned on stopping back late afternoon to sign the contract. However, I was delayed. It was late but I decided to take a chance. If she was still open we'd get the paperwork out of the way." Pad paused, anticipating questions. Being met with silence, he continued. "The house was lit up like a Christmas tree. As I started up the walk, I noticed the door was ajar. My training kicked in. I entered the building to secure the scene before calling it in."

"Rob mentioned your credentials. It seems you're well trained for these types of situations."

"Yes, sir. I have over ten years of experience."

Hank nodded.

"Upon entering, the building appeared deserted. I discovered Ellie's car was parked by the back entrance, her handbag on the kitchen counter. I called out to her and after a few moments, I heard a faint voice from inside the closet. Ellie had been locked in, and as I helped her out, she fainted. I called 911. Once your officers arrived, my sole focus was Ellie. After the ambulance left, I stayed and answered questions."

"I'm puzzled. Why are you here? Bell and Greene filled me in on the details."

"Sir, with all due respect, I don't think this was random. Ellie told me there has been a black car with tinted windows lurking, and the vandalism was methodical. Whatever the perp was looking for, they didn't find it, however they destroyed a Winifred Simpson painting."

"I would agree with you. What do you want to do about it?"

"I asked Cari if I could poke around, basically work behind the scenes."

"Do you think my officers are incapable of solving this crime?" Hank's eyes narrowed.

"Absolutely not, but Ellie wants to go home, and neither her parents nor I think that's a wise idea. I'm sure Ellie's in danger, and Cari's worried about her daughter. I revealed the basic details of my past and volunteered to protect Ellie."

Hank snorted. "That's an understatement, Mr. Stone."

Pad chose to ignore the implication. "Nevertheless, she would agree if you'd vouch for me. I'm here to ask you to make a phone call and tell Cari I'm a stand-up guy."

Hank leaned forward, elbows on the desk. "I can do that. On the condition, you turn all information over to the department. Keep in contact with Officers Bell and Greene. This is their case which you'd do well to remember."

Padraic slid a business card across the desk with a single name and number on it. "This was my boss. He'll answer any questions you feel are appropriate. Once you confirm I am who I say, call Cari Davis. Ellie is being released today, and she plans on going home."

Hank stood up, pulling himself to his full, imposing height. "I'll do just that and let you know if you get the green light."

Pad shook the chief's hand and stopped at the door. "Chief, this guy isn't done, and I don't like that he attacked a defenseless woman." Padraic Stone stormed out.

🍷

*P*ad stepped off the elevator. He wondered how anyone could rest with the constant paging and people rushing around. The smell of antiseptic clung to his clothes. For people who were really sick, it probably didn't matter since they slept most of the time. He noticed a housekeeping cart outside Ellie's room.

"Excuse me," he said to a man who was gathering sheets from the cart. "Was Ms. McKenna moved to a different room?"

"Nope, she was discharged." He left Pad standing in the hallway to go about his work.

Through a clenched jaw, he muttered, "I should have gone to the gallery first." Pad stopped at the nurses' station. "Excuse me."

An older woman glanced up from the paper she was reading. "How may I help you?"

"I was looking for Eleanor McKenna. Has she been discharged?"

Glancing at a chart, she surveyed the notes. "Yes. I believe she left with her mother."

"Thank you." Pad started to leave and turned back. Casually he asked, "Ellie had quite a gash on her head. Do you know if the doctor determined what was used?"

"I'm sorry I'm not at liberty to disclose any information about a patient."

Pad flashed what appeared to be a police badge. "I'm working with the local PD on the case, and it would be helpful to know if it was an object of convenience or something the intruder brought with him."

"Well…" Glancing up and down the hall, the nurse dropped her voice. "Since you're a cop I can tell you. It appears to be something round. The doctor thinks it might be a heavy flashlight or a stick, you know like what cops carry."

Pad kept a straight face. "Thank you and I won't tell anyone. It's just between us."

The nurse's expression was grave. "That poor girl, the wrong place at the wrong time. I've always said if someone wants to break into my apartment I hope I'm not home. They're welcome to whatever they can carry."

Padraic thanked her again before stepping into the elevator. His cell vibrated in his jacket. He didn't recognize the number.

"Stone here."

"Hello, Padraic, this is Cari. Cari Davis."

"What can I do for you, Cari?"

"Ellie and I are at the gallery, but we haven't gone inside yet. I'm wondering if you have some time could you come over? It would make us both feel more at ease, if we didn't go in by ourselves. I tried to reach my husband, but he didn't answer."

"I'll be there in ten minutes." Pad started to jog through the parking lot.

"We'll wait for you in the car." Cari paused. "By the way, I spoke to Hank Booth."

"No need to say anything more. I'm on my way." Pad knew what Hank Booth said; the call said it all.

Not knowing which side streets were short cuts, Pad stuck to the main road. There might have been a bit of traffic this time of day, but it was quicker than getting lost. At a stoplight, Pad flipped up the back seat to confirm his pistol lockbox was handy. He didn't expect to need it but he was always prepared.

Cari's SUV was in the driveway, and Pad crossed the grass to where the ladies sat in Adirondack chairs.

"Ladies, sorry it took a bit longer than I anticipated." Pad glanced at the door, for the first time noticing a new door handle had been installed. "Your husband's handy work?"

"A carpenter comes in handy at times." Cari didn't attempt to get out of the chair.

"Would you like me to go in first and look around?"

Ellie grabbed the back of the chair to steady herself. "I'm coming with you."

Pad frowned. "All right, stay behind me and if I tell you to go out, don't ask questions just do as I say." He studied Ellie's deep blue eyes. "Understood?"

Ellie gave a curt nod. "Lead the way, Mon Capitan."

In single file, the three went to the front door. Cari passed Pad a key; it turned easily in the lock. Pad took one last look at Ellie before pushing open the door. He could see Ellie's face was ashen. Pad hated whoever did this to her. No one had the right to take away a person's feeling of safety in his or her home or place of business.

Pad flipped on the lights; despite the sun he wanted to alleviate any dark, lingering shadows. He took Ellie's hand, helping her step over broken glass and pottery.

"Mom," Ellie cried. "They smashed the beautiful cranberry glass vase that was Gram's. Remember, she gave it to me last year for Christmas." Ellie blinked back a tear. "This destruction is senseless." Crossing to the desk, she punched open the register. "My credit card's here. It's a small comfort but it just doesn't make sense."

Her fingers hovered over the keyboard on her laptop. "Pad, is it okay if I turn the computer on. I'd like to check the security camera."

"Go ahead. We can get a copy to the police station later."

Ellie tapped a few keys and it sprang to life. "Pad? It's ready."

He looked over her shoulder as Ellie fast-forwarded to the point when she got up from the desk. The camera caught her standing at the front door. The footage was a little dark due to low interior lighting, but it was easy to make out what happened in the next few moments. The door flew open and a figure dressed in black pounced. Ellie hit the floor. Pad watched as she scrambled up, attempting to get away.

Cari gasped. "Oh, my stars, Ellie!"

Ellie clung to her mom's arm. "Mom, we have to watch. It's the only way to find out who did this to me."

Pad was impressed with Ellie's inner strength. "She's right, Cari. I understand this is painful, but it's necessary."

Cari remained glued to the screen as the footage rolled.

"Look, right there! That's when I got clobbered! What is that?" Ellie pointed to the screen.

"It looks like a big flashlight," Cari exclaimed.

Pad leaned in closer and grimaced. "It reminds me of a police issue flashlight; they're heavy and can be used like a baton. They're less lethal. A lot of people have died after being hit with a night stick."

"My gosh, he drags me to the closet and just tosses me in like a sack of potatoes." Ellie stifled a cry. "What is he doing now? He's looking around the room for some-thing...wait! He's coming to the desk. What's he doing with my laptop?"

The answer was evident as the screen went blank. The threesome was speechless, unsure what to say or do next.

"He shut down the cameras. Ellie, do you remember if you locked your computer when you got up?"

Pad turned her away from the screen. "Think, close your eyes and replay those few moments."

"I never lock my screen. It has a fifteen minute delay to auto lock."

Cari piped up, "The attack didn't take fifteen minutes so your computer was easy to access and gave the intruder opportunity to fool with the security system."

Ellie chewed on her lower lip. "Mom, I wouldn't have thought this would happen, not in a million years."

Pad interrupted, "Ellie, your mom's right and you'll need to make some changes. One will be a camera facing the front walkway. You might have seen him coming and a video screen will sit on your desk and it will be live at all times. I can get that installed for you."

"How do you know about all this stuff?"

"I've met some people who were really good at security while bumming around." Anxious to change the subject, Pad suggested, "How about we take a look around? Once we confirm the police have gotten all the evidence there's a fair amount to be cleaned up. You can take inventory and contact your vendors."

Ellie rubbed the back of her neck. "Those aren't going to be fun conversations, and I can't forget to call the insurance company."

"I'll grab my camera from the car so we can document everything. The pictures may be helpful as this gets sorted out with the insurance company too."

Pad retuned carrying a large black bag. "Camera equipment." He set the bag on the floor and pulled out a camera, fiddled with some settings. "Ready when you are."

Methodically, the two walked through the gallery, Pad

taking pictures and Ellie making notes of each artist's display and the damaged pieces.

"So much of a person's soul goes into their work, I don't want to make the phone calls."

Hopefully my vendors will understand.

Ellie stopped in front of the painting, simply titled, 'Waterfall.'

Her voice cracked. "Do you think it would be okay with the police if we took this down?"

Pad watched the range of emotions race over her face. "What do you plan to do with it?"

"I'm going to take it back to Winnie. I can't tell her over the phone. She was so gracious the first time we met. It's the right thing to do, especially as it is so valuable. It might sound stupid, but I wished another painting had been slashed. I got the feeling this one was very special to her."

Pad spoke softly, "Would you like me to go with you?"

"No, thank you. This is something I'll need to do by myself."

Pad could see Ellie's eyes were puffy.

"I really appreciate you being here today. Mom and I could have done this by ourselves but, well, you rescued me and in those first few moments after you opened the closet door you made me feel safe." Ellie touched his arm. "I'll never forget that."

Pad's skin tingled underneath her fingertips. Unnerved, he replied, "It's not a big deal. I didn't do anything special."

Ellie pulled back her hand and cleared her throat. "After I speak with Officer Greene would you put the painting in my car? If he says it's okay I'll drive out tomorrow."

6

*E*llie answered more questions from two police officers after she turned over the surveillance footage and the shop had been straightened up. Mom was making supper, while Ellie filled out paperwork for the insurance company. A door slammed. Not one to typically be on edge, she went to investigate.

Ellie briefly closed her eyes and flung open the back door. "Mom, Ray 's here."

Ray Davis was tall and lean with killer blue eyes enhanced by dark hair with a dash of gray at the temples. Ray said, "Hi Ellie, tell Mom I'll be right in. I want to take a look around."

Ellie smiled when Ray finally came into kitchen, wrapped his arms around her mom, kissing her upturned lips. "Did you two get everything cleaned up?"

Ellie gave him a thumbs up. "Padraic Stone helped us. He's getting a camera installed that looks out over the front and back along with a new monitor that will be on all the time."

Ray said, "Hmm, you seem to be smitten with this young man."

"No, I'm not. But it does make me wonder. Mom, do you think Pad is just a nice guy, or do I need to be careful around him too? Maybe he had something to do with all of this." Ellie looked towards the front of the house. "This started after the first time I met him."

"I wouldn't have called him if I had any concerns. He's a good man and it seems like he has the time and experience to be helpful. Pixie, don't try to control everything; for once just go with the flow."

*E*llie pushed back from the table and walked into the family room.

🍷

"*H*ey, kiddo." Ray sat next to Ellie on the couch.

She looked up from the computer. "Did Mom kick you out of the kitchen to check up on me?"

He grinned, "No, that was my idea."

"No need. I'm fine."

"If you say so." He handed Ellie a glass of iced tea. "Mom said you got the surveillance footage over to the police."

Ellie took a sip. "Yeah. I'm not sure how helpful it will be, though. The guy was smart enough to shut the camera off." Ellie got up and stretched. "The gallery will be pretty secure after Pad's done."

"It sounds like Pad spent most of his day here. Doesn't he have a job?"

"He's a photographer, a really good one too. Have you seen any of his photos?"

Ray shook his head and smiled. "If I were to guess I'd say some will be hanging on these walls?"

"If he doesn't change his mind." Ellie crossed the room. "Come look. I have a few now. The light is excellent, reflecting off the walls without casting shadows. He hung a few smaller photos, and I'm hoping tomorrow he'll drop off a few landscapes. They're stunning."

Ray pointed to the vacant space. "What are you going to do about the Simpson painting?"

"Pad put it in my car. I'll talk to Winnie, and if she decides she wants me to return the others I'll understand. Her paintings are worth a lot of money, and I don't even know how I'll pay for this one if the insurance doesn't cover the cost."

Ellie shrugged her shoulders. "I never expected anything like this would happen."

Ray brushed a tear from her cheek as she looked up. "Why would anyone do this to me? I don't have anything to steal and if this was just vandalism, did they have to make such a huge mess? It's taken me all day to clean it up, and I've to stay closed another day since I need to call my artists."

"I don't know, El."

Ellie squared her jaw, and a glint shone in her eyes. "This jerk could have looked around all he wanted and not break anything. After all I couldn't have done anything since I was locked up."

Ray let out a hearty chuckle. "Only you, Eleanor McKenna, would think an intruder should be tidy! But I don't think absorbing artistic expression was on his mind."

Ellie smiled, happy to have a bit of light heartedness

shine into an otherwise dark day. "Did you notice what Mom's cooking for dinner? I'm starved."

"Let's see if it's ready. I wouldn't want you wasting away from hunger." Ray draped his arm over his petite step-daughter's shoulders. "If you finish your dinner maybe we'll walk down to Scoops for an ice cream."

"Ray, I'm not twelve." Ellie grinned. "But if you're buying count me in." She tapped her forehead. "I'm thinking a double scoop of butter pecan with chocolate sprinkles on a sugar cone."

They were bantering over the best flavors as they entered the kitchen. It never ceased to amaze Ellie the bond she had with Ray. To outsiders, they acted like father and daughter. When Ellie looked back over, her childhood, Ray had always been a father figure for her. He lent a strong male presence when needed, just as Mom had done for Ray's son Jake, trying to step in as a mother figure when he needed advice about girls. The McKenna and Davis family had formed long before Ray and Mom made it official.

"What are the two of you plotting?" her mom asked.

Ellie giggled. "After dinner, we're getting ice cream."

"Really?" her mom teased. "And whose idea was that, Raymond?"

Ray wiggled his eyebrows. "Well, sweetheart, you know ice cream fixes everything, and Ellie does have seven staples in that pretty little head. It makes sense we need a double scoop from Scoops."

"That's right I have a lot of staples, so that means several trips, don't you agree Ray?" Ellie batted her eyelashes in his direction.

Her mom got into the spirit of the conversation and

quickly agreed. "We should hurry and eat in case Scoops runs out or maybe just skip dinner altogether."

The trio sat down to salad and grilled chicken when the gallery phone rang. Her mom glanced up. "Do you want me to get that Ellie?"

"No, I'm fine." Ellie left the room.

"Hello, The Looking Glass, this is Eleanor, how may I help you?"

A brief pause and they could hear Ellie say again, "Hello?"

Ray came into the room.

"Who is this?" Ellie demanded. "What do you want?" Nearly hysterical, she dropped the phone.

Ray picked it up.

Ellie shook her head. "They hung up."

Ellie stepped into his open arms, and he waited until she stopped quaking. "Who was on the other end?" Ray asked.

"I don't know. It sounded like a man and he asked if I got the message. Yesterday was just the beginning unless I made a few changes."

"Mom, will you call the police? And Pad too, maybe he can come over."

Ray sat Ellie on the couch, rubbing her icy hands. "It was just a phone call, El. I won't let anyone hurt you."

"Ray, I'm not scared. I can take care of myself but this person wants me to change something about my gallery. I have no idea what." Fire burned in her eyes. "It's obvious this jerk doesn't know who he's dealing with. I'm not a pushover."

A sharp rap on the door interrupted her. Ellie crossed the room, but Ray reached the front door first. Looking through the side windowpane he unbolted the door.

Officers Bell and Greene entered the front room and gave a curt nod.

Officer Bell said, "Ms. McKenna, are you okay?"

Before Ellie could answer, Ray stated, "Ellie received a disturbing phone call. I think it's the person who broke in."

"Ms. McKenna. Can you tell us exactly what you heard, any background noise, anything at all that might help us?"

Ellie paced the room, recalling the conversation when loud footsteps pounded up onto the front porch.

Ellie raced to the door. Seeing Pad, she cried, "He called me!"

Pad grabbed her arm. "Slow down and tell me what happened."

Ellie nodded in the direction of the police. "It's good you're here so I won't have to repeat myself. I was about to tell them what happened."

Ellie stood behind the desk. She took a few deep breaths with her eyes closed. When she opened them, she repeated what was said, verbatim.

Pad watched her carefully, waiting to see what questions the local cops would come up with. They were busy jotting down notes and not interrupting.

Pad glanced at the two local cops.

"Ellie, sit down on the stool and close your eyes again." Pad knelt down. "Now think for a minute. Are you sure it was a male voice? Take your time."

Ellie's eyes flew open. "I'm not sure. It was sort of distorted. It could have been female."

"All right, what was in the background, was there any music anything unusual or distinctive sounds?"

Ellie closed her eyes again and let the call replay again.

"Um, there is traffic in the background. Not close but I did hear a horn."

"Good. Now anything else?" Pad prodded.

"I don't think so, but whomever it was demanded I do something, but didn't say what." Ellie opened her eyes. "I'm sorry it was such a short call and I panicked."

Officer Greene spoke. "You have caller ID on your phone?"

"Yes."

Greene picked up the hand-set, "I'd like to scroll through the list, if you don't mind."

"Sure."

"A blocked caller, and by the looks of your call history you've had several over the last few days. Is this typical?"

"I don't look at the ID when I answer. This is a place of business I'm not going to screen my calls," Ellie snapped, her patience wearing thin.

*

*P*ad gestured for the officers to join him outside. He looked at Ellie. "I'll be right back."

Greene and Bell glanced at one another before they followed Pad.

"I'm assuming you've spoken with Chief Booth about my involvement in this case?"

"Yeah, apparently you're some big shot from out of town, and we're supposed to give you access to every-thing," Officer Bell said.

"Well that isn't exactly the case. I am experienced and since I am working with Ms. McKenna it gives you a set of trained eyes on what is going on behind the scenes." Choosing to ignore the territorial dance, he continued.

"Did you have an opportunity to review the security footage?"

"Before we left the station."

"Did you notice anything odd?"

Officer Bell rested her hands on her belt. "No. Why?"

"I think we may be looking for a woman. The person had a slight build and moved more like a female than male. That's why I asked Ellie about the voice."

"Well that isn't conclusive. There are men with small frames," Officer Greene said.

Pad took a new approach. "You're right but I think we should consider all possibilities."

Grudgingly, Greene agreed. "What's your next move, Stone?"

"I'm going to hang around, see if Ellie gets any more phone calls tonight, and tomorrow I'll oversee the security upgrade."

"She's not staying here, is she?" Bell asked. "It's not wise for her to be here alone until we get a better handle on the situation."

"Understood and her parents are staying with her tonight." In addition, I plan on keeping an eye on things. Obviously, this person isn't done yet." Pad flashed a stern look. "I'll keep you up to date on anything that happens and I assume you'll extend me the same courtesy?"

With a mock salute, Greene said, "As per the chief's orders."

Pad waited until they were gone and did a visual sweep of the area before going inside. He hissed under his breath, "You can hide for the moment, but I will get you!"

Pad strode into the room.

Ellie asked, "They're gone?"

Pad looked at the three faces staring at him, fraught

with concern. "Yes, but if anything comes up they said to call."

Cari reached for Ellie's hand. "Pad have you had dinner? We have plenty if you'd like to stay."

"Well that's an offer I can't refuse and it beats eating alone in a restaurant. Thank you, Cari."

"Ellie do you feel up to eating?"

"Mom, of course. I need to be in top form to beat this jerk at their game. The stronger I get, the faster this will be in my rear-view mirror."

Pad nodded while Ellie talked.

"Pad we're going to Scoops for ice cream, well Ray said he was buying if I eat all my dinner."

Pad chuckled. "Scoops? Sounds intriguing."

Ellie laughed. "I guarantee it's the best ice cream in the north east."

The foursome sat down to enjoy what was left of the evening, despite recent events.

Ellie glanced at Pad. "Pad, tell us, you seem to be fairly knowledgeable about security systems and police stuff. This personal experience, is it from the right or wrong side of the law?"

Pad choked on a piece of chicken. Gulping down water, he frantically thought about the best way to answer without giving too much away or opening himself up to a barrage of questions.

"I travel around a great deal, and there have been a few times I've helped out local law enforcement. You can see a lot of detail through the lens of a camera, once you develop an objective eye. It's proven to be helpful to officials a time or two."

"Why did you become a photographer?" Ellie resumed eating.

"After college my job sent me around the world, and I saw some unpleasant things, nothing that should be discussed over this delicious meal." He smiled at Cari and continued. "I picked up a camera as a way to disconnect from the stress of my job, but in doing so I discovered a new way to look at my surroundings, seeing people doing everyday tasks, living life, and the beauty of the countryside. I was inspired to capture it on film, and an old friend encouraged me to show my work to their agent. To my surprise, people were clamoring to have my photos in their homes. I was still working my day job until I was forced to take a leave of absence to fully recover. That's when I decided to do what I really loved, full time. The rest is history as they say."

"You take amazing photos. In fact, there is one of Tuscany I'd like to buy and send to my sister and her husband. Don's family owns a winery in the Finger Lakes region, and it would be perfect for Kate's new restaurant. She's opening after their baby is born."

With a gleam in his eye, Pad said, "I'm sure we can work something out."

Ellie cheeks flushed deep pink.

"Um, thanks."

Pad smirked. "I plan on spending a lot of time here, so I'll help you pack it up later this week. I want to be here when the security company sets up the cameras."

"I don't need a babysitter, Pad. Or for that matter you two." Ellie scowled and pointed at her parents. "It's time everyone gets back to a normal schedule. I'm done dancing to a tune I don't know."

"Ellie be reasonable. You got a threatening phone call less than two hours ago, and yesterday you were knocked unconscious. The next time you might not be as lucky. If I could, I'd wrap you in bubble wrap...you're my baby girl." Her mom's voice cracked.

"I'm sorry you feel this way, Ellie. I've spoken to Chief Booth, and we agree since I have time to hang around I'm going to help out. For your sanity, you might want to agree. It will make it easier for everyone."

Ellie snapped, "I don't take orders from you or anyone. So, you'd better get used to that!"

The tension was thick in the air as two strong-willed people held their ground. Ellie looked up from her plate and smiled sweetly. "Well I guess you can hang around. I could use someone to help me get a few things fixed. That's if you're handy with tools?"

"I've been known to swing a hammer from time to time." Not fooled with the quick about face, he grinned. "I'm at your service, Miss McKenna."

Under her breath, Ellie muttered, "This should be interesting."

7

*E*llie watched the sun's rays go from pinkish-red to brilliant yellow. Sleep had eluded her for the first time in her life. Was this something she had to look forward to—sleepless nights filled with worry? Would she ever feel safe again? Ellie's feet touched the cool, wood floor. Leaving the warmth of the downy soft comforter behind, she hastened through her morning routine. She wasn't supposed to jog yet, but a short, brisk walk down Main Street would be nice. She paused in the hallway. Hearing the gentle sounds of snoring, Ellie tiptoed down the stairs and pushed the front door closed with a soft click.

Ellie drank the fresh morning air deep into her lungs, eyes closed, tilting her head back under the warm sun. The morning breeze teased her skin. A dog barking a few houses over caused her to glance around—nothing wrong with being cautious, she mused. Placing one foot in front of the other, she followed the familiar route, down the brick and cement sidewalk to What's Perkin'. Dani and Luke would be opening the shop soon. Ellie arrived before it was open. The lure of the park was too strong. A loop or two around the perimeter would be a slice of sanity. There were plenty of people out jogging or walking, most of whom would recognize her, and Ellie liked the idea of safety in numbers.

Headache free, Ellie decided to make one last loop before breakfast. Rounding the last corner, she noticed a jogger up ahead. Unnerved, she stopped and pretended to tie her sneaker. From under her ball cap, she kept a watchful eye. There was something vaguely familiar about him. He turned and began to run toward her. Ellie got a good look—Padraic Stone. Well, that explained his physique, she thought. Before he got too close for conversation, Ellie fled. Her head was starting to throb, so it was time to head to What's Perkin'.

The bell above the door jingled as Ellie entered the bright, sun-filled space, a place she had spent more time in as a child than at home. "Good morning, Luke."

"Ellie, it's good to see you." Luke came from the back of the counter and gave her a squeeze.

"Cari told us what happened. It's good to see you're feeling better."

"Thanks, I still have a little headache, but you know me, nothing's going to slow me down." Ellie laughed. "Since you heard about my little incident, you must know Mom and Ray are staying at my place. I thought I'd surprise them and pick up breakfast. I'll take three orders of whatever Dani's whipped up for the daily special and an assortment of muffins."

Luke called out the order to Dani and winked. "I'm assuming you want me to include a few blueberry and chocolate chip?"

"You do know this family well. Chocolate has always been my weakness."

"I should, it's been almost two years." Luke wrapped up a few extra pastries as Ellie passed him her credit card.

Luke frowned. "I'm not supposed to take money from the family."

"Mom isn't here and what she doesn't know won't tick her off."

Ellie jiggled the card. "Please, Luke. Just swipe the card."

Dani came out front with a bag. "Hey, Ellie, here you go."

Ellie peeked inside. "Just couldn't resist adding fruit too. My sister would be proud."

Dani giggled. "I'm carrying out strict orders, when I'm cooking for you, or anyone in the family, I'm to provide you with a balanced meal."

Ellie laughed. "I'll be sure to let Kate know you're providing a full range of fruits and veggies."

"Ellie, would you give your mom a message? Tell her we have everything under control and to enjoy the day with you."

Ellie tucked the credit card into her armband. "Thanks, guys. I'll let her know, and Luke," she pointed at the register, "our little secret, right?"

"I'm certainly not going to rat you out. Cari's tough!"

Ellie laughed and backed up into a muscle-bound wall. She dropped both bags. "Oh shoot, I'm really sorry." Ellie bent over to pick up the bags and didn't notice who towered above her.

A deep voice, smooth like aged whisky, drawled, "Are you okay?"

Ellie stopped mid-sentence and gazed up into deep

amber eyes. "I'm fine, Pad, thank you," Ellie stuttered. "You're up early." Pretending like she hadn't just ignored him in the park.

"Some habits are hard to break, and I like to get my run in early before I get, well, distracted." His eyes studied her face.

Her mouth went dry. "I hear ya. I love running early. The air is crisp, and it's just me and the pavement." Ellie held up the bags. "Can I interest you in breakfast?"

Pad said, "Your mom fed me dinner and now you're offering me breakfast. I'm capable of getting my own meals."

Ellie spoke softly "Oh, I didn't mean anything, just trying to be friendly." She looked up the street. "I need to get home. I'll see you later?"

"You've rescinded the breakfast offer already?" Pad smirked and Ellie saw the twinkle in his eyes.

"You're teasing me?" She lightly punched his arm. "Well if you're hungry let's go. I'm sure everyone is up at my house and wondering where I am."

Pad took the heavier bag and fell in step with Ellie, matching his long stride to her shorter one. The pair strolled down the sidewalk.

"Where are you staying while you're in town?"

"I have a room at the Village Inn. It's pretty comfortable."

"That's a nice place. But rumor is, it's haunted. Have you seen any ghosts?" Ellie tilted her head and looked up.

"Nope, and I don't believe in ghosts, other than on the big screen. I'm a firm believer when people leave this earth they move on to the next plane."

"You don't think souls can get stuck between here and heaven?" Ellie's heart pounded. What would Pad think about her mother, sister, and now her talking to her father's ghost?

"I guess I can't answer that question with one hundred percent accuracy, but, no, I don't think they could."

"Here we are." Ellie bounced up the front steps.

A smile reached her mom's eyes while she clutched Ray's hand.

"Morning!" Pad called out. "I hope you don't mind. I bumped into Ellie and she invited me to breakfast." Pad held up the bag he carried. "I can't take credit but it came from the best eatery in the county."

"Flattery will get you invited to a lot more meals, Pad." Her mom chuckled. "Can I interest you in a cup of coffee?"

"I just finished my run. Any chance I could have a glass of water first?"

Her mom's eyebrow arched. "Ellie, please don't tell me you ran this morning. You know the doctor said to wait until your staples are removed."

"No, I walked, just to stretch my legs." Crossing her fingers across her heart, she said, "Promise."

Ray took the bags from Ellie and Pad. "Are we eating inside?"

Her mom pulled a small, wrought iron table away from the corner. "We can eat out here. It's a gorgeous morning. We don't get many perfect days like today."

Ray set the bags down and went inside to get plates and utensils with Pad following him.

---

*R*ay glanced over his shoulder. "You ran into Ellie in the park?"

"No, she was just coming out of What's Perkin'. I

think it's a good idea for me to spend more time with her. She needs to get comfortable with me hanging around. It's the best way for me to catch this guy before he strikes again."

"I should caution you. Ellie's very intuitive, as are all the McKenna women, and there are times where they know what you're thinking before you do. If Ellie thinks you're hovering, she'd escort you to the door and lock it behind you."

"That is quite an image. I'll remember your advice." Pad gulped down a glass of water and filled it up again. "Does Ellie have someone special in her life?"

"Are you asking if Ellie has a boyfriend?"

Pad shrugged. Not that her relationship status was any of his business, but he wanted, no, he needed to know.

Ray's smile quickly faded. "No, she doesn't, and if you trifle with her emotions you'll answer to me." He glanced at Pad. "I'm sorry if you think I'm coming on too strong. Ellie may not be my biological daughter, but in every way that matters she is my daughter."

"Understood."

Ellie's voice drifted inside. "Ray if you don't get out here, I'm eating your muffins!"

"That's our cue. Ellie is a woman of her word."

Ellie sat with her back to the street. Pad seemed to enjoy the food and company but she noticed his gaze kept straying to the cars passing by.

"Tell me Pad, you've been a bit vague about life before photography. Care to share your deep dark secrets?" Ellie made another attempt to get him to open up. She knew there was more than met the eye and longed to know what made the man tick.

"Really there isn't anything to tell. Other than I observe

human nature through the lens of my camera, catching images to be preserved for eternity."

"Ellie," her mom chided. "If Pad wanted to tell you more, he would."

"Mom, you know how I like to get all the facts and Pad, no disrespect but since you have walked into The Looking Glass, my life has been a little topsy turvy."

With a raised eyebrow, Pad stated, "I get it, but I've found accepting people and getting to know them without a lot of ancient history distorting an opinion is a better option."

"Whatever." Ellie scraped her chair across the deck, "I'm going to take a shower." Glancing at Pad, she said, "What time will you be back as I assume you'll be hanging around?"

Swallowing his laughter, Pad glanced at his phone. "Let's meet here in say," he paused, "an hour."

"Fine." Ellie stomped off and did her best to clomp up the carpeted stairs.

❦

*W*aiting until she was out of hearing range, Cari leaned in. "Ellie wants us to go home and let her handle the situation. Do you think she's safe?"

"That's hard to say. I don't think she should be here alone. I intend on being here a lot, but she'll get suspicious with me hanging around all the time. I've decided I'm going with her to Winnie's."

Ray blinked. "How are you going to pull that off?"

"It's simple. I'd like to meet her. Of course, Ellie will need to call first."

Cari bit her lower lip and then lowered her voice. "I'm

glad she's not going to be on some lonely country road, but what if Mrs. Simpson says no?"

"Trust me, when Winnie asks who Ellie wants to bring out there, she'll say yes."

Pad leaned back in his chair. "Winifred Simpson will be fine with me tagging along. Ellie will take it at face value. While we're together, I'll ask a few questions about the car that's been hanging around here."

Cari crossed her arms. "You seem rather sure of yourself." She glanced at the clock as it struck the hour.

Pad said, "If I'm going to be back in time I need to take off."

Cari waved her hand. "We'll be here when you get back."

With a curt nod, Pad jogged down the walkway and disappeared toward town.

"Ray, I hope we're doing the right thing. Putting our trust in this man."

Ray laid his hand over Cari's. "What is your intuition telling you?"

"That we're on the right track. But Ray, it's my baby girl." A lump filled Cari's throat. "I couldn't bear it if anything else happened to her."

Ray gathered Cari in his arms. "Nothing will happen to her. I promise."

Ellie cleared her throat. "Hello…. You do know I live here, right?" Teasing, Ellie put her arms around them. "Group hug!"

They pulled her in and held on tight.

Cari carefully straightened the hat Ellie was wearing. "Trying to cover the bump?"

"It was hard to blow dry my hair this morning with the staples, so the hat solved a case of bad hair." Ellie stepped inside and peered into the hallway mirror. Grinning she said, "Besides, don't you think I rock this hat?"

"Yes, you do, kiddo." Ray tweaked Ellie's pert nose and turned to his wife. "I need to get to work."

Ray kissed Cari full on the lips.

"See you both at dinner."

Ray hopped into his truck. Giving one last wave, he backed out of the driveway.

"Mom, you two don't have to stay here tonight. I'm sure you miss sleeping in your own bed. I'm fine, really."

"Ellie, I'll sleep better if I'm here. Do you really think I can go home and forget about what happened? I need to know you're safe."

Ellie shook her head. "I don't need a babysitter." Ellie caught sight of Pad coming up the walk. "Speak of the devil. Pad," Ellie called out. "Mom is insisting she's staying again tonight. Tell her I'll be fine."

Pad held up his hands. "I don't think it's my place to get between a mother and daughter. But if you're asking my opinion, I happen to think it's a good idea, at least until we have a better idea what's going on."

Ellie scooped up the last of the dirty dishes. "I thought you'd be on my side!" She stormed into the kitchen.

*P*ad followed Ellie. "Eleanor," he said sharply. "You've already spent one night in the hospital. I'm sure you don't want to have a repeat visit, and the next time you might not be so lucky."

Ellie slammed the cabinet doors shut repeatedly. The assault on dirty dishes was next. Pad leaned against the counter.

Ellie's frustration began to recede. "Padraic, I'm sorry. I've never been the kind of person who wants to be dependent on anyone. This situation makes me feel like I'm disrupting my parents' lives and even yours. Can you understand?"

"More than you think. For now, try not to be pigheaded and let your parents, who care about you, stay."

"Fine." Ellie threw the dishtowel on the counter. "I need to get out to Winnie's."

Pad asked, "Can I tag along? I'd love to meet Mrs. Simpson and check out her studio."

Ellie stopped short. "I don't know if she'd like company." She looked at him out of the corner of her eye. "But if you're serious I guess I could call her."

"Absolutely. I hear her place is amazing. It was her husband's family home, and it was built in the mid eighteen hundreds. Old architecture is fascinating, don't you agree?"

Ellie fiddled with her hat. "You like old houses?"

Pad smiled. "It's one of my secret passions, to purchase an old house and restore it."

"Give me a minute." Ellie watched Pad move around the room, catching his eye from time to time while he checked out various displays.

Pad was impressed. Ellie wasn't an artist, but she had an excellent eye for color and space.

Pad heard Ellie say, "Thanks, Winnie, we'll see you soon."

Ellie tilted her head. "Surprisingly enough, Winnie said she would love to show you her studio. And before you ask I didn't tell her about the painting. I need to do that in person."

"Great, I'll drive."

Ellie pulled herself to all of her just over five-foot stature and announced, "No, I don't think so, but thank you for offering. I'll get my bag and meet you out front."

Ellie saw Pad check his cell and slip it back into his jeans. She escaped to the safety of her bedroom. Ellie paused in front of the mirror. Picking up the blush, she swished on a few strokes. She turned from side to side, pleased with the desperately needed extra touch of color. Typically, she was fair-skinned with rosy cheeks, but with her head starting to throb, her natural color was drained.

"Ready?" Ellie watched Pad pull the door shut, and he gave the handle a push to make sure it was secured.

"Remember Winifred Simpson is famous but doesn't like people to fawn over her. Treat her just like she's an every-day person."

He said, "Of course. I'll treat her like I've known her my entire life."

"Mom," Ellie yelled. "We're leaving."

She popped out from the side of the house and waved enthusiastically, sporting gardening gloves. "Be careful driving and have fun, you two."

Ellie leaned into Pad. "Mom's happiest when she's playing in the dirt, planting flowers or vegetables. Maybe I'll take you out to our house and you can see, she doesn't have a green thumb, she has a green hand."

"I've never done much gardening, but I could take some photos…that's if your mom doesn't mind."

Ellie's hand rested on the door handle of a small SUV. "I'm sure she wouldn't, her roses are stunning. She has a Madame Hardy bush. My grandparents gave her a piece of theirs the year she married my dad. It's a long bloomer and has the most amazing fragrance. The flowers are double-cupped, and have a small green button in the center." Ellie blushed. "Sorry, most people don't find roses to be that interesting. They go into a store and buy them but never take the time to really see the delicate beauty, or learn the history."

"Maybe I'll be here when they bloom."

"We should get going." Ellie slipped behind the wheel and waited for Pad to buckle up.

8

_____

*T*he drive to Winnie's was uneventful. Pad kept a watchful eye but nothing struck him as out of the ordinary. Ellie drove fast, hugging the corners like a race car driver while her passenger enjoyed the view inside the car as much as out.

In contrast, Ellie drove cautiously up a long, tree-lined, brick paved driveway. "To call this a house is an understatement. It's really an estate," she said, peering through the windshield. "Look at the flower beds, they're stunning!"

Pad looked around. "This is beautiful. I enjoy landscaping that doesn't look like it's trying too hard, if you get my drift."

"I agree. Do you think she takes care of the gardens herself?" Ellie jumped when she heard a woman's laughter.

"No, Eleanor, I have someone who takes care of weeding and such, but I do love to dabble in the dirt when I have time. Flowers are excellent subjects for painting."

Winnie kissed Ellie on both cheeks. "It's good to see you." With a twinkle in her eye, she took Pad's hand. "And who is your young man?"

"Winifred Simpson, this is Padraic Stone. He's the man I called you about. Pad happens to be a famous photographer and a new friend."

"Padraic is it. That's an unusual name."

"Please to meet you Mrs. Simpson." Pad grasped her hand in his. "Call me Pad. My friends and family do."

"Well then you can call me Winnie." Her warm smile reached her eyes. "Shall we go inside for some iced tea? I'm sure I have some cookies. We can enjoy them on the back terrace. It's a lovely day."

Ellie looked at the ground. "Winnie, this isn't a social call."

She tugged the large framed painting from the back of her SUV. "I wanted to tell you and show you, in person."

Pad took the unwieldy canvas and carried it towards the house.

Winnie looped her arm through Ellie's. "Whatever is wrong dear can't possibly be as horrible as you think."

"You might want to reserve judgment until you see the painting," Ellie murmured.

Pad waited for Winnie to open the door, and the ladies entered the house first. He stepped into the large foyer and hesitated. "Where can I prop this up?"

"Let's go into the kitchen and you can lay it on the table." Winnie walked down a short hallway and stopped. Pointing down, she said, "Watch your step the floor drops here."

Pad laid the painting on an oversized oak trestle table and stepped back, letting Ellie take over.

"Winnie, I should have called you yesterday, but I didn't know what to say. I'm just heartsick and after seeing this if you want to remove your work from The Looking Glass, I'll completely understand. No hard feelings." Ellie's fingers trembled as she folded the brown paper back to expose the damaged painting.

Winnie fell silent. Turning away she said, "I guess someone didn't appreciate my technique. Let's take our refreshments to the terrace and then you can tell me everything." Winnie busied herself, pouring tall glasses of tea with sprigs of mint. She artfully arranged cookies on a floral plate. "Pad, would you mind carrying the tray?"

Pad took the tray, following their hostess out the French doors. Carefully, he set the tray on the round, glass-topped table and waited for Winnie to take a chair and then Ellie.

Winnie waved her hand at an empty seat. "Please sit. I can see you were raised with impeccable manners."

Ellie began to speak and Winnie held up her hand. "Eleanor, unless you tell me you destroyed the painting, I see no reason to withdraw my support from your lovely establishment. So, we won't speak of that again. But I would like to know what happened."

Ellie perched on the edge of her chair, hands folded in her lap. "I'll try to make the story brief."

"Take your time, I'm in no rush." Winnie gave her a warm, encouraging smile.

"Two nights ago, I was working late in the gallery. I went to close up and someone pushed their way in, knocked me unconscious, and dragged me into a closet. Then they proceeded to ransack the gallery, and I'm sorry to say, they cut your canvas from corner to corner."

"My goodness, are you okay?"

Ellie touched her hat. "When I woke up in the closet, my head was bleeding. I'm not sure how long I was out, but thank heavens Pad stopped by to sign some papers and found me. If it wasn't for him I'm not sure how long I would have been locked in, most likely until morning."

Winnie made soothing sounds and patted Ellie's hand. "You must have been terrified."

Ellie's eyes welled up with tears. "I was scared. But now the most important thing to me is I want to pay for the painting." Ellie bent over and withdrew a check from her bag and handed it to Winnie.

Winnie looked down. "This is from your personal account." She ceremoniously ripped it in half and handed it back to Ellie. "I won't hear of any such thing. I paint for the love of it, not to make money, and I will not accept your generous offer, however I'm impressed by your integrity." Winnie looked at Pad. "What is your part in all of this?"

"Ma'am, I'm helping Ellie upgrade her security system, and I did a little cleaning with her yesterday."

Winnie nodded, obviously pleased with his response. "All good steps. Eleanor?"

"Yes?"

"In my humble opinion, you need to keep Pad around as much as possible. Have him stay in your guest room. If anything like this were to happen again, he would be close by, and with a male present, the intruder might think twice. After all he looks pretty tough to me."

"I can't ask Pad to divert his life to babysit me," Ellie protested. "And I'm fine, my parents are staying with me."

"Pad, what are your plans for the next couple of weeks? Anything that can't be changed?"

Pad said, "I was going to use Loudon as home base

81

and take some day trips for photography. In fact, if you'd agree, I could do a day in the life of an artist? It would keep me close by for Ellie, and I've never seen anything about your life in a pictorial. What do you think, would that work for you?"

"I don't think you should impose on Winnie. She's busy and I'm sure doesn't want someone snapping pictures while she works," Ellie admonished.

Winnie put up her hand. "It's all right, Eleanor. I can speak for myself. I have two conditions."

Pad and Ellie waited.

"Pad, you will put the photos on exclusive display at Eleanor's gallery, and Eleanor, your parents will return to their home with the assurance that Pad will stay with you for the next several weeks."

"But Winnie, I don't think that will work." Ellie chewed her lower lip. "We have our own lives."

"That's my offer, take it or leave it. It will be good for both of your respective careers." Winnie's eyes sparkled. "I can see the press release now,

Reclusive artist's studio unveiled at The Looking Glass.

"Now that will be a high-profile exhibit." Winnie looked at her guests. "I'm not being pompous, but you have no idea how many times I've been approached for something similar and I've turned everyone down. Until now." Winnie gleefully rubbed her hands together. "This will be so much fun. More than I've had in years."

Winnie held up her tea glass to toast. "To our joint venture."

Without hesitation, Pad raised his glass. With an eyebrow arched in a challenge, he said, "To our first joint venture."

Ellie sighed. "To us."

After enjoying a relaxing visit, Ellie was anxious for Winnie to unlock her studio.

As if on cue, Winnie stood up. "I'm sure you must wonder where the images in my head spring to life. Would you like the nickel tour?"

Ellie interrupted, "Shall I bring the damaged painting?"

"I guess we should move it out of the kitchen. Pad, be a dear and carry it for me?" Winnie turned on her heel and ascended the grand mahogany staircase.

Winnie led the way down a long hallway toward a door at the end. Ellie peeked into several lavishly furnished bedrooms and gazed at one closed door. No explanations about what was behind the door were forthcoming.

Grinning, Winnie paused at a set of double doors. Throwing them open, she announced, "Welcome to my haven."

Pad and Ellie stepped into the light-filled space. Large, floor to ceiling windows dominated the exterior walls. Scattered about the room were canvases in various states, some looked finished, others were blank. A large canvas sat on the easel which overlooked the lush rolling lawns. Ellie's mouth fell open. Pad gave her a nudge and she closed it.

"I never dreamed it would look well, chaotic. Do you spend a great deal of time here?" Ellie whispered reverently.

"I do, except when a few friends or my nephew comes to visit. Otherwise, I spend up to ten hours a day immersed in colors."

"I had no idea you would need so many things to

paint." Ellie's fingers trailed the length of a long counter, pausing to look at tubes of paints, brushes, and mysterious containers. Large bolts of linen lined one wall and lengths of board were carefully stacked on open shelves.

Ellie glanced at Pad. "Have you ever seen anything like this?"

"I think at some point in time I've been inside a room very similar. It's overwhelming to the non-painter." Pad crossed the room. "What are you working on now?"

Winnie stood beside him. "I love flowers. A few weeks ago, I went to Harvey Park and took pictures of the rose gardens." She smiled at Pad. "Nothing like you would take, but have you been to the park?"

"I don't believe I have." Pad frowned at Winnie. "Do I need to see the gardens to appreciate your paintings?"

Hearing the tone in Pad's voice, Ellie rushed over. "Pad I've seen them and they're stunning. I'm sure Winnie was just trying to be polite." Ellie gave an apologetic smile to the older woman.

"Eleanor, its nothing, I was just reminiscing how romantic they can be. If my husband were still alive, he'd say I fell in love with him in that very park." With a pat of Pad's arm, she crossed the room to where Ellie had been looking at the fabric.

"Did you know I make all my own canvases? Someday I'll bore you with the process. But if you both will excuse me I do need to get back to work. Do you think you can find your way out?"

Ellie stuttered. "Of course, we can. I'm sorry if we took up too much of your time."

"Not at all dear, I enjoyed your visit and I hope you both can come again soon for a purely social call." With a slight nod of her head, she continued. "Pad, I'll look forward to working together."

"I will as well." He paused. "Winnie."

Winnie leaned it to give Ellie a kiss on each cheek. "Eleanor, I know the incident with the painting upset you, but please remember things can be replaced, people can't."

With that, Winnie closed the door to her inner sanctum.

9

*E*llie and Pad chatted easily on the drive back to town. Since Winnie coerced them into being roommates, even if it was just for a few weeks, they wanted to learn more about each other.

"Where did you grow up?" Ellie spoke as she sped down the long driveway. "Your past seems to be pretty mysterious."

"There isn't much to tell. I grew up an only child with terrific parents. They lived in Virginia."

"Was it lonely growing up without brothers or sisters? I can't imagine what life would have been like without Shane or Kate teasing me, being there for me, and they helped me get through the best and worst times of my childhood." Ellie stared straight ahead as tears hovered on her lashes.

"Were you very young when your father passed away?"

Pad's gentle tone almost caused the flood gates of tears to open.

"I was five. He had a brain aneurysm and that was it. I

never got the chance to say goodbye. It took us a long time to get past the gaping hole in our family." Ellie shrugged. "Maybe you never really do; you just get used to the emptiness. Kind of like a scab on a really bad cut. It gets hard but then something snags it, you bleed and feel the pain again. Over time it gets less and less."

"I'm sorry. It's never easy to lose a loved one but when you were so small, well I can't imagine. Ray seems like a great guy. I can tell by the way you guys talk to each other there is mutual respect and love. When did he and your mom get married?"

"Ray and his son Jake lived next door to us for as long as I can remember. Shane and Jake were best buds. As single parents, I think they were a support system for each other. Then a few years ago Ray's ex-wife came to town and long story short, she held him at gunpoint. Mom wrestled her to the ground but during the struggle, Ray was shot. While he was in the hospital, Mom realized she was in love with him and vice versa. It was all very romantic. A few months later they were married and we became one big, happy family that's living happily ever-after."

"That's a great story, I mean, not the part where Ray was shot but that your mom and Ray found each other. What happened to the ex-wife?"

"Apparently, Vanessa, Ray's ex, thought she killed her husband Stan, and came here expecting Ray to provide her with an alibi. It turns out she is suffering from bi-polar disorder. I don't think anyone has seen her since she went to jail, not even Jake. Vanessa won't allow any visitors."

Ellie glanced at Pad. "You know, I'd give anything to have just one more minute with my father, and Vanessa could see her son and her grandchildren but she's cut all ties. I never could figure out how Ray could have married someone so cold-hearted. He's such a good man."

Pad shook his head. "It takes all kinds of people to make up the human race. Some people, like Vanessa, are cold and distant. In my experience, most times, they're the most fragile. Keeping themselves isolated prevents them from feeling emotions. You'd be surprised to what lengths people will go to protect themselves."

Ellie gave him a hard look. "Are you talking from personal experience?"

Pad raised his eyebrows. "I have the feeling we have that in common, Ellie. You are an independent woman, and other than your family, you keep yourself at a safe distance from emotional noise. You avoid relationships and bury yourself in work. You have friends but you don't let anyone get too close, feeling in control makes you feel safe."

Ellie snapped back, "Who are you to make assumptions about my personal life? And for the record, I have friends and if I choose, I would have a relationship. At the moment, I'm busy getting The Looking Glass in the black."

Pad looked out the window. "I'm sorry, Ellie. I didn't mean to poke my nose into your business."

Ellie parked the car and leaned back in the seat. She exhaled slowly. "I'm sorry. I'm a little touchy today. Maybe it's a delayed reaction from the other night. Apology accepted."

Ellie stretched out her hand. "Friends?"

Pad gently took her small hand. "Friends," he said, giving it a light caress.

Ellie's hand warmed to his touch. "Um, I'm going inside." Pushing open the door, she looked at him, her brow creased. "Are you coming?"

"Well you heard Mrs. Simpson. I'm supposed to be your bestie now. Do you think we should call your mother?"

"No, have dinner with us tonight, and we'll fill them in. You can start babysitting duty tomorrow. Mom won't mind fussing over me for one more night." Ellie's face was tight.

"Let's start beefing up your security system, checking with the police and if you're comfortable being alone, I'll go for a short run and check out the neighborhood, what seems normal and what doesn't."

Ellie nodded, her blue eyes wide. "Do you think whoever it was will be back soon?"

"I don't want to alarm you, but yes this is a serious situation."

Squaring her shoulders, Ellie marched inside, with a flip of her head. She saw Pad watching her. "Well? We have work to do!"

❦

*T*hinking of all the things he would like to say to this spitfire, Pad held his tongue. Pad stopped short on the top step. The hair on the back of his neck prickled. This hadn't happened to him in a very long time —not since he left the agency. Casually looking around he muttered, "Make no mistake, I will find you and you will be held responsible for what you've done."

"Pad," Ellie called out from an upper window. "Did you say something?"

"Nothing important. Hey, I'm starving can I raid the fridge?"

Laughter answered him. "Make me a snack too. I'll be right down."

Pad stood in front of the refrigerator. What the heck? Chick food. How could he pull together a decent snack with cottage cheese, yogurt, and fruit? Peering into the freezer, he was thrilled to see a pint of ice cream, and wait, happiness in a box, a meat-lovers frozen pizza. He turned the oven on and rooted in the cabinets for a sheet pan. Not finding one, he decided to slide it in on the rack—crispy crust was better anyway, he thought.

The first thing Pad noticed when Ellie padded into the kitchen, was her bare toes sporting deep pink polish.

"What did you find, I'm starving?" Ellie dropped the box in the trash. "Pizza. That's more like lunch and not a snack."

"I'm a man and need a man-sized snack. By the look of your food supply, we're going to need a grocery store run. This man can't survive on yogurt alone." He grinned and held up a pad. "I've started a list. Feel free to add what you want. When I go back to the inn to shower, I'll stop by the store."

Ellie stole the pad. "Well this looks packed with nutrition, chips, roast beef, bread, ice cream. No fruit?"

"I'll get strawberry ice cream. That counts, right?"

Ellie just shook her head. "Mind if I go with you? I don't need lots of junk food hanging around. I might just dive in head first and come up for air with five extra pounds."

Pad looked her up and down. "You'd wear it well."

He could see Ellie squirm under his gaze and a flush crept over her cheeks staining them crimson.

The timer buzzed. "It's ready," she said.

An idea flitted through Pad's brain. Could the attraction be mutual? "I'll grab the plates." He pulled open the cabinet and took out two plates and glasses and then guessed correctly which drawer held forks.

Taking them from Pad, Ellie set the table and then proceeded to cut the pizza into quarters. "I should warn you I have a huge appetite and won't politely give up the last piece unless I'm full."

"Duly noted, Miss McKenna and if need be we can always split the last slice."

Pad waited until she sat down.

A string of melted cheese slid onto Ellie's chin. "Wow this is cheesy." Before she could say anything more, the front door banged open. "Excuse me for a minute." Ellie pushed back her chair.

Pad hovered at the door, listening before curiosity drove him out front.

Ellie was escorting a man of slight build and red hair flecked with gray, around the shop. "As you can see we have art in many forms on display. I've taken the opportunity to feature the artists at various stages in their careers. Some are unknown, as is the sculptor Jeremey Case, to the very well-known Winifred Simpson."

The man nodded enthusiastically. "You have an eclectic space and I must say, somehow it seems to work."

Pad stood to one side. The man fawning over Ellie seemed vaguely familiar, but Pad couldn't recall where he had seen him.

The newcomer glanced at the front door and then to Pad. "Does that gentleman work for you? He seems a bit out of place with the art."

Ellie patted a tweed, suit coat covered arm. "No, he's a friend, but I will be displaying his photos in this section." Ellie gestured to an empty space. "Mr. Stone captures the human element in his work. This exhibit will be simply titled, 'Life in Motion.'"

"Ah, I see." Stuttering, he said, "Well if you will excuse me I must be going."

With a potential customer walking out the door, Ellie piped up, "May I take your contact information so I can add you to my mailing list? Mister...? I'm sorry I didn't catch your name."

"No, I don't think so. I don't like to be barraged with junk mail. However, I will keep an eye on the newspaper, and if there is something that interests me, I'll be back." With an old-fashioned dip of his head, the man hastily left the shop.

"Well he's seems like an odd little man, don't you think?"

Ellie and Pad watched from the door as the man hurried down the walkway and disappeared around the corner.

Pad said, "He does and he was a little over dressed for this time of year. Strange, I feel like we've met before."

Pad stepped onto the front porch and studied the street. After several long minutes, Pad returned to the kitchen. "I'm sorry I was trying to catch a glimpse of the car that man drove."

"For heaven sakes, why? He was just an odd little man with faded red hair and a fuchsia handkerchief sticking out of his breast pocket, and well, tweed this time of year, I'll admit is not something you see every day. It's not a big deal and you'll see lots of people just like that coming and going just browsing."

"If you say so, but I'll feel better once the new system has been installed and is fully operational." Pad gave Ellie a stern look. "And promise me that it will be on at all times."

"Of course, it will be, not to worry. Jeez you sound just like Shane." Ellie chomped on her second slice. "If you don't start eating you're going to leave hungry. Good news for you, there is always plenty at dinner." Ellie hopped up. "I forgot to call Mom, be right back." She dashed out front to find her cell phone. "Um, Pad? Can you come here a sec?" Ellie's voice was shrill.

"What's the matter?" Pad's eyes surveyed the shop, scanning for something amiss.

"Look!" Ellie pointed at the desk. "On the stack of papers." She slipped behind Pad.

Snorting, Pad walked over and said, "What, the spider?"

"It's not just any spider, it's a brown recluse. They're poisonous." Ellie shuddered. "And I hate spiders. Kill it!"

Pad grabbed a rolled-up newspaper and slammed down, obliterating the arachnid. He lifted his weapon of choice and pulled Ellie towards the desk. "See, he's dead."

Ellie's voice quivered. "I wonder how he got in here. I have the exterminator come every three months, just so I don't have to deal with crawling things."

"More than likely, he didn't see you had rolled up the welcome mat." Pad grabbed the remains into a tissue and started to throw it in the garbage.

"No!" she cried. "Don't throw him in there, you have to flush him down the toilet. Just in case he comes back to life."

Glancing at Ellie, Pad noticed the terror lingered in her saucer-sized eyes. "Okay, I'll give this critter a proper water burial."

Using a pencil, Ellie pushed papers around on her desk before picking up the phone.

"Hey, Mom, I'm not sure what you're making for dinner but we're having one more. Pad is staying," she announced.

"See you later." Ellie disconnected. She placed another call.

Ellie frowned and said, "Hello, this is Eleanor McKenna, owner of The Looking Glass on Main Street. I'd like to schedule an emergency appointment with the exterminator. I found a brown recluse spider in my shop, and if a customer found it that would be extremely bad for business. If someone could come today perfect, if not I must insist someone is here tomorrow." Ellie left her cell number and hung up. Pad was leaning against the door jamb.

"Spiders really scare you, huh?"

"You have no idea. When I was a little girl, Mom was taking us to the lake. I was in the back seat and Shane was in the front. I felt something on my leg, and when I reached down to scratch it, I saw a huge spider. I started stamping my feet on the floor and screaming at the top of my lungs. I think it scared Mom half to death. She pulled over and I was sobbing and scrambled out of the car as fast as I could. I wouldn't get back in the car until she said it was dead."

"How do you know she killed it?"

Ellie folded her arms across her heaving chest. "Because she had it squished in a tissue." Reliving the terror made her head ache.

Pad found himself longing to pull her into his arms and reassure her that she'd never have to be frightened of

94

anything again. Shaking his head, he pushed the image away.

Ellie took a deep breath and dropped her arms next to her sides. "I'm sure I sound unreasonable and ninety-nine percent of the time they don't bite. I just don't like the creepy crawling sensation of all those legs." Ellie stood tall. "I'm sure you have something you're scared of too," she challenged.

Softly, he said, "Everyone has an Achilles heel, El." Without elaborating Pad reached out to touch her cheek. "As long as I'm around, I promise to kill all spiders and dispose of them properly."

"I appreciate that, now let's talk to a man about a security system." Pointing out the van in the driveway, she said, "They're here."

Pad's smile was slow and easy. "Spiders and security systems are my specialty of the day, Miss." Giving a half bow, Pad left Ellie sitting at the desk.

.

10

*E*llie tossed and turned, unable to sleep. The back of her head ached a bit, but she knew that wasn't the real issue. She threw the covers aside and then padded to the window seat, grabbing a robe. She settled onto the cushion. Moonlight surrounded her in a soft comforting glow.

Watching the leaves on the trees stirred by a light breeze, she thought, why isn't Mom upset that I've invited a virtual stranger to live in my house? Ellie replayed the dinner conversation over again. Her mother had been completely at ease hearing Pad was taking up residence even offering to help make up the other guest room for him. Ray had interjected once and told Pad to let them know if he needed anything. Pad grinned like he had won the lottery.

I wish I hadn't agreed to this arrangement with Winnie. Ellie rolled her shoulders and neck while watching a cat skulk across the lawn.

"Hi, little one." A voice as smooth as warm milk and honey floated in the air.

Ellie jumped. "Daddy?" she cried.

"Yes, Honey, it's me. I thought you could use some company." Her father crossed the room in his fashion and perched on a small wooden chair near Ellie. "You seem troubled. Would you like to talk about it?"

"I thought you were a figment of my imagination brought on by the head injury. However, since I'm fully awake, it's safe to say you're, sort of, real." Ellie focused on the soft outline of her father. "You don't really look like how I remember."

"You were so very young when I died. At that age, it is hard to store a memory. I can assure you I'm as real as you want me to be."

"Do you know how I got into this mess? Well you know what happened the other night." Tears dampened her cheeks. "Why did you leave me? One minute we were talking and the next, you abandoned me, again."

"I never left you, I stopped talking. Your friend came and found you. I knew you were safe. If it makes you feel better, I stayed until they took you to the hospital."

"You did? But I couldn't see you." Ellie's voice cracked. "Why didn't you ever come back before now? There have been so many times I needed you. Did you know I cried myself to sleep every night when I was little? Praying I could have just one more day with you."

Ellie turned away, hiding the raw emotion that bubbled just under the surface of her tough exterior. "Kate and I knew you came to Mom all the time. Shane never really believed it, but we did."

"I was trying to help your mother move on with her life. My death crippled her in so many ways. I wasn't able to come to you until you really needed me, for something more than mere comfort. You had your mother and grand-parents to fill the void."

"Do you think they could take your place? I needed you!" Her temper erupted. "Do you think making an appearance now makes up for the last nineteen plus years?" Ellie stood up quickly, and a wave of dizziness washed over her. "Well it doesn't!" Ellie grasped the wall for balance.

"Eleanor, please I don't have much time left. I need to talk about why I was pulled to you, now. We can rehash the past another time." Dad began to fade. "There are things you must know. Things I can help you understand if you'd give me a chance."

"Daddy, I loved you with all my heart, and it broke when you died." Her voice cracked. "Then when I was older and really understood you came to Mom, and only Mom, pain filled my heart again. Lastly, when you appeared to Kate, one more time my heart broke. How many times do you think I can take you leaving me? Needing you to be in my life has left this huge gaping wound, and I just can't keep bleeding. I won't allow myself to ever open my heart to the potential of love, only to be left with searing pain. I just won't." Crossing her arms over her heart, Ellie pulled herself to all of five feet two inches. "You can come back or not, either way it won't change anything."

"Oh, Pixie." Dad spoke her childhood name in a whisper and was gone.

Frantically, Ellie searched the shadowy corners of the room. "Daddy, where are you? Don't leave me…"

Flinging herself across the bed, a river of tears flowed from the depths of a daughter's broken heart.

*C*ari woke with a start and felt a light breeze on her cheek. She glanced at the window but the curtains were still. Carefully sitting up, not to disturb Ray, she heard the sounds of muffled crying. She slipped out of bed and tiptoed down to Ellie's door. Pausing on the threshold, she listened. Without knocking, Cari entered the moonlit room.

"Sweetheart?" Cari pulled Ellie into the warmth of her arms.

"Mommy, I can't do this anymore."

Murmuring under her breath she smoothed Ellie's hair. "What are you talking about?"

"Daddy. He was here and left me again. He always leaves me. What did I do to make him go away?"

"Oh Honey, he didn't leave you. He was taken from us before he was ready. He comes back as he has unfinished business with you." Cari continued to hold Ellie as if she were a shattered porcelain doll.

"But Daddy used to come and talk to you all the time. He never came to me until a few nights ago."

"I think you're forgetting all the years he came to me I was very withdrawn, and I'd built an impenetrable shell around myself. I wouldn't allow myself to have a relationship, until Ray. Once we married, your father's visits stopped. It was time for him to move on just as I had done. Then, two years ago, he went to Kate. She was slowly destroying her marriage, and he helped Kate realize life was precious and what she really wanted out of this life was Don. I don't think he's visited Kate since she moved to Crescent Lake."

"How come Shane has never seen Dad?"

"I think the McKenna women are more sensitive. If Shane had the opportunity, I'm sure he would welcome the chance at one more conversation with Dad. But at least for now that's not in the cards."

Soft hiccups peppered the night air. Cari waited for Ellie to dry her tears. "Do you think you can sleep now?"

"I'll try. Do you think Daddy will come back? I was a real brat and told him I had a broken heart and I didn't want to talk to him. It just made everything worse."

"If there is one thing I know for sure, your father won't give up until he's finished what he started. Your dad has a single purpose and until you know what it is, be prepared for him to just pop in at any given time. Usually it will be when you're receptive. At least that's how it happened for me. I'm not sure about Kate. We never talked about the specifics."

Ellie was quiet for a time and said, "I hope he comes back. I wasn't very nice. At least I can apologize, even if he's a ghost I'm sure he has feelings."

Cari said, "I'm sure he'll be delighted to get an apology." Early streaks of the sunrise were bathing the walls in light. "Even if he is a ghost." She pulled the covers back and tucked the blankets around Ellie.

"You don't have to treat me like I'm a baby, Mom."

"You'll always be my baby. I know you have a tender side, even if you pretend to be tough. I'll soothe your hurts as often as I can." She kissed Ellie's cheek. "Pixie, sometimes everyone needs some tender loving care from their mom."

"Mom?"

"Yes Pixie?"

"I love you very much and thanks for sitting with me." Ellie rolled over and promptly fell asleep.

Cari watched her baby girl sleep. An owl hooted at what was left of the moon. Silently, Cari retraced her steps down the hall.

*W*hen Ellie woke, the sun was streaming in the windows, and the air had a touch of humidity. Stretching, Ellie glanced at the clock. It was barely eight. Wondering why her alarm hadn't gone off, Ellie walked into the bathroom and took a hot shower to ease out the kinks. She carefully chose her outfit, wanting to look nice but not like she was trying too hard. Pleased with the sleeveless cotton blouse and a flower print wrap skirt, she skipped barefoot down the back stairwell, the smell of coffee welcoming her into the kitchen.

Making an entrance, she called out, "Good Morning."

"Good Morning, sleepyhead," Ray said as he walked to the coffee pot. "Have a seat. Mom went down to the café, and so I thought I'd stay and have breakfast with you." Ray winked and passed Ellie a mug. "It's rare when I get time alone with my favorite Pixie."

"Ray, I'm sure you have a job, somewhere."

"Jake has everything under control, and I hired a helper so I have plenty of time to spare. Remember Mom and I are getting ready for semi-retirement."

"This smell good." Ellie grinned as Ray set a plate of crispy bacon, scrambled eggs, and toast in front of her.

"I hope the eggs aren't too dry. I tried to time it perfectly once I heard the shower turn off." Ray sat down and picked up his fork. Seeing Ellie staring at the plate, he asked, "Is something wrong?"

"No. I was just thinking if my dad was still alive would he have wanted to have breakfast with just me."

"I'm not sure where this is coming from, but your dad was a close friend. He was a good man and he loved each one of his children deeply. He would have been over joyed to have breakfast with his little girl, no matter how old she was."

"You don't have to say nice things to make me feel better, Ray. But I appreciate it anyway." Ellie's smile was tight.

"You know I never had girls, but I think of you and Kate as my daughters and I couldn't love you more if I was your real dad."

Ellie laid her hand over his. "You're a great dad and I'm lucky Mom chose you to be a part of our family. Maybe we should eat breakfast before it gets totally cold."

The sounds of a slamming car door drifted in from the driveway. "Who in the world is here now?" Ellie pushed open the back door and chuckled. "How much stuff are you bringing? This was supposed to be for a few days."

Pad held a cardboard box perched on one hip and a large duffel bag slung over his shoulder. "Would you mind?" He handed Ellie a small black bag.

Ellie grabbed the handles and stepped inside.

Ray jumped up. "Hey, let me give you a hand." Setting the box on the floor, he said, "Do you have more in the car?"

"Yeah, there's a backpack and my camera equipment." With a twinkle in his eye, he winked at Ellie. "I figured there was no sense in keeping my room when I'll be staying here for the foreseeable future. You don't mind, do you?"

"Me? Mind? You need your stuff. To be honest I still don't understand why we agreed to Winnie's scheme."

"I get the distinct impression what Winnie wants, Winnie gets." Standing in the midst of his stuff, he shrugged. "Any chance you can point me towards my room? I'd like to stow my gear."

"Sure, follow me." Leading the way up the back stairs and down a short hallway, she stopped at a large airy room overlooking the back yard. "I thought you might like this one. It has a nice breeze and it's quieter than the others." Ellie opened an adjoining door. "This is the bathroom."

Pad dropped the duffel bag and placed another bag which Ellie presumed to be a computer on the bed.

"Where's your bedroom?"

Ellie's eyebrow arched. "My room overlooks the front yard. I love the morning sun."

"Good to know." Pad glanced around the room. "I'll bring up the rest of my stuff and get settled. Then I'll fix some breakfast if you don't mind."

"Not at all, in fact there's plenty of coffee in the pot and make yourself at home. As you know the refrigerator is stocked."

"Thanks, El. I'll be down in a bit."

Ellie withdrew from the room and liked how the house hummed with Pad's presence. Slowly she walked down the stairs to discover Ray taking a mug out of the microwave.

"Hand me your coffee and I'll nuke it."

Ellie handed off the cup. "Do you think this is a good idea?"

"What, the coffee?" Ray asked.

Ellie jerked her head toward the stairs and hissed, "No. Pad."

"I think it's the best possible solution. You want your mom and me to go home. The police haven't found the guy who broke in and Pad seems more than capable of taking care of himself, and we'd feel better having this guy hang his hat here."

"How do you know he's okay? We don't know him," Ellie whispered through clenched teeth. "Why don't you guys think that maybe he's the bad guy."

Ray let out a hearty chuckle. "Did you forget how your mother operates? She called Hank Booth and had him checked out. If Hank said he's okay that's good enough for us and should be for you as well."

Grudgingly, Ellie relented. "If you say so I'll stop complaining. But I don't have to like it."

Ellie heard footsteps thump down the stairs and then Pad appeared in the kitchen. "The mugs are...?"

Ellie pointed to the cabinet next to the sink. "Over there. When you're done make sure you load the dishwasher," she snapped. "I'm not picking up after you."

Grinning, Pad bowed low. "Fear not, fair maiden. I'll be so tidy you'll think I'm a ghost, not leaving any evidence of my presence."

Ellie visibly grew pale at the mention of a ghost.

Pad touched her arm. "I'm sorry, did I say something to upset you?"

Ellie shook her head. "No. I have a bit of a headache," she fibbed.

Ray interjected, "How about I whip up some fresh eggs? I can take the cold ones to Gifford." He continued, "You have to meet my dog, Pad. He's a big lump of fur and thinks he's a sixty-pound lap dog."

Ellie, who was beginning to regain color, heard Pad reply, "I love dogs. While I'm in town maybe I'll get the chance." Pad steered Ellie to a chair. "Why don't you have a seat and eat something, it might help you feel better."

Giving him a wan smile, she said, "Yeah, I guess." She held the coffee mug to her lips and took a small sip. "Relax, I'm fine."

Ray set two plates on the table and handed a jar of salsa to Ellie. "A little spice will put the pink in your cheeks, Kiddo."

Pad chuckled. "Better leave some for me. Salsa and eggs are a must, but please tell me it's at least medium heat?"

Ellie passed him the jar with a spoon sticking out. "Hot," she challenged. "If you're going to spice things up, might as well really kick it up."

"I couldn't agree with you more. If this keeps up we're going to be great roommates." Pad scooped up a forkful. "After we eat what do you want to do?"

"I have phone calls to make and you need to start thinking about hanging a few more photos in the shop. After that, maybe we can talk about the photo-shoot at Winnie's. I'd like to set that up soon. I'm closed on Tuesday and Wednesday each week, so I'd like to pencil it in for next week if you're game. If not the following week for sure."

Pad nodded as she ticked off ideas for the shoot. "I'll need bright days to do the garden shots. I know Winnie says someone does the bulk of the work, but if I were a betting man I'd say she likes to get her hands really dirty. Gardens don't have that kind of grandeur without some serious hands-on work daily and usually it's from the owner. I've seen gardens that are left to professionals.

They're impersonal and too perfect looking. These have a personal touch."

"You might be right. I wonder if she'll let me have another large painting on consignment. You know to replace 'Waterfall' that was the centerpiece of her display."

"Give her a call and ask. All she can say is no, right?" Pad scraped his plate clean while Ellie frowned and pushed her eggs around the plate.

"Gimme a break, I was starving."

"Don't think you're going to eat my breakfast."

Ray watched as the two bantered and plotted. "Well if you kids don't mind I'm going to head out. I want to check on Jake, and there are a couple of new jobs I need to quote." He dropped a kiss on Ellie's head careful to avoid her staples. "If you need something call my cell and Mom is just down the street." Ray shook Pad's hand. "Keep an eye on things here and we'll talk later."

After Ray was out of earshot, Ellie poked Pad in the arm. "What did he mean to keep an eye on things? Is there something going on that I don't know about?"

"I'm not sure what you mean. I'm here to keep unsavory characters from darkening your door."

"I guess, but I think there is more to this story. Something doesn't add up." Ellie carried dishes to the sink and began to load the dishwasher, wheels turning. She spun around and demanded, "Are you a cop?"

11

*S*he was closer to the mark than Pad wanted. "No, I'm not a cop. I'm a photographer who happened to be in the right place at the right time. Based on a request from your parents, and your new patron Winifred Simpson, I'm hanging around for a little pro-bono bodyguard work. I have the time, and my travel schedule allows me to go where and when I want."

He peered out the window. "I'm going to run upstairs and get my camera bag. I want to go to the park, and I need to make sure I have all the right lenses and such." Pad ducked up the stairs before Ellie could hammer him with additional questions.

Pad shuffled his bags around to make some noise, just in case Ellie came snooping up the stairwell—his story needed to hold water. "Ray's right, she's pretty intuitive," he mused. "How do I keep tap dancing around the topic of my past when we're going to be in close quarters?"

Slinging two bags over his shoulder, he wandered down the hall to the top of the front stairs, taking the opportunity to get the layout of the second floor. He paused at the partially open doorway, Ellie's room. The feelings that caught him off guard when he laid her on the bed and discovered her head bleeding surfaced. It was as if they were kindred spirts. Pushing them aside, he noticed the linens were different and surmised the blood had caused a permanent stain. Pulling the door back to the original position, he quietly walked down the broad staircase.

*E*llie was perched on a stool, intent on the screen, muttering to herself. "So many unanswered questions, Pad Stone. How could anyone not have a digital footprint? Everyone was on the Internet somewhere, other than his darn website."

"You won't find any dirt on me, Eleanor, at least not online." Pad spoke, his voice deepening with each measured word.

Ellie quickly closed the browser. "I was just checking the long range weather forecast. To see if next week might work…" Ellie's words trailed off as her excuse sounded hollow even to her ears. "Besides, you must think pretty highly of yourself if you think I'd waste precious time stalking you on the internet."

Pad gave a hearty laugh. "It's not how I think of me, but you're a very inquisitive person by nature and to not have every last question about me answered is driving you bonkers." Pad set his bags down on a long, wooden trestle table and began to spread the contents over the polished surface. "If you want to know the person behind the camera, you should take the time to get to know me. I think you'll find the personal touch more satisfying than anything you'd find on a computer." With a wicked grin, he said, "Who knows you might even come to like me."

Flushing bright pink, Ellie felt an unexpected quickening of her heart. His eyes. They're different every time I look at him: amber, copper, almost wolf-like. I'd like to run my fingers through all that dark wavy hair...

Pad's cell phone buzzed, snapping Ellie out of her fantasy. She watched him step outside to take the call.

Ellie peeked her head out and heard, "Stone here." She returned to her desk.

Deliberately not asking about the phone call, Ellie said, "Do you mind if I tag along with you this afternoon? I'd like to walk since I still can't run per doctor's order. My body's turning to mush from lack of movement."

"You don't look like your morphing into a blob, but sure, I'd love the company. Maybe you can point out interesting spots that might make for some good shots."

"Do you like boats?"

"Yeah, I love being on the water." Pad's eyes widened. "Why, do you own a boat? You don't strike me as the boating type.

"I don't but my brother has a small boat docked at his house. I'm sure we could borrow it; you might get some great shots of the cranes."

"That sounds like fun. It's a date." Pad started to walk toward the door and stopped in his tracks. Ellie wasn't walking with him. "What's the matter, do you see something?" Pad twirled around, his eyes scanning the street.

"Ah, no. I didn't see anything." Ellie croaked, her mouth dry as a desert. "I'm fine."

Pad looked at Ellie. He put out a steadying hand. "Are you sure? We were talking about the boat and you went pale. If you're not a fan, we can skip it."

Ellie wasn't about to admit the word "date" in conjunction with Pad caused her knees to knock. "I'm not feeling well. I'm going to go upstairs and rest for a while. Would you mind keeping an eye on things?"

🍷

*P*ad watched Ellie run up the main staircase, to the safety of her room. "She isn't moving like she doesn't feel well. I wonder…"

The remainder of the morning was uneventful. Pad readied his equipment and placed a few phone calls, canceling hotel reservations that were booked for the next month. He had been in the police business long enough to know cases were never solved like on television. It took time to ferret out the unsavory characters in the game of life. Around lunchtime, Ellie found her way back downstairs.

"I'm going to make a sandwich. Would you like something?" Pad waited for Ellie to look up from her laptop. "Earth to Eleanor McKenna." Pad tapped the top of the screen.

"Sorry, I was looking at this footage online about spiders. You know like the one you killed?"

"And, what did you find out?"

"First, they are not native to the Northeast, so it is highly unlikely it was a brown recluse. Second, they only have six legs, not eight. There are a bunch of common spiders that people often mistake for the brown recluse but aren't. So basically, we may have over reacted, and now I'm wishing you hadn't given it a water burial so we could take a closer look." Ellie pointed to her screen. "See the map? I think we were safe."

"Good to know. We should stop discussing spiders and talk about lunch. Are you hungry?"

Ellie stretched her arms high above her head. "Are you good at making sandwiches?"

"Depends on your definition of good," Pad teased. "You'll never go hungry when I cook."

"Well then, lead the way and I'll judge your skill."

Pad pulled out deli meat, cheese, and bread from the refrigerator and Ellie grabbed some vegetables and pickles. She passed them to Pad before grabbing plates and glasses and setting them on the counter.

"Why don't you sit and I'll take it from here." Pad glanced at Ellie. "I'm concerned you're still experiencing headaches. Have you thought about calling the doctor and get checked out? Maybe your head injury was more severe than he thought."

Ellie waved her hand. "I'm fine. It was just a momentary thing. Once I laid down for a few minutes it went away. I think it is stress from the situation as opposed to the injury."

Pad's eyes narrowed. "I thought we'd head over to the park around four. Does that work?"

Ellie picked up a plate overflowing with a sandwich and chips. "You forgot the pickle." She held her plate out while Pad pushed the chips into a pile and placed two large dill pickles on the side.

Ellie took a seat. "Four's good. I was thinking starting next week I should stay open until six, and open at eleven. I think those would be better hours. What do you think?"

Pad tipped his head to one side. "If you want my input, you'd capture lunch time and after work shoppers, which is good for customers. I've never really been much of a shopper. But if I had a regular job having someplace open after five might help me out if I needed to pick up a gift."

"This afternoon Victor, the potter, will be by with a few pieces to replace the broken vases, and I'm going to insist he take a check. I've filed the insurance paperwork so no matter what, Victor needs to be paid."

"That is admirable and good business ethics."

"Well if the insurance doesn't come through, paying the artists will eat away at my savings, but if the shoe was on the other foot, it's what I would hope a business owner would do for me." Ellie shrugged her shoulders. "I never expected something to happen so soon. I don't think I can afford it if the insurance company raises my rates. But, there's nothing I can do about it. I'll just have to wait and see."

Pad crunched a chip. "Seeing the way you feel about your artists confirms what I felt the first time I met you."

"Oh, and what's that?"

"You're the kind of person I can trust, and I believe the others are going to feel the same way. We've put our trust in you and you're delivering. You're a good person, Miss McKenna."

Color flooded Ellie's cheeks. "Stop, you're going to embarrass me."

"You're cute when you blush."

Ellie gobbled the last of her sandwich and hastily put her plate in the sink. "If we're going to be out of here at four I'd better get busy." The door buzzed and for the first time, Ellie was grateful they had installed the noisy thing. "Gotta go." She fled the room.

"Hello, Victor." Ellie greeted the older man wearing spattered pants and shirt holding a wooden crate in his hands. "Please, come in. I'm happy to see you. I wasn't sure you'd be back given recent circumstances."

"I was sorry to hear you were hurt and despite the trouble I wanted you to have a few more pieces." Victor set the crate on the floor and unloaded four new pieces of pottery onto the counter.

Ellie picked them up one at a time. "These are lovely." She smiled. "Let me log them in and give you a receipt."

Ellie handed Victor a piece of paper. "Here you go."

He took it, and after telling her she should go outside for the afternoon, he left.

Ellie slipped up the front stairs to change for her walk with Pad: yoga pants, and a loose t-shirt, sneakers, and on top of her head an old frayed baseball cap with her pony-tail pulled through the back.

She walked down the hall to see what Pad was doing. His bedroom door was open and he sat in front of the computer.

"Hey, what are you working on?"

Leaning back, Pad turned the chair. "I was curious if there had been similar break-ins in the surrounding towns. So, I've been scanning the news reports, nothing's popped on the radar. The attack on you seems to be isolated. Then I got to thinking, is it possible the attack's related to one of the artists you have on consignment? Also, I jotted down a few other ideas... types of display, vendors used for construction, invitee list for the cocktail party and staff. There has to be a connection to one of these people, but I'm not any closer to figuring it out now than when I sat down.

Looking at the clock, Pad said, "Ellie, sorry I lost track of time. I see you're ready." He slung his bag across his body "But I'm ready now."

"Not a problem." Ellie said. She skipped down the back stairs with Pad on her heels and started out the front door.

Pad stopped and held up a finger. "Be right back." Pad returned from the kitchen with two bottles of water. He held them up for Ellie to see and stuck them in the side pockets of his camera bag. "Now, I'm really ready."

Laughing, Ellie said, "About time."

Pad tugged the shoulder strap. "I've got it all under control. Sometimes the best laid plans get derailed for a reason." He held the front screen door open and waited for Ellie to jiggle the handle.

"I doubt anyone would try to get in now. The place is locked up tighter than Fort Knox." She slipped a chain with the key dangling off it over her head. Ellie stepped off the front porch and then down the path.

🍷

"It's pretty warm out," he commented. Pad loved the heat and humidity of a summer day. "Have you lived in Loudon all your life?" He wanted to get Ellie to open up. He had never been overly curious about the people he met with the exception of capturing a great photo.

"I was born here. My parents moved to Loudon after they got married. Mom thought it was a great place to raise a family. She lives on the other side of town in the house where I grew up. As you know, Shane lives with his family on the lake. My brother Jake, I'm not sure if you met him yet, but he and Sara and their triplets live on the outskirts, and of course my sister Kate lives in Crescent Lake near Don's family."

"What about you? I think you said you lived in Virginia?"

"I had a sister, but she died as a baby."

"I'm sorry to hear that. Do you have a home base somewhere?" Ellie quizzed.

"I have an apartment in a small town south of Seattle, but I'm rarely there. It's just a permanent address."

"I would feel lost if I didn't have a place to call home." Ellie and Pad walked down the flower-lined trail toward the center of the park where a small pond was barely visible. Passing a wrought iron bench, Pad sat down.

"Hold up a minute, I want to get my camera ready. The park is really beautiful. See those kids running over there? That'll make a great shot. From this distance you can't see their faces specifically but it's just what I'm looking for, total abandonment in the moment of a summer day. The lens captures everything."

Pad became lost behind the camera lens. It made small clicking sounds while he stayed light on his feet and moved slightly from one angle to another. Then Pad whirled around and continued to click what they had just passed, the flowers and gazebo. After changing the lens, he knelt next to a bed of hydrangeas, bringing the flowers in for a close up. He moved back and then forward again, all the while totally oblivious to anything other than what he saw in his viewfinder. Pad turned, his eyes sought and found Ellie's.

"Are you ready to finish our walk?" Pad asked.

Ellie fell in step beside him. "I am. Did you get what you wanted?"

"I did and more." Pad patted his bag.

Ellie chattered on about facts of the town and the people who lived there, many families for generations. She was talking about farms that dated back over two hundred years and was asking Pad a question when he realized a response was needed.

"I'm sorry what did you say?" He was enjoying listening to the musical sound of her voice and temporarily forgot conversation was a two-way street.

Pad gave her a dimpled smile.

Taking a deep, she said, "I was asking if you'd like to go out to the Bennett farm and take pictures. They raise horses and have some of the best-maintained original barns in the area. The kind built from timber and pegs. I can call Liza Bennett and see if she'd mind. That is, if you like horse farms. I think they have ducks and chickens too."

"I'd like that. Horses are magnificent creatures. Do they have people who work with the horses, or just family? It would be good to have people around too. The communication between man and horse is powerful, all from a touch or a look."

Ellie involuntarily shivered. The way Pad's voice said "touch or look" had Ellie thinking what it could be like to have a tender look or a mere touch of his long fingers on her skin.

Ellie's voice squeaked, "Yes." After clearing her throat, she gulped water from the bottle Pad offered her. "Yes, they give riding lessons as well as working them for therapy horses. In the last year or two, they've taken to rescuing miniature horses and use them with children of abuse or other disabilities. A full-grown horse that stands sixteen hands can be intimidating."

"You seem to know a lot about the place." Pad stopped, pulled out his camera to capture pictures of a flock of birds that had just taken flight from the trees.

"Liza and I were in high school together and occasionally, when I wanted a break from the books, I would go out and ride or just hang out and groom a horse. It was…" Ellie looked into Pad's golden eyes, "therapy for me too."

Pad's voice was tender. "Was it tough?"

Ellie watched the path as they strolled to the pond. "At times, sure. Mom did her best but I spent a lot of time trying to catch up to Shane and Kate. They're five years older, and we just never seemed close until we got older and even then, Kate went off to college and Shane was a guy. He didn't want his little sister tagging along after him. That's when I made up my mind to be the smartest kid in school."

Pad took Ellie's small hand in his, and they strolled along the path.

Ellie pulled away. She said, "Will you take my picture?"

She plastered on a goofy smile, and Pad obliged clicking away.

Pad lowered the camera, and in a husky voice, he said, "I got it."

12

---

*S*everal days passed without an incident. Pad and Ellie settled into a routine of sharing meals and her workspace. Customers were beginning to trickle in and sales were increasing. Ellie replaced all the damaged art, and to her credit, not a single artisan withdrew. It seemed everyone had faith in The Looking Glass.

Pad glanced up from his laptop. "I'm going to call Winnie later and see if next week will work for her photo shoot. Do you still want to come?"

"Absolutely. Can you suggest one of the days the gallery is closed?" Ellie got up and stretched. A frown crossed her face. "I have a follow-up appointment with the doctor first thing tomorrow."

"Not a problem, I can drive you and maybe we can swing by the grocery store again. We're almost out of cookies." Pad didn't reveal his true motivation, that he didn't want Ellie driving around alone. Too many lightly traveled roads, and the police weren't any closer to catching the intruder.

"Sounds like a plan." Ellie came over. "What are you working on now?" She peered over his shoulder.

Pad minimized the pictures he had taken of Ellie at the fountain. He turned the screen for her to get a better look. "Park pictures. I'm reviewing to see what I want to work with now and what will be filed away for another day or maybe even deleted."

"You delete pictures you take, why? I'm sure every picture you take is wonderful."

Pad gave a hearty laugh. "I take lots of bad pictures. The light isn't right or something in nature moves. It's all part of the job, but I appreciate your vote of confidence. I'll remember that the next time a critic gives me a bad review." Hm, it was strange, Ellie's opinion matters more than any other woman I've met.

Ellie smirked and headed into the kitchen. "Well you just tell them to call me, and I'll set them straight."

Out of the corner of his eye Pad could see Ellie standing in front of the open refrigerator. "We've got nothing for dinner. We can either grab a pizza or better still, I'll call Mom and see what she's fixing. We could crash their dinner."

"I don't think I should invite myself to your parents but feel free to go. I'm fine here." Pad studied the screen and muttered, "I like to get lost in my work, when I'm creating a new portfolio." Pad stared at a photo of Ellie. He wondered if she would let him take pictures if she knew the camera didn't lie; he could peer into her soul and see a lonely young woman, holding the world at arm's length, unwilling to let herself be vulnerable.

Ellie popped into the room. "Great news, roomie."

"What's that?"

Pad shut the laptop cover.

"Mom invited both of us for tonight and asked if you'd bring your camera. She said Ray is working with some reclaimed wood and thought it might interest you."

"Ellie, I told you I wasn't going to impose on your parents."

"You're not. I invited myself and then, Mom told me to ask you too. So, it's all set. We should be over there around four."

Pad shook his head. "You are sounding more like an agent lining up shoots for me than a temporary roommate."

The doorbell rang, signaling a new customer. "You need someone to expose you to neat stuff around town." With a flip of her hair, Ellie walked away.

"Good afternoon…"

Pad returned to his work but he was unable to concentrate. Out of the corner of his eye, he watched the petite blonde. He swallowed hard. She wore a simple blouse, a short, straight skirt that highlighted her shapely legs, and impossibly high-heeled sandals featuring bright pink toes. He couldn't stay there much longer. He was getting attached and enjoyed seeing Ellie across the breakfast table each morning. He wasn't even going to begin to think about how many hours of sleep he'd lost since staying in her guest room. He'd better find out who had broken in and why, and get Winnie's photos completed before he lost all sense of direction. Falling in love was not part of Pad's plan. He enjoyed the role of hapless drifter far too much to settle into small town life.

Pad returned to email. There was a new one from Officer Bell, and he scanned the contents. Leaning back in the chair, he reread the email one more time. Judy's current hypothesis: the intruder was female. She noted, just as the camera was turned off, it caught a glimpse of the eyes, and the person seemed to be wearing false eyelashes. Pad closed the email. Unsure what to think, Pad wandered through the front to visualize the events again. How could a woman burst through the door with enough force to cause Ellie to hit the floor, hit her over the head, be strong enough to drag her into the closet and then shut the cameras down? He glanced at Ellie, surmising she couldn't weigh more than one hundred and ten pounds. He thought about the blood smears on the floor and it clicked. It wouldn't take a lot of strength to break things or even destroy the waterfall painting.

Pad returned to his computer and drafted a short response, requesting to review the footage himself. He snapped the computer closed.

"Hey, Ellie, I'm feeling a little keyed up. I'm going to head out for a run. But if you need me just call and I'll head back."

Ellie closed the register and snapped. "You're not my babysitter and you don't need to let me know where you're going. I've told you I'm fine alone."

"I never said you weren't capable of being alone, Ellie, but someone attacked you, and until they're caught your parents need some reassurance you have muscle around. And that my new friend, would be me."

"Well I guess if I have to have a bodyguard, you'll do until someone else comes along. Now get out of here, you're making me jealous going for a run while I'm still on the DL."

"Ah, I like it, a reference to America's favorite past time."

Pad stepped into the bright sun. Slipping his shades on, he jogged off at a slow pace, letting his muscles loosen and finding his rhythm. The music playlist set the pace for his long stride. With each step came a renewed sense of clarity as he mulled over his feelings toward a certain young woman. What he felt was a simple reaction from the way she looked at him with those big, blue saucers graced with long, dark lashes. Maybe it was because Pad had never stayed under the same roof with a girl for any length of time, and their relationship had been built on respect and friendship first and not lust. There had been girls who stayed with him for a few weeks at a time depending on where he hung his camera bag, but nothing to make him feel this unfamiliar churning inside.

Coming around a bend, Pad stopped in his tracks. A dark Charger with black out windows was parked on the side of the road. Cautiously Pad approached, wishing he had some type of weapon on him other than his hands.

Rapping on the window, Pad stood just behind the door. The window slowly eased down and a pimple faced boy grinned. "Hey man, what's up?"

"Is this your car?" Pad demanded.

"No, I'm just borrowing my older brother's wheels. Cool, huh?" The teen's head bounced in time to the loud rock music blaring from the interior.

"Turn down the music please and step out of the car."

"Dude, are you gonna make me or what?"

"I'll haul your butt out of there. It would be embarrassing for both of us. Now step out of the car."

The kid tried to jam the car into drive while Pad reached through the open window and slammed it into park. The car jerked to a halt.

"Dude, you are in so much trouble. My brother is going to kill you for dropping the tranny."

Pad pulled open the driver's door. "As I said, let's wait

for the police together." Pad pulled his phone from the protective sleeve and dialed.

"Greene, I have a suspect driving a car that may have been outside Ellie's shop. Care to join me?" Pad listened and said, "Okay and call a tow truck. The car has a little transmission problem."

"Now what do you say you and I start over. My name is Stone."

"Good for you." The teen sulked. "What was I doing that had you acting all super cop on me?"

"Your first mistake? Driving an expensive car and using the oldest line in the book: it belongs to my brother. Second mistake, you tried to run. That, my young friend makes you look guilty of something. So now we wait and find out just what you're running from."

The teen boy shrunk with each sentence. "I didn't mean any harm. The car was just sitting there with the keys dangling in the ignition. I figured it wouldn't hurt to take it for a spin. It's some hot set of wheels. I was gonna return it, honest!"

"What's your name, kid?" The picture was becoming clearer, but Pad wanted to keep the boy talking in case he saw something that could be helpful.

"Kenny."

"Kenny, do you have a last name?"

"Oh man, I'm gonna catch it when I get home." Kenny shrugged his shoulders. "Martin."

"Do you have a driver's license Kenny?"

"No."

"You were driving without a license?" Pad's voice was firm.

"I didn't drive it, all I did was sit in it. I thought about it, but I swear this is exactly where I found it. Just sitting on the side of the road."

"You did put it in drive," Pad reminded him.

"Technically you parked it, so I never really drove it and it moved what ten feet, maybe. Can't you cut me some slack on this man? My folks are gonna be furious as it is. They'll never let me get my license if they think I've really messed up."

Before Pad could answer, a cruiser rolled up and parked amid swirling road dust. Officer Greene got out from the driver's side.

Giving a curt nod, he said, "Stone."

"Hello, Officer Greene. Allow me to introduce you to Kenny Martin. He has been telling me he found this vehicle sitting on the side of the road, abandoned with keys in the ignition."

"Well, Mr. Martin. It seems you're in a bit of a predicament. What do you have to say?" While Greene was asking questions, Officer Bell surveyed the outside of the car, writing down the plate number and taking pictures of the car.

"Be straight with me, Kenny," Greene's voice held a warning tone. "You were walking down this road and just happened to find a car and decided to sit in it?"

"Well I didn't just open the door and sit down. I knocked on the window first, thinking maybe someone was inside, ya know sick or something. When no one answered, I tried the door and saw it was empty. I hadn't been sitting in it for more than ten minutes when this guy," Kenny jerked his finger in Pad's direction, "came knocking and I got scared."

Paul glanced at Pad.

"Oh, and that Stone guy dropped it in park, and I'm

pretty sure its gonna need a new tranny and I'm not paying for it."

"Tow truck's here," Bell announced.

"Kenny, you should come down to the station and give a statement. We have been looking for a person of interest in a break-in who we believe was driving a car just like this one."

"Will you have to call my parents?" Kenny's voice cracked.

"You can call them when we get to the station. To be clear, you're not under arrest, we just need your help." Officer Bell put her hand on Kenny's arm. "Let's get you in the back."

Kenny looked at Pad. "Stone, ya gotta help me. Ya know I didn't do nothin'. Say something man, please. I'll tell ya anything just don't make me ride in the cop car."

"Kenny, you're not under arrest. Think of it this way, maybe if you help bring the bad guy in there will be a reward as a good citizen."

The boy brightened at the idea of a reward and walked to the cruiser.

Greene turned his back on the boy. "Do you think he's telling the truth?"

Pad nodded slowly and glanced around the wooded area. "Take a look. I think whoever left the car was looking for a couple of things. One, if the car was picked up and taken for a joy ride, something like this would happen, or they could come back and use it again. Lots of ways to get to the car without being seen. This part of town is pretty quiet, and the road is not well traveled."

"I hate to admit when you're right but this time you're dead on." Paul glanced around. "Did you get the email from Judy? About the intruder's eyelashes?"

"Yeah, I emailed her asking if I can see the footage. It might help me if someone comes back to the shop or starts hanging around Ellie. I don't think this was random, Paul."

Greene stood a little taller as Pad shared his comment. "Judy," he nodded toward Officer Bell, "and I have the same feeling. This was personal. I just hope we find out who before something worse happens." Paul sauntered toward the car and called back over his shoulder, "I'll let you know if Kenny tells us something interesting."

Pad gave a salute and started a slow jog back to Ellie's, trying to decide if he should fill her in on this new development but decided this afternoon's events weren't that important, yet. Pad was deep in thought, when he jogged up the walkway.

"About time you got home." Ellie got up and handed Pad a glass of water. "I was beginning to wonder if you had pulled a Forrest Gump and just kept running."

Pad avoided her eyes. "Sorry, I was enjoying the solitude. I'm sure you discovered the joy when you began running. Just you and the road, one foot in front of the other following the pace of your breathing, I mean, after the feeling that your lungs are going to collapse goes away."

Ellie chuckled. "I know what you mean. When I started, it was just about knowing I could run. But eventually I found it gave me a lift, and I began to look forward to it every day. I'm anxious to get back at it, and soon."

Pad filled the glass one more time and headed to the stairs, pausing one foot on the bottom step. "I won't be long and then it's off to your parents. Should we stop and pick anything up like wine or beer? I hate to show up empty handed."

"Mom would like that." Ellie smiled at her unexpected friend. "You're pretty nice, Mr. Stone."

"Thank my mother."

✿

*E*llie wiped off the clean counter and looked around the room. The little bell on the front door jingled, and Ellie admonished herself for not locking the door, again. She thought about calling Pad but changed her mind and went out front.

"Karlene, this is a surprise!" Ellie gave her former boss a warm hug. "What brings you to Loudon?"

"The same as usual, I've been trying to convince Winifred Simpson to let me host a small show for her. She mentioned about the trouble you've had, and I just had to stop and see for myself that you're okay." Karlene babbled on, "She told me you'd been hospitalized and needed staples in your head. You poor thing, it must have been quite a scare."

"It was a little scary, but the single most infuriating thing was the intruder destroyed Winnie's painting. It was over here." Ellie walked to the space which was bare. "On this wall. I wish you could have seen it. The entire place seemed to vibrate, almost as if you could hear the rushing waters and smell the flowers."

"I have seen pictures of it and it did look exquisite. I can't imagine what it must have been like in person." Karlene studied the room. "I'm very proud of you. The gallery is amazing. I love how you've utilized the space to enhance each artist. You learned well from your time in my employ."

"Thank you. From you that is certainly high praise. I

127

can't ever repay all you did for me, taking me under your wing. You were the best mentor I could have hoped to work with."

Karlene's cheeks had a hint of pink. "You have talent, Ellie, pure and simple. I hate to ask, but have they caught the guy who did this? You must be scared living and working here, most of the time by yourself."

On cue, Pad strolled into the room, hair damp from his shower, dressed casually in jeans and a short sleeve shirt. "Ellie isn't living alone, well at least not anymore." Pad slipped his arm around Ellie's slim shoulders and tenderly kissed the top of her head, avoiding the staples. He looked deep into her blue eyes imploring her to play along.

"Ah, no," she stuttered. "Karlene, this is, um, Pad."

Karlene looked from Pad to Ellie's face, unsure what was going on. "Ellie, I didn't know you were dating anyone let alone living with a man." Karlene held out her hand. "Karlene Johnson, Ellie's former boss and I must say, you're quite a surprise."

Pad clasped her hand. "Pad Stone, Photographer, and we've had a long-distance relationship for quite some time but kept it on the down low, you know in case the circumstances proved to be too stressful. I'm sure you can understand how difficult it is to keep a relationship going living in different parts of the world. But I'm back, and it seems just in the nick of time. My sweet Eleanor was attacked on the same night as I returned. If I had arrived a bit sooner, we would have had him red-handed. I'm just grateful Ellie was only mildly injured and will make a full recovery."

Kissing Ellie's forehead, his amber eyes narrowed. "But rest assured I will find out who did this and hold them accountable."

Karlene shivered. "Ellie, you certainly do have a

formidable boyfriend." She glanced at her watch. "Just look at the time. I need to get back to my own gallery." Karlene lightly kissed Ellie on both cheeks. "Good luck with everything, and I'll be in touch soon."

Ellie and Pad watched Karlene leave, and Ellie hissed through clenched teeth. "What do you think you are doing? Pretending to be my boyfriend?"

Pad dropped his arm and Ellie turned to face him. "I've been doing a lot of thinking, and if we can get the word out that I'm living with you it will give you a level of protection when I'm not around. Whomever this was, didn't just break in because they had nothing better to do. There was a point, and until we know why and that they've been arrested, I will do what I feel is necessary to protect you. After all, you can always say later that I was too arrogant for you to stay in a long-term relationship with me."

Ellie half-listened while Pad talked. It had felt amazing when he put his arm around her in front of Karlene. Like he was protecting her. She had never felt that safe before. Hearing her name brought her back to the present.

"Ellie. Are you listening?"

"Of course. I'm sorry, Pad, you're right and we'll do this your way."

"Finally. Now we're going to be late."

Ellie paused. "Does this mean you have to drive us around now? Just not sure how this relationship stuff works."

Pad chuckled. "You can drive, my little control nut."

13

$\mathcal{T}$he next few days passed with little fanfare. Ellie's staples had been removed, and she and Pad settled into a routine of sharing the cooking and cleaning duties for all common areas, and they were starting to run together. As promised, Ray and Mom let Pad take as many photos as he wanted of the workshop, gardens, and What's Perkin'. The shoot was set for Winnie's studio and Ellie talked about the horse farm again. Pad was mulling over the idea of going out to the farm and taking some pictures.

At breakfast one rainy morning, Pad's phone vibrated on the table. Ellie looked over the newspaper to see why Pad hadn't picked it up. She glanced around to see he was looking out the window into the back yard.

"Your phone is buzzing."

"Ellie, have you ever looked around out here? There are a lot of places where someone could hide. Do you think Shane might come over and clear out some of the hedges, and it would provide a little less cover if someone did want to creep around?"

Ellie stepped in front of him. "Where?" I don't see anything."

Pad pointed, directing her attention to the back corners both of which bordered on the property of an antique store and the neighbors were only around on weekends. "People aren't really around much to see someone sneaking across the yard. Maybe a motion detector light would be good too."

"If you think it's necessary, I'll call Shane. He'll send someone over. Heck he might even come take care of it himself. And I can give Ray a call to find out about an electrician." She titled her head back to look at him. "Do you think this is urgent?"

"No, but you shouldn't put it off too long either." Pad took another sip of the hot coffee. "Is the shop open today?"

"Nope, it's mid-week." Ellie frowned. "Remember, my busy days are Friday through Monday."

"Honestly, it's pretty easy for me to lose track of days. I do it all the time when I'm traveling. That's why I rarely fly. I don't have to be on someone else's schedule."

"I love schedules and routine. I don't think I could do what you do. Have you always been this way?"

Pad went back to the table and Ellie trailed behind him.

"There was a time I worked eight hour shifts and loved what I did, but I got burnt out. Life is short and there was no way to tell if I would have a tomorrow. I quit, hit the road, and never looked back."

"What did you do exactly?" Ellie's big, blue eyes watched Pad closely.

"I worked with the men and women in blue. Nothing special."

"I knew it! You were a cop," Ellie shouted. "Was it in a small town or were you big city?"

"Ellie, being a cop is the same no matter where you live. There are good guys and bad, and some days filled with crime and other days not so much." Pad shrugged his shoulders. "Do you mind if we change the subject? It was a life time ago."

Ellie tapped her forehead. "It's all coming together, how you knew the jargon when you talked to the police and why Mom and Ray are okay with you staying with me. I do have a personal bodyguard."

Ellie sniffed. "Are we only friends because they're paying you?"

"El, I can assure you I am not getting paid to be here. I felt awful that night, when I found you locked in the closet, carrying you up the stairs and everything. You looked so defenseless, and I hate people that treat others like they are disposable." A dark look came over Pad's face and was gone just as quickly. "I promise, we are friends, real friends, and I'll be here until I know you're safe."

Pad reached across the table and rested his hand on hers causing Ellie's pulse to quicken.

Ellie casually withdrew her hand. "So why a photographer? That seems to be quite a departure from a cop." Ellie could see deep lines appear between his eyebrows, which she realized happened when he was deep in thought. "

Pad hesitated. "When you're a cop you see all types of people in situations when they're typically at a low point, a speeding ticket, victim of a crime, or car accident. I started taking the time to really look at people, not just the surface. Many times, it helped me to ferret out the truth. After I ended up with a fractured ankle, I had to take time off to recover. Since I didn't want to hang out around my apartment, I headed to Jamaica. I picked up a camera and started snapping pictures. When I got home I was looking at them and a funny thing happened. I saw my vacation with new eyes. Although someone might have a smile on their face, their eyes told the real story. I was drawn to the truth the camera revealed. I was hooked. When I went back to work, my job was less satisfying, and I realized I was burnt out. I resigned and I've never looked back."

Ellie was dumbfounded. "You still went back to it, to being a cop? How did you get injured, specifically?"

"I shared my epiphany with you about photography and all you can focus on, was the injury?" He chuckled. "If you must know, I fractured my ankle while chasing a suspect. I was running after him and to slow me down he was tossing stuff in my path, garbage cans, chairs whatever he could toss and run. I can assure you it isn't like the movies where you leap over everything and catch the bad guy. In the end, it was a kid's tricycle that tripped me up. It wasn't serious and my partner was able to apprehend him. Everything turned out for the best."

Pad gave her a warm smile. "In more ways than one, the trike helped me find my way to Loudon and meet you."

"Well it was more like you rescued me, and for that I am in your debt, kind sir." Ellie spoke in a proper English accent and followed it up with a mock curtsey.

Laughing, Pad mimicked her. "My lady, I am at your service."

The little spot between her eyes wrinkled. "Do you miss it, the thrill of police work? Chasing the bad guys and everything?"

"Someone has been watching too much television. It's really not like that at all. What made you decide to become an entrepreneur? Karlene seems like a bright business woman."

"Her gallery is very traditional with specific exhibits that open and close. Karlene has a few favorites of course. I think that's pretty normal, you know the ones that pull in the buyers, and people seem to like her no-nonsense approach. When she wants a new artist to succeed, they usually do. She is the best at writing press releases, and she certainly taught me a lot. Karlene was very supportive when I came up with the idea of this gallery. I wasn't sure what to expect, but I was able to keep working with her while Ray and I rehabbed Abby's house."

"I didn't realize you did the grunt work too, for some reason I thought you were the brains behind the operation," Pad gently teased.

Ellie flushed bright pink. "Everyone underestimates me. I can swing a hammer and a crowbar as good as anyone. Ray even hooked me up with my own tool belt." Grinning, she said, "But he had to make extra holes in the belt part. The first time I put it on it kept sliding off my butt."

"I would like to have seen that."

Ellie wasn't sure if he was flirting. "We should clean up. Do you have anything on your agenda today?"

I think I'm going to finalize plans with Winnie Simpson for tomorrow. I have a list of pictures I want to take in the studio and depending what the lighting is like outside I may take some shots there too. What are you up to?"

"I'm going to get a pedicure and stop and have a late lunch with my mom." Ellie glanced up through her lashes. "Do you want to go out for sushi or Thai tonight?"

Pad's eyes gleamed. "Sounds like a plan."

Beaming, Ellie said, "Let's meet back here at five and we can decide then."

"All right." Pad hesitated. "See you later." Ellie's gaze followed him as he jogged up the back stairs taking them two at a time.

In the kitchen Ellie admonished herself. "What possessed you to ask Pad to have dinner, like a date? I know it's the twenty-first century and women can ask men out for dinner, but why this guy?"

Ellie moved around the kitchen tidying the space before going upstairs to get ready for her appointments. It was her day, and she just might get in a little shopping too. She could always use a new blouse and maybe she'd wear it tonight. Walking up the front staircase, she changed her mind about wearing something new. If Pad knew, he would think she was trying to impress him and get the wrong idea.

❧

*P*ad was driving down a familiar road, not paying much attention to his surroundings, deep in thought. Was tonight a date or just two friends sharing a meal? Why did he spend so much of his time thinking about how not to date Ellie? This was an odd situation for sure, to be living under the same roof, offering protection and developing feelings for the petite blonde. Her eyes were so blue, at first, he thought they had to have been contacts, but after seeing the family photos on Cari's mantle, he discovered Ellie had her father's eyes. At the entrance to Winnie's home, he took a few minutes to look around and make sure Winnie's fans weren't lurking about. He turned up the long drive, enjoying the meticulously manicured lawn and shrubs. Each time he came up the driveway, he always had the same feeling that everything was right in the world.

Before Pad could get out of the car, the front door flew open and Winnie waved, calling out, "Hello!"

Pad hurried up the brick path and hugged her warmly. "Hi, Aunt Winnie."

"Hello, my favorite nephew. I see you're alone today. Where is the lovely Eleanor?"

Grinning, Pad ushered her inside. "I'm your only nephew. If you have coffee, I'll tell you all about it."

"I do and I had hoped to see your handsome face, so I baked a lemon pound cake. If I remember correctly it's your favorite."

"It is and if I hang around here too long I'm going to start gaining weight." Pad chuckled and draped his arm over his aunt's shoulder. "Between eating regular meals with Ellie and what Cari fed us the other night, I'm eating a lot more than I usually do."

"You could use a bit more meat on your bones. You're all muscle and bone. Did I hear you say something about Cari? I assume you're talking about Cari Davis."

"You did and I was. Ellie and I went to her folks' house for dinner. I took some pictures of Ray working in his shop. The lighting was quite interesting, and I found some great angles. I've taken a quick look on the computer too, and I'm pretty sure there are a few nuggets in the batch."

Winnie gestured for Pad to have a seat while she fussed over him, pouring a large mug of coffee and setting the cake platter in the middle of the table. She handed Pad a generous slice and gave herself a sliver. She started to sit down and then bounced back up to get the cream pitcher and sugar bowl.

"Tell me how are things going in the investigation? I've been dying to talk to you but can't call as that would raise suspicion since you still haven't told Ellie about our connection."

"I've wanted to tell her a bunch of times. You know why I didn't in the beginning. I wanted her to think she got both of us because we believed in her vision for The Looking Glass. Now the longer I hold back the truth the harder it becomes. I figure it won't be a big deal when I hit the road. She'll have Winifred Simpson and Padraic Stone's work in her shop. I know I sound like a hot shot but if she promotes both of us, she'll have a nice steady business for all her artists."

"Well Pad Stone, you do sound egotistical. If I didn't know you, I'd think you were way too full of yourself," Winnie scolded.

"It's the truth and you know it. Our names are well–known, and it will help her." Pad popped a hunk of cake in his mouth. "Aunt Winnie, this is just like I remember."

Pleased with his empty plate, she gave him one more slice. "Eat and then we can talk about tomorrow. However, before we do, I want to know what is going on between the two of you. Is there a budding romance? Did you take her to Harvey Park yet?"

"Auntie, I'm not living with her because we are romantically involved. I'm there to keep her safe." Pad diverted the conversation. "I haven't had the chance to tell you about the car I came across. I was out for a run the other day, and there was a car that matched Ellie's description of the car that had been hanging around. When I tapped on the window, some teenage kid rolled it down and then tried to make a run for it. He was taken in for questioning, but he didn't jack the car, and he certainly isn't who we are looking for in connection with the break-in. The car was dusted for prints, but we came up with nothing. I feel like I'm missing something that is right in front of my face."

"There you go again, getting that look you get. Maybe you're too close to the situation?" Winnie prodded.

"No, I don't think so, but I will figure it out." Pad drained his coffee cup and pulled out his notebook. "We need to talk about tomorrow, so here is what I have planned. I'm going to do a series of pictures in the studio and then move out to the perennial gardens. That is if you want to do some gardening tomorrow."

"I would like to show off the vegetable garden too. I'm growing some heirloom varieties of tomatoes and peppers. The colors are amazing." Winnie beamed. "Let's go outside and have a look."

"I trust you, Auntie. Every year you have the most amazing gardens." As requested, Pad followed his aunt out to the garden and gave the compliments it deserved.

"Do you want to take a few things back with you? You can have some fresh tomatoes for dinner."

"Thanks, but Ellie and I are going out tonight."

"You are, like a date?" she teased. "Where are you taking Eleanor?"

"You're incorrigible, it's not a date. Just roommates eating in a restaurant."

"Excuse me young man, in my day that would be considered a date." Winnie stalked back to the house.

"Aunt Winnie, I'm sorry. I didn't mean for that to sound, well, rude. But I have a life on the road, and you know how that works out. Relationships usually buckle under the stress of being separated for long periods of time. You know how much I come home now. I have a lot I want to accomplish before I set down roots anywhere."

The last thing Pad wanted to do was bruise his only living relative's feelings. After his parents and his uncle passed away, all he and Winnie had was each other.

"You have always been so stubborn. I think you're afraid to fall in love because you would want to give up your gypsy lifestyle." Winnie linked arms and walked Pad out front. "I hate to push you out, but I have work to do and you need to go by the police station and see if there are any new developments, or however you say that, and do yourself a favor, review everything with a fresh eye. Approach it like you're giving me the details. You never know it might help." Winnie stood on her tip toes and kissed his cheek. "See you tomorrow." She turned on her heel and sauntered back into the house.

Pad watched her go, thinking there was a bit more bounce in her step than normal. "She must be excited about this new painting. I'll make sure to see it tomorrow. Maybe it will be a good replacement for Ellie's shop."

Pad drove directly to the station. Winnie was right; he needed to review everything again. There was something he was overlooking, and then he would go to Ellie's and walk through that night one more time.

14

*E*llie walked into What's Perkin', sporting freshly painted, hot pink toenails and shopping bags dangling from her arms. It had been a whirlwind shopping extravaganza. Ellie had justified her purchases with the reasoning she needed new clothes for work.

"Hey, Luke, is Mom around?" She greeted her mom's counter guy, but that was an understatement. Luke had quickly become Mom's right hand and Dani, her sister's replacement, was the left. Now her mom had time to spend away from the shop with Ray.

Luke beamed. "I see someone is keeping the local economy humming." He took a couple of large shopping bags and set them behind the counter. "Your mom's in the kitchen getting more cupcakes. They're selling like hotcakes today."

"What's the flavor of the day? I might have to sample one." Ellie grabbed a glass, filled it with some fresh squeezed lemonade, and drained half of it. "I'm parched; shopping is thirsty work." She grinned. "That's good, not too pulpy and I like the tartness. Someone forgot to put sugar in there."

Luke flushed bright red. "Well that explains the half empty glasses. I'll fix that right away." He hurried through the swinging doors, holding the door while Ellie's mom came through carrying a tray of cupcakes and cookies.

"Hi sweetheart, what brings you in?" Her mom set the tray down and began filling the case. "Can I interest you in something sweet?"

"Absolutely, are those oatmeal cookies?" Ellie wrinkled her nose.

Her mom smiled. "They are."

"What's in the cupcake? I asked Luke but he was focused on his tart lemonade."

"I haven't tried one yet but Dani said it's a white chocolate cupcake with a raspberry frosting. They're selling so fast I don't know how she is keeping up. Would you like one?"

"That sounds decadent. I'll take one now and pack a few to go? Pad has a sweet tooth."

Her mom handed her a small floral plate and tucked two in a small pastry box along with a couple of cookies.

Ellie licked the top peak, savoring the burst of fresh raspberry in sweet creamy frosting. "Oh wow, I've never tasted anything so good." Ellie giggled. "Well except the peach cupcake Dani made last week. Where does she come up with these ideas?"

"The shop she worked for back in her home town had lots of different flavors on the menu. She took the basic recipes and put her own twist on them. I can tell you I never thought cupcakes would be such good sellers."

Her mom glanced at the stack of bags. "Been doing a little shopping?" She peeked inside. "I thought you were putting yourself on a shopping moratorium for a few months?"

Ellie shrugged her shoulders. "I just wanted to pick up a couple of things, like scarves, a couple of basic tops and Threads is having a great sale. You should stop in and check it out. Before I could help myself, I was leaving with all these bags."

Ellie slipped off the stool. "Check out the cute dress I bought." Ellie dug around in the bags. Holding it up, she gushed, "Isn't this a beautiful shade of blue, not quite azure, and feel the fabric, it is so soft. The best part it was seventy-five percent off so I just had to buy it." Ellie held it against her body and twirled. "What do think?'

"It's beautiful but a little dressy for work." Her mom touched the hem. "Wow, that is soft, what's the fabric?"

"Organic cotton. I always thought cotton was a bit stiff until it was washed several times, but when I put this on I was like, hold the phone, I have to buy this dress."

"It's the perfect color with your eyes and hair. Now you just need an occasion to wear it."

"Well…" Ellie blushed. "Maybe I'll wear it tonight. Pad and I are going to dinner, either Thai or sushi."

"I guess you two are becoming good friends. It's to be expected living under the same roof. And I'm glad you're getting out and doing things. You've worked hard this last year getting the shop ready to open and while working for Karlene."

"Do you think the dress is too much, you know, too dressy for dinner with a friend?"

"El, is he really just a friend or do you like him?"

"He's hot, don't you think?" She giggled. "His eyes are so intense and an amazing color. Every time I look at him they're a slightly different shade." Ellie frowned. "But he isn't interested in staying in Loudon. Although he hasn't said anything specific I think he's getting closer to figuring out who assaulted me."

"What makes you say that?"

"It's not what he says specifically, but the cops aren't sure if the person on the video was a man or a woman, but Pad thinks it might be a female. The big question is why?" Ellie glanced at her watch. "I gotta run. I want to be ready on time for a change." Ellie threw her arms around her mom and squeezed. "I'll call you tomorrow."

*P*ad jumped up from the chair when he heard fumbling at the back door. "Hey, let me help you." He took the bags and held the door open as Ellie stepped inside.

Ellie glowed when she saw Pad. "Thank you." Ellie set her handbag on the table. "I'm going to take these bags upstairs."

"I'll run them up." Without waiting for a response, Pad easily picked up all the bags and dashed up the front stairs.

Pad returned in a flash. "I saw Winnie today, and we're all set for tomorrow. You know I think she's looking forward to it too."

"That's good, right?" Ellie's eyes sparkled as she said, "Did you tell her you've been taking pictures all over town while you play one of the Hardy Boys?"

Pad laughed. "I filled her in on the high points of the last few days. She said to come over as early as we want, and she plans on serving lunch. Do you mind if we leave around seven? I'd like to catch the morning light in the studio."

"Not at all. I'll be ready. I appreciate you letting me tag along. I've never been to a professional photo shoot, and I'm looking forward to it."

"I hope you're not disappointed. Most of the time it's pretty boring, a lot of moving the camera looking through the lens, take a few shots and then move it again. It's not like taking portraits."

"It's all new to me. I promise not to get in your way."

"I like having you around." Pad's face was flushed. Clearing his throat, he asked, "Um, have you decided where you want to have dinner?" He checked the time. "I can be ready in fifteen, if that gives you enough time."

"I thought we agreed to five thirty. I know what I'm wearing so we can leave soon."

She paused. "The choice of food is all yours. I'm easy." Ellie blushed. "Meet you back here."

Pad watched Ellie dash up the stairs and heard a door slam. The tension between them was palpable. His mouth felt like cotton. Pad reminded himself, Dude, remember she's just a friend.

Pad did a double take as Ellie walked into the kitchen. "You look amazing." She wore a blue sleeveless dress with a deep V in the back and a slight scoop neck, and the hemline seemed to float as she walked, caressing bare legs. Her honey blonde hair was piled high on her head, exposing the curve of her lovely neck. His gaze traveled from her pert nose, over lush, rose-colored lips, down to pink toes and impossibly high heels. He leaned in and with his voice husky said, "Nice perfume."

His mouth went bone dry. "Ah, are you up for Thai food tonight?"

"You'll really like Siam, the food is cooked to perfection. In fact, that's where Mom and Ray had their first date. It's a funny story and I'll tell you over dinner, if you'd like."

Ellie dangled the keys. "Would you like to drive?"

Stepping lightly, Ellie reached for the door handle.

Pad touched her elbow. "Allow me."

She stepped to one side as he held the door.

Ellie said softly, "Thank you."

Pad jumped into the driver's seat and buckled up. He glanced over. "Ready?"

Ellie nodded, the lengthening shadows didn't hide her flushed cheeks. "This restaurant is really good," she babbled. "And they have the best coconut ice cream. Sometimes they shave bittersweet chocolate on the top, but I don't think that's a traditional garnish from Thailand."

"I would agree that definitely sounds like an American twist. Do you have a dish you would recommend?

My favorite appetizer is the steamed vegetable dumplings, and then I usually order either the pad Thai or the paradise shrimp. You can't go wrong with any of the main entrées."

Ellie pointed. "There's a spot."

Pad slipped the SUV into the vacancy and turned the car off. "You've really peaked my appetite with all this talk of food.

"Then we should get inside," Ellie said with a giggle.

She opened her car door. Pad's gaze traveled the length of bare leg to her painted toes.

Ellie stood at the door, and Pad ushered her into the dim interior. It took a few moments for their eyes to adjust to the lighting.

The hostess approached. In a heavy accent, she asked, "Table for two?"

Ellie glanced around. "We have a reservation, McKenna."

The petite Asian woman nodded and chose two menus. "This way please." She stopped at a booth. "Will this be okay for you?"

"Do you prefer a booth or a table?" Ellie didn't want to assume Pad would like to sit in a romantic booth.

"Booth, please." Pad waited for Ellie to slide in before taking a seat.

The hostess set the menus down and said someone would be over.

"That usually means they want us to order everything at the same time," Ellie whispered.

"Let's surprise them and order one thing at a time, drinks a couple of appetizers, and then our main course. If you don't mind letting me take the lead."

"They do like to keep the tables turning."

Pad scanned the room. "We're the only ones here and its mid-week."

"At the moment that's true, but it is tourist season and they could get busy. I would hate to hold up a table."

"If they get busy we'll take dessert to go."

A young waiter approached their table. "I take your order now?"

"We're not sure what we'd like for dinner so we'd like to start with…" Pad glanced at the wine list and said, "A bottle of Pinot Grigio, the third one on the list will be fine."

Over the top of the menu, Ellie whispered, "What are you going to do when he asks us to order food."

"Just watch and learn Ms. McKenna, the subtle art of slowing down the dining experience."

The waiter returned and went through the formality of pouring a sample for Pad. After receiving the customary nod, he poured Ellie a glass and then filled Pad's.

"You order now?"

"We're still perusing the menu. Can you give us a few minutes, and then we'll be ready to order our appetizers? We want to have a leisurely dinner this evening. It is a special occasion for the lady and me."

The waiter gave a slight bow and backed away.

"I think he might have gotten the hint." Pad grinned. "Let's relax and enjoy the evening. After all I did just say it was a special night for us."

"He probably thinks we're celebrating an anniversary or something."

"I'm sure he does. Look, he's over there with the hostess gesturing and giving us pointed looks. They're speculating if we're getting engaged or something."

Ellie choked on her wine.

Pad leaned forward. "Are you okay?"

Ellie tapped her throat. "Went down the wrong pipe," she croaked. "I'm fine."

Pad watched Ellie's color return to normal. "If you're sure."

She looked down and drank a miniscule sip of water. "I'm fine. Thank you."

Pad reached over and put his hand on top of hers. Heat flooded his veins. "Good."

"I'm having a wonderful time."

"Me too. Let's take a look at the menu and decide what we should start with. I'm sure it will make our waiter pleased to bring us something to eat." Pad's eyes squinted as she let out a loud chuckle.

"Well in that case we should make his night. Order

whatever you'd like as long as you get an order of the veggie dumplings, the steamed ones."

"As you wish, my lady."

After the waiter slipped away, Pad asked, "Ellie you never talk about a boyfriend. Is there someone special in your life?"

Ellie looked at him square in the eye. "No one special. I don't really date much. I've never had time."

"Really? You're a beautiful girl. I would think guys would be beating down your door."

She looked down at her clasped hands. "I've got some great male friends, but I've never met anyone I'd want to date."

"What about you, anyone special waiting for you somewhere in the world?"

"It's hard to make lasting relationships when I travel so much, and I've never found someplace I'd want to permanently hang my hat."

In a soft voice, Ellie said, "Oh. I've never thought of living anywhere but Loudon. It's a great town with easy access to the ocean, mountains, and Boston or New York City. I think we have access to the best of everything."

"Loudon does have a lot to offer." He continued. "Close proximity to so much culture and adventure is a bonus."

With a grand flourish, their waiter arrived. Setting small plates in front of them, he placed the appetizers and specialty sauces on the table, and then left them to enjoy their food.

Pad said, "So tell me about yourself?"

Ellie quietly exhaled. "There's not much to tell. I graduated from high school early and took a bunch of college courses, so I was able to shave off about a year and a half from college."

"Where did you go to college?" Pad paused his hand mid-way to his mouth. "These dumplings are good."

Ellie speared the last one before Pad claimed it. "There's a small liberal arts college about an hour north; most of the time I commuted. Occasionally I'd crash with a friend but housing was expensive, and I didn't want to waste money boarding at school. I graduated early and got a job at Karlene's gallery. After a while, I decided to open my place. I think art is so much more than paintings. It takes on many forms and depends on who is appreciating it. I think the name The Looking Glass reflects back to how you feel about something."

"I think the name suits your gallery. You believe art should be accessible to all not a select few. In all sincerity, that's what drew me to your shop." Pad wiped his mouth with the linen napkin and smirked. "That was delicious. I think we're ready for our next course."

The waiter swooped in and whisked away the plates.

He looked from Pad to Ellie. "Dinner, now?"

Pad placed their order. The waiter slapped his pad shut and bounced away.

Pad leaned in. "Guess I made his night."

Ellie giggled and took a small sip of wine.

Pad leaned back. "So how did you pick the house for your gallery? It doesn't seem like the most economical investment."

"I didn't buy the building. I'm sure I mentioned it belongs to my sister-in-law, Abby. When she and Shane married, they decided to live at his place. I wanted to have a shop where I could live onsite, and it would save me money. I talked it over

149

with Shane and Abby, laid out my ideas for an apartment and the gallery. Thankfully she agreed." Ellie's eyes danced. "The only stipulation was she gets a discount on all purchases."

"It sounds like it was a perfect solution for everyone. I seem to recall you had Ray do some work and you were knee deep in construction debris too."

"I was, and it was a blast. I discovered I love demo but not the reconstruction part. It is way too time consuming." Ellie giggled. "Patience is not my forte, but, I hung dry wall, filled nail holes, and then I was the official painter of walls but not trim. Ray has a steady hand and didn't need to use that blue painter's tape. Before I knew it, I moved in. Then it took time to find the artists who wanted to be a part of the eclectic space."

"How did you land Winifred Simpson?"

"That was very odd. A day before I opened, Winnie showed up. We had a nice conversation and she informed me, she was giving me several paintings to display. And that was that."

"She must have great faith in you."

"I never thought of it that way. But I would love to know how she even heard about my little establishment." Ellie nibbled on a jumbo-sized shrimp. "Maybe someday, over a cup of tea, she'll tell me."

"Maybe she will."

15

"*P*ad!" Ellie' said.

"I'm sorry. What?" Pad's eyes captured Ellie's.

"I guess regaling stories from my youth was a bit boring. I asked if you wanted dessert?"

"No, you aren't boring at all. I was just trying to remember the last time I've had so much fun, and since I'm coming up empty, I guess it's been a while."

Pleased to hear Pad's comment, Ellie felt her cheeks get hot. She was certain they flushed to a deep shade of pink. "I'm having fun too. You're very easy to talk to."

Ellie imagined how his lips would feel on her's. She dismissed her train of thought to focus on what Pad was saying.

"I think we should take ice cream to go. If what you say is true, I don't think we should miss out."

"You won't be disappointed." Ellie smiled at the waiter, which prompted him to rush over.

Pad ordered two servings of ice cream and asked for it be doubled-bagged with a small baggie of ice. The waiter placed the check on the table and hurried off. Ellie reached for it when Pad scooped it up. "I've got it."

"No, you don't. I asked you out, so by rights I should be picking up the check."

"Where I come from the man always picks up the check on the first date." Pad said, "My mother raised me with impeccable manners."

Ellie smiled. "This was an official date?"

Pad's breath was ragged. "Is that okay? I like you, a lot, and despite that we are living under the same roof in odd circumstances, I rather enjoy the idea of getting to know you on a more personal level." Pad waited half a beat. "But if the idea of dating me is too close for comfort we can be just friends. The choice is yours."

"I'm glad you're not looking at me like a damsel in distress. "A shy smile played over her lips. "I like the idea of this being our first date." Ellie burst into giggles. "I guess we won't have that awkward moment at the door when you take me home tonight. After all, we live together."

"Well, I could walk you to the front door, see you inside, and then park the car and come in the back. Would that make it less weird?" Pad teased.

The waiter approached the table carrying a large bag. Pad handed him a credit card and peeked inside. "This must be the best well-packed ice cream I've seen."

The waiter returned and waited while Pad signed a slip of paper and wished them a good night. "That's our cue." Pad held out his hand to Ellie. Once standing, Pad's voice was barely audible. "I'm sure you've heard this many times but, you have the most captivating eyes."

Ellie blushed. "I can honestly say no one has ever said a word about my eyes." She didn't want to say that she had never been this close to a man before tonight. Otherwise he might think there was something wrong with her.

"I'm glad I am the first," he said for her ears alone.

Ellie shivered. "We should go."

Pad was the perfect gentleman and let Ellie walk ahead of him.

"Would you like to go for a ride before we head home?"

"There will be a beautiful sunset." Ellie pointed to a turn up ahead. "Take the first left and then the next, and we'll be on Lake Drive. We'll circle around and it will bring us back to town."

Pad turned and within minutes, Green Lake came into view. "How big is the lake?"

"I'm not one hundred percent sure. Shane could tell you exactly. He loves facts and figures. But over five hundred acres, I think, and in some spots, it's over sixty feet deep. Did you know he has a house on the water?"

"You told me."

"That's right I did. It's a great spot. When we were kids, there was an old guy, Mr. McIntyre. Shane used to ride his bike out to the north end just to mow the lawn. Well anyway after old man McIntyre passed, the house became a shack and Shane bought it. Spent a couple of years working on it and now it's amazing. In the summer, our family tends to gather at Shane's for barbecues and during the winter we get together at Mom's."

"It must be nice to have a close family. I'm pretty close to my aunt but that's about it for me."

Ellie studied his profile. "That's too bad. What about your parents?"

"We've had our moments."

Pad pulled over to the side of the road. "Look." His

voice was filled with awe. "There's geese skimming across the water. I think they're going to land."

Pad took Ellie's delicate hand in his. Hand in hand they sat in silence, enjoying the beauty and simplicity of the moment. Darkness crept in from the shadows and the geese rose, breaking the mirrored surface, flying to a safe haven for the night. With the spell broken, Pad released Ellie's hand.

"We should go. It's getting late and tomorrow will be busy."

Caught up in the spell the evening had cast, Ellie didn't speak until they were driving down the darkened road.

"I had a really nice time tonight." She clasped her hands in her lap. "Driving out here was wonderful. Maybe another time we can borrow Shane's boat and putter around. Unless you water ski, we can do that too."

"Just trolling around sounds nice, very relaxing. There are times I have to be reminded to slow down and enjoy life."

"I know. I get too focused, and before I start to enjoy summer, the winter holidays are upon me."

Pad pulled up the driveway and put the car in park.

"I forgot all about the ice cream, it might be melted."

Ellie laughed. "I did too. Well maybe we can refreeze it or enjoy cool, sweet, coconut soup." Ellie picked up the bag at her feet and opened the door.

Pad followed her up the short path and stopped her. "Wait, I want to walk you to the front door. After all it is a date."

Ellie fumbled with the keys. "Huh?" She smiled. "I forgot."

"A date walks you to the front not the back."

Ellie reversed direction. Pad reached out and slipped

his hand over hers. "Just in case there is a loose stone or something."

She looked at him through her lashes, vowing to savor this moment, praying he would kiss her like she had never been kissed.

The couple stepped up on the front porch, and Pad gently drew Ellie to his chest. Slipping his arm around her tiny waist, he held her tight, his mouth hovering mere inches from hers. Ellie could feel the warmth of his breath. With heart racing, she leaned in, beckoning him closer. Pad's mouth grazed her quivering lips. Ellie stepped closer, knees weak. Warmth flooded her body. Losing herself in the sensations, she urged Pad to kiss her deeply with matching desire.

Ellie's tongue teased his lips with a feathery touch.

A loud crash broke the spell.

*P*ad thrust Ellie behind him. "Stay behind me," he hissed.

The doorknob turned easily. Pad hesitated and opened the door a crack. He felt a flash of heat and the dim interior was bright with orange light. "Call 911, now!" Pad raced into the house.

"Pad, wait. Get the fire extinguisher." Ellie screamed.

In a few long strides, he was at the counter. Reaching down, his hand struck the metal holder. With one fluid motion, he pulled the extinguisher off the wall and pulled the pin. Feet planted, he directed the nozzle at the base. Fanning back and forth, he worked to suppress the flames. It was enough. The fire was out.

Pad called out, "Ellie, where are you?"

Sirens in the distance were growing closer.

"Ellie!"

Silence.

Pad ran toward the back of the house and discovered her heels discarded in the driveway. He took off down the road. Just as he was ready to reverse direction he spotted her, limping towards him. Pad ran to her and wrapped his arms around her. Holding tightly, he demanded, "Where did you go?"

"Someone ran out the back door so I followed them. Unfortunately, they were too fast and got away."

"Don't be stupid and do something like that again."

Ellie stiffened. "You can't tell me what to do."

Before an argument could develop, Ellie hobbled down the sidewalk with Pad falling in step beside her. Police cars and fire trucks were in front of her home, water hoses crisscrossing the lawn.

Crossing the dew-dampened grass, Ellie called out to a fireman. "Brian! Have you been inside yet?"

The fireman came over to where they stood. "Hey, El, yeah. The fire was small. It looks like you got home just in time. It could have been really bad. Good thing your friend here acted fast and knew how to handle a fire extinguisher."

Ellie looked at Pad. "This is Brian Gallagher a friend from high school."

Pad shook the guy's hand. "Pad Stone. Wish we could have met under better circumstances. Are you sure we got the embers?"

"We laid down some suppressant and that will smother anything. Other than a mess that needs to be cleaned up, everything is all clear."

Ellie started to walk up the steps before Pad stopped her.

"We'll have to wait. This is a crime scene, and it needs to be processed first."

Ellie plopped onto an iron bench resting her head in her hands. The sounds of tires screeching caught Pad's attention. Ray and her mom got out of the car and ran to Ellie. Dropping next to her daughter, Cari wrapped Ellie in her arms and the tears started to flow.

Ray snapped. "What happened here tonight? I thought Ellie would be safe with you."

"Ray, hold on a minute. We went out to dinner and had just gotten home. We heard a crash, and when I tried the door, it was unlocked and I saw the fire starting to spread. Ellie gave chase to the intruder. I couldn't take care of the fire and watch her too."

Ray shook his head. "I'm sorry. I know she is pigheaded and you're right, putting out the fire was your first priority." Ray glanced towards the house. "Did you get a look at the guy?"

Pad shook his head. "Unfortunately, no. But I'm hoping Ellie got a good look. Whoever did this, wants us to know this is personal. Someone has a grudge against Ellie, and we need to figure out why and stop them before this really gets out of hand.

Ray stalked away.

Pad saw Officers Bell and Greene had arrived and went over to give a statement.

With a curt nod, Paul said, "What happened tonight?"

Pad relayed the story succinctly, giving them the pertinent details, but he left out the part about kissing Ellie. He didn't feel it was relevant to the situation.

"You didn't notice any cars or anything out of the ordinary when you pulled up?" Paul's pen was poised over the pad.

"No, we were talking so I didn't see anything. With everything having been pretty cool lately, my radar hasn't been on high alert. But it will be now."

Judy asked, "Pad are you losing your objectivity?"

Pad didn't answer.

"We need to talk to Ellie. Are you coming?"

"Let me ask the questions. I saw her right after she chased the perp, and I might be able to draw out some details."

Bell and Greene exchanged a look before nodding in agreement.

"Remember she's a witness."

Pad growled, "I know she's a witness. I don't need to be reminded of anything."

Pad approached Ellie. "Are you ready to tell the officers what you saw both before you took chase and after?"

Ellie hopped from one foot to the other

Pad asked, "Are you cold?"

"The grass is freezing but it doesn't matter. I'm done playing around, and it was time to end this thing, whatever it was.

"Of course. Where do you want me to start?"

"You and Pad were on the front porch?"

Ellie glanced at Pad. "Yes."

"Then what happened?" Bell spoke in a soothing tone.

"We had just come from dinner at Siam, and we were on the porch talking. Just as we were going to unlock the door, there was a loud crash." A sob in her throat threatened to escape. Ellie rested a hand on her chest and continued. "Pad told me to stay behind him. He tried the door and it opened. It made a funny creaking sound, so I think it must have startled whoever was inside." Ellie flinched and cried, "Pad, I know the door was locked when we left. I always make sure!"

Pad grasped her hand. "I know it was too."

Greene said, "I'll check the locks, front and back, to see if they were jimmied."

"Then I saw this flash of orange and heard a whoosh. Pad pushed me toward the door shouting for me to call 911. I was scared to be inside or stay out here too." Her voice quivered and she tore her eyes from Pad. "Fire scares me to death."

Ellie squeezed Pad's hand. "I'm sorry. I should have stayed to help you."

"You have nothing to be sorry about. I didn't want you in the line of fire, literally."

Ellie took a deep, shaky breath. "I saw someone, dressed in black run down the driveway. I called for them to stop but they kept going. I started running after them but my heels slowed me down. I kicked them off and ran."

"Just one person?"

"Yes."

"Did you see his face; can you describe what he was wearing?"

Ellie closed her eyes trying to bring up a mental picture. "The person was in very good shape, thin and athletic looking like a runner. You know someone who has a long stride?"

Greene's gaze encouraged her to continue. "Was the person wearing a hat?

"Yes, pulled down over their ears."

"Male or female?" Bell prodded.

Ellie shook her head. "I'm not sure. It was so hard to tell it all happened so fast."

Ellie looked at Pad. "Did you see anything?"

"By the time I got outside you were gone. I ran after you and by sheer luck I chose the right direction."

"I had to stop running. My head was starting to throb and I was getting dizzy." Ellie looked from Bell to Greene. "I should have kept going. Maybe I would have caught up to them."

"You did the right thing, Ellie. Now let us do our job." Greene flipped shut his pad. "Bell, let's take a look around the outside."

The police walked away and Ellie sank into Pad's arms.

I'm sorry I snapped at you before. This is like a nightmare that I can't wake up from, and I'm constantly thinking about what will happen next."

"We'll catch him. He'll make a mistake and we'll be there."

Her mom said, "Ellie, I think you and Pad should stay at our house tonight."

"Thank you, Cari. Ellie will stay with you but I'm staying here. Once Greene and Bell give the high sign, I'm going to look around, and I want to be here in case we get a return visitor." Seeing alarm flash over Ellie's face, Pad quickly reassured her. "I don't think they'll be stupid enough to come back."

Ray said. "Honey, take Ellie home. I'm going to stay and see if I can help."

"I don't want to leave. Mom, this is my home," Ellie protested.

"Ellie, you said your head was throbbing and you need to get a good night's rest. You'll be back bright and early. Humor me for a change. Pad and Ray will make sure everything stays safe.

Ellie looked at the three faces watching her. Knowing it

was futile to protest, she agreed. "I will be back bright and early."

Pad chuckled. "I'll be waiting for you."

Ray handed her mother the truck keys and gave her a quick kiss. "I'll call you if we hear anything, promise."

Pad watched the truck pull away from the curb.

"Stone! We found something," Paul bellowed.

Pad turned to Ray. "Ready to investigate?"

"Lead the way. Let's get this SOB."

16

"Over here."

Paul was poking through a small pile of burnt ash. "What do you make of this wooden box? My guess, it was used as the flash point."

Pad bent low. Using a pen, he pushed things around. "Looks like an old fruit crate, notice the wire holding the slats together." He pointed to what was left. "This was brought here. Ellie didn't have anything like this."

"Why do you think they used a box?" Judy said as she approached from behind. "Isn't that odd?"

Ray was standing to one side. "This whole thing is a little weird. Why is someone targeting her?"

"Sir, if we knew the answer to that we would have caught them by now." Greene looked around the room. "At least this time nothing appears to be broken or destroyed."

"You're kidding right? This whole place could have gone up in smoke if Pad and Ellie hadn't come home when they did. I can't believe your blasé attitude."

He swung around. "Pad, you're not saying much. What do you think?"

Pad studied the room and then walked into the adjoining kitchen and noticed the broken pane of glass. "This is how they got in, but why unlock the front door? Easy route of escape after the fire had been started?" He came back into the room and did a complete survey of the scene. Standing next to the burnt box, he turned and studied the room from all vantage points.

"I can see out most of these windows. If whoever was watching they would have seen my headlights come up the drive. I think the timing was deliberate. I don't think the fire was meant to get out of control, but instead wait until it could be put out."

Bell and Greene walked to where Pad stood, studying each angle.

"Judy, Pad might have something. If the perp didn't want to get caught they had a means of escape. It didn't matter which door Pad came through, hence unlocking the front. They chose the center of the room, waited until the perfect moment, caused the crash, lit the paper and then took off out the back. I think the only thing they didn't anticipate was Ellie chasing them."

"So where does that leave you now?" Ray demanded.

"It tells us quite a bit about the perp, they're looking to scare Ellie."

"Hell of a scare tactic." Ray left the room to find a broom and box to clean up the mess.

After he was gone, Pad said, "The person seems to know Ellie's routine or at least her plans. Someone is watching her. We have to figure this out soon. What if she had come home alone and tried to put the fire out. This could have been a disaster."

"I'm sure we all agree it's time to step this up. I want Ellie to come in tomorrow and talk with us about people who have been in the gallery with a similar build and maybe even hair color. For that matter, have you seen anyone that fits the description?"

Pad thought for a moment. "There was an odd fellow that was in a few days after the first incident. He reminded me of someone, but I couldn't put my finger on it at the time. Come to think of it, he had a reddish mustache tinged with gray and had a slight build. I wouldn't take him for a runner, but he could have been pretending to be a little slow."

"Will you come in tomorrow with Ellie?"

"I will, but we need to go somewhere first and that will take the morning and maybe part of the afternoon. Is late day okay?"

Judy interjected. "We start at four so if you come in around shift change we'll have some time to talk."

Ray cleared his throat. "Is it okay if I clean up? I'd like to get the smell of wet, burnt paper outside not to mention the disgusting soup of soot and foam."

"You should wait for the insurance company if you plan on filing a claim," Paul stated.

"Ray, we can call the insurance company first thing tomorrow. I'm sure if Ellie requests they come right over they'll agree. But if you think it's minor, we can clean it up without involving them."

Ray said, "I just want to make this all go away for Ellie. But since this is a criminal case, we need to involve the insurance company. I'll wait for them since you have the shoot tomorrow. Possibly, by the time you get back everything will be right as rain again."

"I know Ellie appreciates your help." Pad turned his attention to the two cops. "If I think of anything else I'll give you a call."

Pad informed Ray, "I'm going to look around. I'll be back."

❦

*R*ay gave a wave and went in search of coffee and his cell phone. He wanted to check on his wife.

Cari answered the phone on the first ring. "Hello?"

"Hi, Honey."

"Ray, I was getting worried. How are things at the house?"

"The police just left and they think the person waited until the kids got home before lighting the fire." Ray paused. "The timing was too coincidental."

"Does Pad agree?"

"Yeah."

"Where is he now?

"Outside, I think he's looking for evidence. He should be back soon. The police and Pad want the insurance company to come out and take a look before I clean up. I'm going to clear my day and wait for them and then get things back in shape. There doesn't seem to be much damage, but I don't want Ellie to come home to a mess. She's already had one to deal with and she doesn't need this again. Speaking of which, how is she?"

"Better than I expected but understandably she's upset."

"That's a good thing. She needs to be strong to get

through this. She's under attack and doesn't know why or how to defend herself."

"She is very strong." Cari released a long, low sigh. "Ray, do you believe we'll find out who this is and put them behind bars? I can't bear the thought of Ellie's dream being destroyed, or worse."

"Cari, we have to trust Pad. He's not going to stop until it's over."

"It's bizarre, we don't really know him and yet we encouraged him to move in and look after Ellie." She gasped. "Ray what if it's him, what if he's doing this to her? After all everything went wrong after Pad came along."

Ray heard the panic in her voice. "Cari?"

Silence from the other end of the phone.

"Cari, stop and think. Hank checked him out, and if he had any doubts he would never have said this was a good idea. Don't let your imagination be fueled by fear."

"I hope we're right."

"If it would make you feel better, call Hank in the morning and fill him in, ask him what his expert opinion is. That'll ease your mind."

"That's exactly what I'm going to do. But now, I'm going to fix Ellie some tea and I'll see you in the morning."

"Sleep well, honey."

"You too, and Cari?"

"Hmm?"

"We will catch him."

"I know, I have faith. It's just a matter of time, and his is running out."

Ray heard a soft click. He sat at the kitchen table wondering what would happen next.

*ad couldn't sleep. He had the car packed with bags of camera equipment and was pouring coffee in a to-go mug when Ellie came bounding through the back door. She didn't say anything about the small piece of plywood inserted where glass once sparkled.

"Sorry I'm late. Give me ten minutes."

"Do you still want to go?"

"Absolutely," she called as she dashed up the stairs.

Ellie came down the back stairs, and her sneakers hit the floor with a thud. "Please tell me there's plenty of coffee?"

Tapping his watch, Pad said, "Just under nine minutes, I'm impressed." He held up two mugs. "And I've packed a snack. I'm sure Winnie will have prepared something for breakfast but I don't like to assume."

Ellie looked at him with eyebrows wrinkled. "What makes you think Winnie will have food. Did she say something when you were over there?"

"No, she didn't say anything specifically but she had coffee cake yesterday. I guess she's kind of like your mom, always feeding people."

Ellie shrugged. "You're probably right." She stood up. "I'm ready, Mr. Stone."

Pad couldn't help but laugh. "You don't look like a photography assistant, more like a teenager hanging out with friends."

She glanced down at her clothes. "Oh, should I change? I thought jeans and sneakers were the right choice."

"No, you're fine. You just look young with your pony-tail pulled through the back of the baseball cap."

Unconvinced, Ellie started up the stairs.

"El, you're perfect just the way you are. I'm sorry if that came out wrong. Most of the time you're, well, a little more dressed up."

"I can see what you mean. I dress so customers and vendors take me seriously. I know I look young. Most people don't want to trust a fourteen-year-old in business."

"Trust me, you don't look like a fourteen-year-old."

Ellie grabbed the coffee mug out of his hand. "We're going to be late," she said, walking out the door and leaving Pad watching the back side of her form-fitting jeans.

"I'm going to have to keep focused today," he muttered and secured the door behind them.

On the drive to the Simpson estate, Ellie peppered Pad with questions about the fire and his theories.

"Let me get this straight. You don't think the fire was supposed to cause a lot of damage. Whoever this was waited until we got home before striking the match."

"I do. We had been gone for hours. While we were, you know, kissing like teenagers, the fire breaks out? I think they waited for the perfect moment so that it wouldn't get out of control."

"Seriously? That is pretty calculated. What if we hadn't, um, noticed?"

"The point was for us to hear it, and we did. The front door was unlocked, and you know it wasn't when we left. It provided quick access, therefore I was able to put the fire out. Oh, you don't know this little tidbit. The fire was built mostly of paper in an old wooden box and set in a metal wheelbarrow, minus the wheels and handles. It had the ability to stay contained but there was a small paper trail leading toward your desk. The potential was there but really designed as an attention getter."

"What do you really think is going on, and I want you to be honest."

Pad looked at her sideways as he pulled to the side of the road and put the car in park. "As you can guess, I've thought about this a great deal. Someone wants to put you out of business is the only reason I can come up with. I don't know why or who but both incidents didn't do serious damage, most of the art survived unscathed." Ellie started to interject. Pad looked at her, one eyebrow raised. "And yes, you were attacked, but your injury, overall, was minor. These are warnings. You need to think about who would benefit by the gallery closing. Could someone from college be envious of your success? What about one of your vendors, has anyone been displeased with your commission or placement in your gallery?"

Ellie shook her head. "There isn't anyone I can think of at the moment, but I'll certainly give it careful consideration. It's just crazy to think that someone wants to destroy my dream." Ellie tried to avert her face, but Pad saw the tears that glistened her eyes.

Pad lightly stroked her forearm. "Ellie, we will get him."

"I know. It just ticks me off. I've worked hard and nothing has been handed to me on a silver platter. If anyone is jealous of what I have accomplished, maybe they should work harder." Ellie wiped her cheeks. In a steady low-pitched voice, she said, "Mark my words, once we find out who is doing this, they'll see The Looking Glass will be successful in spite of their pathetic attempts to squash me like a bug."

Pad squeezed her hand. "That's what I like to see, fire

in those deep blue eyes. It won't be long now before we have someone in custody."

"As long as it's the right person." Ellie exhaled. "We're late so put this car in drive and I'll call Winnie."

Pad did as he was told, mulling over an idea or two about the fire. He would ask Winnie a couple of questions about her gallery friends and who might have it out for Ellie.

Ellie dropped the phone in her lap. "Winnie said to drive safely and she'd see us when we get there. She wasn't in a rush to get started this morning anyway."

"I'm sure she's been up for hours."

Ellie's gaze focused on Pad. "You seem to have a lot of assumptions about a woman you met a few days ago. Are you always this presumptuous?"

"Oh, well yesterday she told me she was an early riser."

Ellie watched the fields of wildflowers out the window. "Sorry, I guess I'm on edge."

Pad slowed the car and saw Winnie standing in the driveway waving. "There she is. Hopefully she's as excited for me to take pictures as she is for us to arrive."

Ellie hopped out and helped Pad carry the cases into the foyer.

"Eleanor, Padraic I'm so glad you're here. Can I interest you in coffee and a sunshine muffin?"

Ellie grinned a knowing smile. "That sounds wonderful."

Pad followed Ellie and their hostess into the kitchen where mugs and a plate of muffins waited.

"Winnie, I hope you're not trying to delay the shoot?" Pad teased his aunt.

"Why would you say such a thing. I firmly believe we need something to give us energy to get through a busy morning."

Pad shook his head and laughed. "Just one muffin, Winnie, and then we work."

17

*W*innie stood in the background with a gleam in her eye. Pad set up a tripod, used a small meter to inspect the lighting, and peered through the lens. She had seen him do this before, fuss over his camera like a mother with a baby.

He nodded. "Mrs. Simpson, are you ready?"

Winnie bit her lip and waltzed over to the waiting canvas. "Is this where you'd like me?"

Pad walked to her side. Noticing that Ellie was distracted by various paintings scattered around the room, under his breathe he said, "Behave yourself."

Winnie smiled sweetly. "But of course."

"Just paint and forget I'm here." Pad took another look through the view finder.

Pad's camera clicked as Winnie became absorbed in the colors of the canvas. Pad could see it showed promise of what was to come.

Ellie watched from Pad's vantage point. Winnie's brush teased the canvas, sometimes tiny movements or larger sweeping strokes. Ellie's voice was almost inaudible when she spoke. "It's like a butterfly coming out of a cocoon."

Pad watched his beloved aunt. As a child, he would spend hours with her in this very studio cajoling the paints on her palette to dance onto the canvas. Often Winnie set Pad up with an easel and paints but more often than not, he would become transfixed by the magic his aunt held over simple items. He was convinced his appreciation of nature was born in this room.

Ellie and Pad were transported into Winnie's world. She stepped back from the canvas, breaking the spell, and Pad started shooting pictures again.

Without turning around, she said, "Did you get what you were looking for Pad?"

Pad nodded, at a loss for words. He had forgotten how this felt, to be here, with Winnie.

Winnie set down the brush and wiped her hands down the front of her smock. "You know I have a nephew, and when he was a child he'd watch me paint for hours." Pointing her finger, she continued, "Eleanor, you are wearing the very same expression. I take it you enjoyed yourself?"

"Very much. Thank you for allowing me to catch a glimpse into your private world."

"Of course, my dear." Winnie turned back to the canvas, and Pad moved around the room taking pictures from various angles. She ignored the camera while she studied the painting.

"Eleanor, do you think this is something you'd like in your gallery? After it's finished of course."

Ellie stammered, "It would be wonderful but I'm sure it would be better at Barton's."

Winnie dismissed the comment with a wave of her hand. "I always decide what goes where, and this will be perfect to replace the one that little monster destroyed." Winnie winked. "We'll show them, won't we?"

"I'm stunned you still want to give me the consignment. At this point there is no guarantee it won't happen again."

"Please stop worrying. As attached as I get to my work, it is, after all, just paint and cloth and a little time. Besides with this young man on your side, I am convinced the end is in sight."

Pad held his breath while watching the two women, one a worrywart and the other the eternal optimist.

Ellie kissed Winnie's cheek. "I appreciate the faith you have in both of us even though we're virtual strangers."

"I know who to trust." Winnie pointed at Pad's equipment. "If you get this picked up, we can have a bite of lunch and then do the garden shoot. But I'll need to change into something more flattering than my old paint spattered apron."

"I can help you with lunch." Ellie glanced at Pad's collection of empty cases. "Or I can help you break down."

"Go with Winnie, you'll have more fun and this won't take me long."

Pad's mouth went dry. How long could he wait before revealing the truth?

The sunroom was filled with light. An old-fashioned tea cart was filled to overflowing with plates of sandwiches, salad, and desserts. A pitcher of lemonade sat in the middle of a matching table, with three floral cushioned chairs. Pad looked out the window and watched Winnie pointing out different flowers in her prized garden. They were headed back toward the house, so Pad poured some lemonade and then grabbed a small bite-sized lemon tart.

The glass door slid open, and the ladies were lost in conversation about tomato plants as they filled glasses. They loaded two small, vine-covered plates with fruit, cheese, and shrimp salad.

"You should see Winnie's vegetable garden, its huge. I don't think a weed would dare to grow in it."

"You don't say?" Pad cocked an eyebrow in his aunt's direction.

Ellie gushed, "And her flower gardens. I don't think I have ever seen such beautiful hydrangeas. The blue ones are breathtaking, and she also has pink and white."

"Eleanor, please," Winnie mildly protested. "You're giving me far too much credit. Once I popped them in the ground, it was up to Mother Nature to do the rest."

"Whoever can take credit, should. Has anyone ever gotten married out there?"

Winnie looked out towards the garden. "Yes, as a matter of fact my sister married the love of her life amidst the rose bushes."

"I didn't know you had a sister."

"I did, unfortunately she passed away years ago."

"What happened to her husband? Did she have children?"

"After Lena was gone, Bruce drifted away from the family, and then he passed away, I believe from a broken heart. They had two children, a son and a daughter."

"Are you close?"

Winnie studied the contents of her glass. "My niece passed away as a child. My nephew and I are close, but he travels a great deal for work so I don't see him as often as I'd like."

Pad stood up, his chair scraped the tile floor. "I think if we're going to get any decent garden shots we need to get started before I lose the light." His voice sounded harsh even to his ears.

"Pad," Ellie hissed.

Pain flashed over Winnie's face. "You're right of course. I'm sorry, you're not here to listen to ancient history." Smiling brightly, she said, "Eleanor, are you coming?"

Ellie picked up the dirty dishes from the table and carried them to the kitchen sink. "In a few minutes. I want to tidy up for you."

"Just put them down, Eleanor. I'll take care of them later."

Ellie trailed behind Pad as he walked through the main foyer. A large framed picture caught her eye. "Is this your sister?"

Winnie stood behind her and picked up the ornate metal frame. "Yes, this is Lena, Bruce, and my nephew."

"He is adorable. Pad, take a look." Ellie looked from the picture to Pad and then back again. "That's interesting he has the same color eyes as yours."

A distant rumble of thunder caught Ellie's attention. "We'd better hurry before the storm hits." She went outside.

Winnie pulled on Pad's shirt tail and hissed. "If Eleanor means anything to you tell her the truth, soon."

"I'm leaving as soon as we nail the guy," he growled and stalked out.

Pad charged toward the gardens. He turned around and started back toward his aunt. Pad stopped in his tracks. She was looking up to the heavens and he heard her say, "Lena, how am I going to get him to see it's time to settle down and start a family?"

Ellie skipped back to the house in search of Winnie and Pad. Finding them standing in the driveway, Ellie called, "Are you coming?"

Pad walked past Ellie headed to the rose gardens. He draped a camera around his neck and had positioned the tripod as the two women walked up arm in arm.

He glanced up from the shot. "The roses are stunning, Winnie. Do you have a secret potion?"

Winnie laughed. "No just rich soil and a great helper. Besides I bet you say that to anyone who let you take pictures of their flower gardens."

"Ma'am, I was raised to be honest and always give a compliment when deserved." He turned back to his camera, slipping into his work.

Ellie said, "Pad, what can I do to help?"

Pad didn't answer her.

*

"*E*leanor, why don't we let Pad do his thing." Winnie led the way through the garden to a large wooden swing. "My late husband built this glider as a gift for me. I've always loved to sit amongst the flowers. I believe roses are filled with magic. Most evenings we'd enjoy a glass of wine and watch the sun set, even in the winter, although those chilly nights a glass of good brandy was the perfect beverage."

Winnie stretched her legs out, wiggled her toes and closed her eyes. Ellie followed suit. A light breeze stirred and the gentle hum of bees could be heard flitting from flower to flower. Pushing the swing in a slow rhythmic motion, Ellie felt the worries of the last few weeks slipping away.

"I would have agreed with Mr. Simpson, this is wonderful, to be able to sit in the sun with this endless view of flowers, meadows, and then forest."

"He'd be tickled pink to know it's still magical. When I'm out here, it doesn't seem like he's gone. Sometimes I forget and expect he'll be walking up, any minute, to join me." Winnie put her hand on her heart. "I remember how he looked at me. Much like the way Pad looks at you."

"Nonsense. Pad is a very good friend, and there's nothing more to it."

"Are you sure?"

"Winnie, stop trying to play matchmaker. I don't need a boyfriend. But someday I'd like to have a garden so I may ask you to give me the name of your gardener." Ellie smiled. "Thank you for sharing this special spot with me."

Winnie lightly touched Ellie's leg. "My dear Eleanor, you're welcome in my haven anytime."

*P*ad kept one eye on Winnie and Ellie as they chatted the hour away. He didn't have to closely monitor what was in his camera lens as he set up the shots expertly, instinctively knowing how to capture each bloom to perfection. It was easy since the gardens were stunning. His cell phone vibrated in his chest pocket. A familiar number was displayed.

"Stone here, have you learned something new?"

"Impatient aren't you?" Paul chuckled on the other end. "I would have thought sharing a house with Ms. McKenna wouldn't be a hardship."

Running a hand over his head, he barked, "Ellie wants

her life back, and I need to get back to mine too. I promised her family I would see this through and I will."

"Hey, relax, I was just kidding you, man."

"Well, have you learned anything?"

"As a matter fact I think we have something very interesting. When can you swing by the station?"

Pad calculated how long it would take to pack up, get back into town, and drop Ellie off. "Ninety minutes?"

Pad knew how the game worked. He was fairly certain Greene had something good.

"Ladies." Pad jogged over. "I hate to cut this short, but I just got a call, and I have to get to a meeting. The good news is I have some great shots, and I got what I need so I'll pack up. Ellie, are you ready?"

"That's too bad I was hoping to convince you to stay. Perhaps you'll come with Pad when he shows me the photos and I'll make dinner."

"I'd love to come, thank you." Ellie beamed. "Excuse me I should help Pad."

"Of course, dear, you run along. I'm going to sit here and enjoy what's left of the day."

*

*E*llie bent to pick up a case at the same time as Pad reached for it. She was unprepared for the effect the mere touch of his hand would have on her. "I'm sorry," she murmured, quickly withdrawing her hand.

"Thanks for the help. Can you grab that small one?"

Ellie stooped down and picked it up. "Is there anything in this one?" She twirled around.

Pad grabbed the case. "Can you be careful! It has the

first camera my mother gave to me, and I don't want it broken."

Ellie's face burned and she stuttered, "I'm sorry, Pad."

Without a word, Pad closed the trunk. "I'm going to say goodbye to Winnie."

Ellie trailed behind him, back to the garden. Silence hung heavy between them. "Do you mind telling me what came up and if it's about me I want full disclosure?"

Pad's steps slowed. "Greene called. It sounds like there might be a break in the case. He wouldn't give me details, but said I should come right over. I'm going to drop you off and go to the station."

"Don't bother, I'm going with you."

"Fine," Pad snapped. "Whether you go or not won't change the fact that I want to stop at the house and drop off my equipment. I don't want to leave it in a hot car since I'm not sure how long it might take."

"You know I'm not a little girl, and I don't need you to protect me." Ellie crossed her arms across her chest.

"I'm committed to catching this person before they do something really bad. As of right now, with the exception of assaulting you, everything has been relatively minor."

"I don't consider a fire, minor."

"Ellie, if someone had really wanted to burn down your gallery they could have started the fire right after we left for dinner. Instead it started when we were standing at the front door. I don't believe that was a coincidence and neither do the police." Pad threw up his hands. "If you want to come then feel free. I'm not going to stop you."

Feeling justified, Ellie looked out the window and remained silent for the rest of the ride.

Pad pulled up the driveway. "I'll be a few minutes. Why don't you just stay put," he barked.

Ellie ignored him as Pad unlocked the back door and made several trips to the car. Each time Ellie was poking in the flower pots. A black, sleek, sports car parked at the curb and Karlene stepped out and embraced Ellie.

"Hi Karlene. Don't you look the perfect picture with your hair tied in a turban, practical for a woman driving her convertible.

Pad joined them. "Hello, Karlene. It's a pleasure to see you again." Pad clasped her perfectly manicured hand.

"Ellie, I didn't know your bodyguard was still hanging around." Karlene winked at her. "Oh, that's right he's not your bodyguard, he's your wayward boyfriend."

"Actually, I was just on my way out. Ellie, are you coming?"

"Oh, I should have called first. I was hoping we could spend a little time together. It seems like it's been ages since we've had time for some girl talk." She batted her blue eyes.

"Pad, you go and we'll catch up later." Ellie jerked her head toward the door.

"I'll pick up a pizza, for three?" Pad looked at Karlene. "What do you like?"

"Oh, thank you, but I can't stay. Besides pizza hasn't touched my lips in more years than I'd care to admit. Unlike Ellie, I don't enjoy exercise or running, specifically."

"Then I will leave you ladies to enjoy your girl-talk."

Pad jogged up the driveway. Ellie watched Karlene lick her lips and study him with a sharp eye. Ellie's stomach flipped.

"That is one fine looking man, Ellie. Have the two of you made permanent plans?"

"Karlene." Ellie blushed

Karlene linked her arm through Ellie's and steered her toward the house. "Tell all and omit nothing."

Her insecure moment forgotten Ellie's laughter rang out.

18

The heavy security door opened easily, and Pad strode toward the desk. The duty officer stood behind the bullet-resistant glass.

"Pad Stone, here to see either Officer Greene or Bell."

The desk officer nodded and picked up a phone. Momentarily, a door to the inner sanctum opened.

Judy smiled. "Pad, thanks for coming in. You'll be happy the new security system was in place."

"Really?"

"We don't know who it is specifically but with this new information, we know we're looking for a woman.

"You're kidding, right?"

"See for yourself."

Judy opened the door to a small office and let Pad enter first. The room was dominated by a large screen, and Paul had a laptop open in front of him.

"Hey, did Judy fill you in?"

"She said we're looking for a woman?"

"Take a look."

Pad leaned in to watch the events unfold and noticed

the time stamp. The person on the screen was wearing tight fitting dark clothing and by the outline it was definitely a woman's figure. She entered shortly after Pad and Ellie had left for dinner. The camera showed her unlocking both doors and then opening and shutting them, confirming access was clear. Then she set up the metal barrel with papers and small pieces of wood. She took a magazine from Ellie's desk and sat down to wait.

"Does she ever remove the mask so we could get a good look at her face?" Pad asked.

Judy shook her head.

Occasionally, the woman would glance at what appeared to be an expensive watch and go back to reading. As the room grew dark, a pen-lite appeared and illuminated the magazine. Pad watched as she glanced toward the kitchen and got up, throwing the magazine on the pile of papers.

"We must have just gotten home."

Pad watched the woman's body turn as Pad and Ellie must have been walking to the front door. After a few minutes, she put a match to the pile, watching the fire spring to life, threw a pitcher to the floor, and took off at a dead run out the back. The camera caught Pad as he rushed in and grabbed the fire extinguisher and Ellie as she pushed past him, in hot pursuit. Pad knew the rest, so he turned away from the video and pulled out a chair.

"It was clear she was waiting for us. But the one thing I find odd, she didn't attempt to cover the camera. We know from the first incident, she knew how to shut it down. But this time, she let it roll, why?"

"You know the criminal type is sometimes hard to figure out. But you're right she wanted to be filmed." Judy looked at her partner. "Why do you think she kept it rolling?"

"It's obvious, she wanted us to know she waited before setting the fire. She was patient, even casual, throughout the entire night and she was well organized. This is a person who wants to be in charge and feels in control of our investigation too."

Pad scraped the chair over the linoleum floor. "Was there anything else?"

"Nope that's it." The officers followed Pad from the room. "What's your next step?"

"I'm going back to the beginning and look at everything again. There is something we've missed and I will find it." Pad's eyes gleamed like hardened steel.

Paul joked. "I'm glad you're not pursuing me."

Pad gave a curt nod. "I'll be in touch if I learn anything and you do the same."

Pad found himself driving out by the lake and wondered if Shane would be home. Adjusting his route, Pad pulled up the long driveway and noted the McKenna landscape truck wasn't there. Before he could leave, a pretty girl came around the side pulling a wagon and a little boy perched in it.

"Hello, can I help you?"

Pad turned the ignition off. "I don't think we've met yet. I'm Pad Stone."

The woman grinned. "The bodyguard. Hello, I'm Abby McKenna."

Pad cleared his throat. "I'm not really a bodyguard. Cari and Ray asked me to keep an eye on things at Ellie's place and help the police apprehend..."

Abby held up her hand, chuckling. "You'd better stop

right there and keep the title otherwise Shane and Jake will not take kindly to you living at Ellie's."

Pad nodded. "I met them at the hospital. If I was in their shoes I'd feel the same way."

"So how can I help you? Devin and I were just on our way down to the water. Care to tag along?"

Pad fell in step with Abby. "Want a hand with the wagon?"

Abby shook her head. "No thanks, I'm fine." She looked at him sideways. "You haven't said why you stopped over."

"Actually, I wanted to talk to Shane. I want to ask him a few questions. I'm hoping he might be able to shed some light on a few things that have been bothering me."

"About the house or Ellie?"

"Primarily Ellie." Pad took a sharp look at his companion. "Would you mind answering a few questions about the house?"

"Not at all. The house is my family's, well mine now. My parents and sister died a few years ago before Devin and I moved back from the eastern part of the state. Originally my great grandparents owned it and eventually my parents."

"It's been in your family for a couple of generations?"

"Yes. Why do you ask?"

"Have you ever been approached about selling?"

"Never. Well someone might have asked Dad. It was empty for almost ten years, but he never mentioned anything."

"Well there goes that theory. I was wondering if someone was using a back-handed approach to force you to sell."

Abby's eyes were the size of saucers. "Do you think that's why someone hurt Ellie, so I would sell the house?"

"No. It was a theory however you haven't been approached, so I'm crossing that off the list."

A slamming door caught Pad's attention, and he looked up to see Shane McKenna jogging across the lawn, looking like a man with a mission.

Abby grinned. "Hi, Honey."

Shane slipped a protective arm around Abby's waist. "Pad."

"Hello, Shane." The two men sized each other up.

"I didn't expect to find you here. Kind of a drive from town."

"I was at the police station. I'm sure you heard about the fire, and we got video from last night. I wanted to ask you a few questions. Stopping was a spur of the moment thing, and your wife has been gracious enough to answer a few lingering questions about the house."

"Such as?"

"Shane." Abby laid a hand on his arm. "Pad wanted to know if anyone had asked to buy it, and I told him no."

"What does that have to do with anything?"

"I haven't told your sister yet but the intruder waited, actually read a magazine, until we got home last night before striking the match. I don't believe the intent was to do serious damage. More of a nuisance."

"That seems odd don't you think?"

"I do, and it got me to thinking about other possibilities. You have a vested interest in your sister's life, but you aren't her mother, so I can ask you some pointed questions."

Shane squared his shoulders. "What kind of questions?"

187

"Shane, why don't we get a cool drink and sit on the deck?" Abby pulled on Shane's arm.

"Yeah, we can go up to the house." Shane pulled the little red wagon and carried a giggling child.

Pad sighed. So, this is what it's like to be part of a large family. Everyone has each other's back at all times. Pad paused to take in the view.

"Great place you have here."

"We like it. It was a shack when I bought it, but the view was priceless." Shane stood at the kitchen door. "Beer or soda?"

"Whatever you're having is fine."

"Shane, will you bring me a water and some for Devin too?" Abby turned to their guest. "Please have a seat."

Devin toddled over to Pad and proceeded to scramble up on the bench beside him.

Pad looked at the little guy and tickled him under his chin. "He sure is cute."

"He has his moments just like all little boys. But we adore him." Abby smiled and continued. "Do you have family?"

"No, my mom died a long time ago, and I was an only child. I'm close with my aunt, her sister, and my dad died a while back."

"I'm sorry to hear that. Do you see your aunt often?"

"Not as much as I'd like but we talk a lot when I'm traveling."

Shane's return interrupted their conversation.

Passing a bottle of cold beer to Pad, Shane took a seat next to his wife and Devin hopped down and ran over to him. Reflex kicked in and Shane scooped up the little boy and plopped Devin onto his lap.

"Tell me, how can I help you find the person that did this?"

"Tell me about her friends, boyfriends, do you know if anyone begrudges her success? That kind of thing."

"Hmm, she's never had a lot of close friends but she is a friend to everyone she meets. If you know what I mean."

Pad knew exactly what Shane was saying. It described her to a tee. "Do you think there is a guy who feels jilted?"

"Nope. When Ellie dated, it was in groups. There was never one special guy. I think she believes in the fairytales that she'll just know when she meets the man of her dreams. I can't think of a single person capable of doing these types of things."

"Abby, what about you? Can you think of anyone connected to either Ellie or you that would be malicious enough to attempt to burn down the house?"

"Pad, I wish I could help you but I'm at a loss too. Everyone around town watches out for each other."

Pad watched Devin squirt water from his straw and giggle. "He sure is a bubbly little guy."

Before Pad could say anything more, Shane's cell phone rang.

"Hello?" Shane paused and Pad could hear an excited female voice from where he stood. "Ellie, everything will be fine. Is Mom leaving for Kate's soon?"

Pad was on alert. "Is everything okay?" He glanced at Abby.

"All right." He put his hand over the phone. "Kate's in labor, and Mom and Ray are leaving and Ellie's ready to go." He spoke into the phone. "Yes. Abby and I can keep an eye on things."

Pad waved at Shane. "Can I talk to her?"

Shane passed him the phone.

"Ellie." Pad was silent. "I'll explain later. I'm on my way home, wait for me." Pad passed the phone back to Shane. "She hung up."

He took off without a backward glance.

*

*P*ad burst into the kitchen, calling out for Ellie. She was standing in the doorway with hands on her hips, her eyes bright.

"Would you mind telling me what you were doing at my brother's house? I thought you went to the police station."

Pad stated, "I took a drive to analyze the information. I found myself out by the lake. On impulse I stopped."

"Do you think my brother or his wife had something to do with all this nonsense?"

"Of course not. Abby owns this building, and just maybe she had been approached to sell it, and saying no ticked someone off. I also talked to Shane about anyone that might have felt rejected by you, an old flame or something."

With some of the wind taken out of her sails, Ellie said, "Well, you could have asked me some of those questions."

"Ellie, most times when there is a jilted boyfriend or business associate, outsiders see things with more clarity."

"Next time, at least you could let me know."

"I will. I'm sorry if I offended you."

Irritation forgotten, Ellie brightened. "I guess you heard Kate's in labor, and I need to take off. I can't wait to meet my new niece or nephew."

"Do you want me to go with you?"

Visibly taken aback, she said, "That's nice of you to

offer but it's an easy drive. All highway and I love driving. I was hoping you'd stay here and keep an eye on things."

"I can do that. It will give me time to do a little exploring with my camera too."

"Oh, I almost forgot, Karlene and I had a great visit. She was telling me about a new painter she hopes to woo. She wouldn't give me any details, but I guess that's how this business rolls, don't share until they're locked up and under contract. I'm thrilled for her."

"Did you like working for Karlene?"

"Absolutely, she taught me so much, how to handle temperamental clients, and I saw first-hand what not to do in my own gallery."

"What do you mean?"

Ellie began rummaging through her handbag. "Now where is that darn phone charger." She pulled it out and grinned. "Can't leave this behind." She put her bag on the table next to the car keys.

"I'm sorry what did you say?"

"You said you learned what not to do. What did you mean by that?"

"Are you interrogating me, Mr. Stone?"

Grinning, he said, "Old habits die hard."

"Since we were sucking face on the porch, you know I didn't start the fire, so I'm not a suspect, and I didn't hit myself over the head and toss me in the closet so we're good. Anyway, her artists are of a certain caliber. She wouldn't branch out. For example, she wasn't keen on photographers but most people love to travel vicariously."

"What does she exhibit?"

"She loves landscapes, oils, watercolors, like Kincaid or Winifred Simpson. Several times she tried to get her under contract, but, no luck."

Ellie glanced at her watch. "I need to go. Can we talk about this when I get back?"

"Sure, do me one favor?"

"Yeah, what?"

"Shoot me a text when you arrive. I'd feel better knowing you got there without any speeding tickets and, of course, I want to hear about Kate and the baby."

Pad found Ellie's tender spot. She stood on her tiptoes and lightly kissed his mouth.

Pad slid his arms around Ellie, pulling her close, and deepened the kiss. Losing awareness of everything other than each other, in those brief moments something changed for Ellie. Pad released her, sliding a finger down her cheek and jaw line. "Please be careful."

Ellie's eyes fluttered opened, her heart hammering. The heat of his kiss lingered on her lips. Very softly, she said, "We'll talk later." It took an immense force of will to step out of Pad's arms and walk away.

19

*E*llie drove on autopilot, as she replayed the kiss over and over. "I can't fall for this guy." She reminded herself for the umpteenth time, "He's leaving."

Ellie flicked on her blinker and hit the speaker phone button.

After the fourth ring, she heard, "Hello?"

"Hey Mom, how are things progressing with Kate?"

"Hi El, slow. The contractions are still ten minutes apart. At least that's what Don said before he went back into the room. Where are you?"

Ellie glanced at the dashboard. "According to my GPS, I'll be there in about an hour."

"All right, there's a chair with your name on it."

"Tell Kate to wait for me."

Her mom laughed. "I don't think that's what she wants to hear. She's ready to have this baby, now. Drive carefully and see you soon."

Ellie's thoughts drifted back to Pad and that amazing goodbye kiss. She hoped there would be time for her to ask Kate's opinion on the date, kissing, and most of all these feelings that were starting to surface.

Ellie pulled into a rest stop to use the facility and buy a cold drink. As she walked back to the car, she thought there was someone sitting in the passenger seat. She turned around to survey the parking lot.

Ellie rushed over to a policeman sitting in a cruiser. "Excuse me."

The police officer's window slid down. "Miss, is something wrong?"

"I went inside for just a few minutes, and it looks like someone is sitting in my car." Ellie's arm shook as she pointed to her car.

The policeman asked, "Miss, the dark green SUV?"

"Yes, in the passenger seat."

"Let's take a look." Ellie stayed one step behind the officer. Without turning, he said, "Is it locked?"

"Yes."

He then walked around the car and tried all the doors. "Can you unlock the car for me. I'll make sure no one is hiding."

Ellie watched as he did a thorough check. "There isn't anyone here. It must have been a reflection."

"Are you sure, Officer?" Ellie's voice quivered.

"Miss, are you okay? Have you been drinking?"

"No, it's nothing like that. I guess I'm just a little jumpy. I was assaulted a few weeks ago, and recently someone started a fire in my gallery. This is the first time I've been truly alone since it all started. I guess it's just nerves."

"That's understandable. Where're you headed?"

"Crescent Lake. My sister's having a baby."

"You have about another hour. Are you okay to drive?"

Ellie forced a smile. "I'm fine Officer, like I said, I'm just a little jumpy."

"Understandable, and we're here to serve and protect." The officer gave her a pleasant smile.

"I'm sorry I bothered you."

"Anytime. Don't forget to buckle up and drive safely Miss…"

"McKenna, Eleanor McKenna."

"Ms. McKenna, have a safe day."

Ellie watched the officer walk away. She heard a soft voice speak.

"I'm sorry, my sweet baby girl. I didn't mean to scare you."

Ellie turned to see her father standing next to the car.

"Daddy?"

Her dad appeared in her passenger seat, and as with the other times she saw him, he was almost transparent. Astonished, Ellie opened the car door, got in, and slammed it behind her.

"Was that you I saw?"

He nodded. "Yes. I thought it would be better to pop in while you weren't driving."

"Well, yeah. This is crazy. I'm talking to a ghost, in a rest stop on my way to see my sister, who is in labor, at this very minute. Waiting until I was parked was a much better idea."

Her father's ghost let her ramble on, until he noticed the police officer walking back toward the car. "Eleanor, you might want to put your seatbelt on and start the car."

Ellie peered out the windshield.

The police officer waited while she rolled down the window. "Ms. McKenna is anything wrong. It looks like you were talking to yourself."

Ellie held up her cell. "Just checking in with my mother, letting her know my ETA."

The officer adjusted his hat and left.

Ellie dropped the car in drive and eased out of the parking space, merging into traffic.

Once at a steady pace, she glanced toward her father's ghost. "I'm not sure why you're here. Shouldn't you be with Kate or in heaven?"

"Kate doesn't need me. Do you remember I was with you in the closet?"

Ellie slowly nodded. "I do."

"You needed me then, and you need me now."

"Why do you think I need you? I'm perfectly fine. My business is open and it's everything I've worked for."

"What about love?"

"I don't have time for all that stuff. I'm too busy."

"Honey, no one is too busy for love."

Ellie exited the highway and found the hospital all without responding. She found an open spot away from other cars and parked. She sat quietly her hands gripping the steering wheel. "I don't want to fall in love and deal with all the nonsense that goes with it. I'm fine by myself."

"Don't you want to have a relationship like Kate and Don?"

"Not everyone gets lucky, Daddy."

"You don't want someone special in your life?"

Ellie glanced at her dad and then out the windshield. "No."

"Eleanor McKenna, don't lie to your father, but more importantly, to yourself."

Ellie put her head down and for the first time in weeks let the tears flow unchecked.

"Daddy," she said with a thick voice. "Since that night

there has been a man in my life. In fact, he's staying with me. Mom put him up to it, sort of, to keep an eye on me since they haven't caught the person trying to destroy my business. I'm developing feelings for him, but he's going back to his life soon, and I don't want to be left with a broken heart."

"Pixie, if you don't let yourself be vulnerable your heart will never be full."

"Daddy, other than stating the obvious, that I'm very much a happily single woman, why else are you here? Do you know who's trying to destroy my business?"

"No, I don't know any specifics about the trouble you're having at the gallery. I visited your mother until her heart healed and then Kate when she and Don were having issues and losing their way as a couple and now it's your turn."

"Now that you mention Mom and Kate, why haven't you talked to Shane? He is your son. Don't you think he needed your help at some point?"

"I don't have the answers. I've been able to watch him from, well, wherever it is I'm stuck, and he's grown into a fine man."

"He's married and adopted a sweet little boy."

"I wish I could talk with Shane. He was good to you and your sister, and the man of the house for your mother. I know it was a heavy burden for a ten-year-old boy."

"Shane is the best brother I could have, and you're right, he was Mom's right hand until Gram and Gramps came to live with us. I don't remember much about the first few years, but I know they were around a lot. Helping Mom with her shop and us kids."

"It was good of Dave and Sue to step in, after…"

Her cell phone buzzed, catching her attention. "Hello?"

"Are you here yet?" Her mom's excitement vibrated through the phone. "It's almost time and Kate's asking for you."

"I just parked, be right up." Ellie touched the empty passenger seat. "He's just in my imagination."

Ellie got off the elevator and looked right and left. She followed signs to the waiting room.

"Mom?" Ellie said. "How's Kate?"

Cari hugged her youngest daughter and said, "Kate's doing great, a little tired, but that's normal. Don hasn't left her side since she went into labor. He's tried to keep her distracted."

"That sounds like Don. Do you think I can see her for just a minute? I want her to know I'm here."

"Come with me." Her mom led the way.

Don's voice boomed. "Are you ready to push?"

Ellie peeked in the room. "Katie?"

Kate pushed Don's hand aside and reached for her sister. "Ellie, come here. I want to see you before I officially become a mother."

Kate grimaced as she breathed in and out. "By the way, labor hurts like heck."

"You look beautiful, Sissy."

"Ah, thanks." Kate shut her eyes tight, breathing deeply through another contraction, squeezing Ellie's hand with all her might. She collapsed back on the pillows, eyes closed.

"Katie?"

Her eyes fluttered open. "It's okay, Pixie, just part of the process to get this little person out of his hiding place."

"I'm going outside, but I'm not leaving until I hold this baby." Ellie kissed her brow and touched Don's arm.

A flurry of nurses came into the room upon Ellie's hasty exit.

She dropped into a chair between Ray and Mom. "Is this how labor is supposed to go? She looks happy and exhausted all at the same time."

Ellie just noticed most of the Price family gathered around the small room.

Kate's mother-in-law, Sherry, said, "It won't last much longer." She grasped Ellie's hand. "I'm glad you're here."

"I wouldn't have missed this for anything. This baby has quite a welcoming committee."

Don came in the waiting room dressed in blue scrubs, walking on air, "I've only got a minute, but it won't be much longer now." Giving thumbs up, he ran down the hallway in booty-clad feet.

"We might as well make ourselves comfortable." Sherry said as she took the empty seat between her husband, Sam, and Don's brother, Jack.

Ellie dropped her voice and spoke only for her mother and Ray's ears. "Pad watched a video of the latest incident. I didn't get a chance to ask all the details, but we're pretty close to solving this mystery."

"Well that's great news," Ray spoke. "When is Pad leaving?"

"Soon, I think." Ellie's face sagged.

"El, is something wrong?" her mom asked.

"Nope, just on edge. All this waiting." She looked up. "I'm going to find a vending machine. Does anyone want something?"

Before she could get an answer, Don burst into the room. "It's a boy!" Don grabbed Sherry and twirled her around the room.

Sam let out a whoop and hopped up, clapping his son on the back. "Another grandson and how's Kate?"

"She did great and the baby is beautiful."

"Don, can we see them?" Cari was anxious to hold her grandson and see for herself, that Kate was fine.

With eyes shining, he said, "Let me check." And he was off down the hall.

Excitement filled the room with everyone talking at once.

Patience was rewarded with a nurse asking, "Mrs. Davis? Your daughter is ready to see your family along with Mr. Price's parents.

"Ellie, are you coming?"

Kate cradled a tiny bundle, sporting a little blue cap, in her arms.

"Hi, Grandma," she whispered. "Here he is." She tilted her arm down as Don hovered over them. "Isn't he gorgeous?"

Her mom's eyes glowed. "Kate, he's perfect." She choked back tears and Ray took her hand.

Sherry clung to Sam. "He looks just like Donovan when he was born."

Sam cleared his throat. "I can definitely see a resemblance to our side of the family."

Ellie perched on the edge of the bed to get a closer look. "Look at all that dark hair. What color eyes do you think he'll have?"

"A baby's eye color changes throughout the first year, so we'll just have to wait and see, but I suspect they'll be brown." Kate placed a tender kiss on the baby's head.

Ray leaned in for a closer look. "Have you two chosen a name yet?"

Kate looked up at Don. "We have."

Placing a hand on Kate's shoulder Don's deep voice filled the room. "We hope you'll approve." He looked from his father to Cari. "Benjamin Samuel Price."

Cari and Ellie's tears fell amid smiles.

Sam was the first to speak. "That's a fine name for your son."

"Mom, if it's okay with you can Ellie hold her godson first?"

Ellie wiped her cheeks with the back of her hand. "You want me to be his godmother?"

"Of course." Kate passed the baby to Ellie. "Now support his head."

Ellie gingerly took the baby and pulled him close. "Like this?" She looked up at her mother.

"You're doing just fine, Ellie." Her mom's eyes glistened.

Ellie took a deep breath, drinking in the sweet smell of the baby. Silently, she vowed one day she'd hold a child of her own in her arms, but until that time little Benjamin would be showered with all her love.

"Mom, do you want to hold him now?" Ellie didn't look up but continued to gaze at the sleeping baby in her arms.

Ellie spoke softly. "Here you go, Mom."

Cari pulled her grandson to her heart and placed a tender kiss on his head. "Welcome to our family, little one."

There wasn't a dry eye in the room. It had been difficult for Kate to conceive, but Benjamin represented faith, love, and hope.

Sherry waited her turn. Accepting the tiny bundle, she adjusted the baby's blanket so Sam could get a better look. "Do you want to hold him, Sam?"

"No, I'll wait till he gets home and I'm sitting down, he's so small I might drop him."

Sherry laughed. "Oh Sam, you never dropped one of our kids."

"I seem to recall they were much bigger than this little fella."

"They weren't but he'll be home soon enough."

"Ray, your turn?"

"Don't mind if I do." Ray beamed. "I think one baby at a time is going to be a breeze." Smiling, he said, "When Jake and Sarah had triplets almost three years ago, that was all hands on deck for quite a few months."

Kate yawned.

"Ray, let's give the kids some privacy. It's been a long day for them."

Ray handed the baby to Don.

"We'll see you later?" Kate asked.

"We're staying with Sherry and Sam tonight, and tomorrow we need to get home. But I'll be back soon." Mom grinned.

"Ellie, we have a room for you too." Sherry extended the invitation.

"Thank you, Sherry. I never thought about where I was staying when I packed my bags."

Ellie slipped off the bed, kissed Don, the baby, and then her sister.

"Sissy, he's beautiful and Daddy would be thrilled to know he has a namesake."

Kate whispered, "When you talk to him, please tell Dad about the baby and that he hasn't been forgotten."

"I will, you can count on it. I'll see you tomorrow."

20

The days morphed into a week, and Ellie relished the time with her sister and tiny nephew. Ellie was scheduled to leave in the morning, but she needed some advice from the one person in the world who knew her best.

Ellie tiptoed over to the cradle and peeked in. "He's beautiful, Kate."

Benjamin was nestled in the cradle in front of the living room windows, exhausted from entering the world. As the baby slept, his tiny mouth was shaped like a bow.

"He looks like a cherub." Ellie's voice cracked with emotion.

Kate checked the open window to make sure there wasn't a draft blowing on him before settling on the over-stuffed sofa. "I think this is my favorite room. I love the sun and access to the deck."

"I never thought I would love another house other than our home in Loudon, but they both have their distinct charm and I have come to love it here."

"Katie, how did you know Don was the man for you?"

Kate's eyebrow arched. Ellie was very private and inexperienced in matters of the heart. She needed to tread carefully.

Kate's gaze drifted to the window. "At first we had a lot of fun together and of course I was attracted to him. He was the most handsome man I had ever laid eyes on. I felt safe when I was with him, but most of all I was happy."

"Safe? How?"

"It was like nothing could ever touch me."

"Did you think he'd leave you? I remember meeting Don and as a teenager even I could tell he was totally hooked on you."

"Sadly, the one man I had loved before Don left. Well at least that was how it seemed at the time."

"I didn't know you had another serious boyfriend?"

Kate spoke in a quiet voice. "Pixie, it was Daddy. When he died, I had a hole in my heart, and I never wanted to feel that kind of pain again. It was hard for me to let anyone get too close. I had you, Shane and Mom and I was always terrified of losing one of you. How could I add one more person to that list? And if you remember, for a time, I kept him at arm's length."

Ellie nodded, the wisdom of losing a parent too young filled her deep blue eyes with tears. "I know exactly what you mean."

"Over time my feelings deepened and I graduated from college, freaked out and thought I had lost him for good."

"I don't remember what happened. Why did you break up?"

"I was young, stubborn and full of my own self-importance. When Don suggested I move to Crescent Lake and work in a restaurant here, I was furious. I thought he wanted me to follow him like a good little girl. Then I blew the interview at Chops, a five-star restaurant in Boston. I thought for sure they'd hire me. Instead, I moved home to lick my wounds and forget about Don."

"And he moved to Loudon to win you back." Ellie grinned. "That is so romantic…"

Kate giggled. "Here we are today, in Crescent Lake, with a beautiful baby boy. I'm opening a restaurant and he's running the winery. I guess it all worked out as it should even if we did take a detour."

"I met someone, Kate." Ellie averted her eyes. "It scares me senseless. I've never let anyone get close and now he's going to leave, and my heart aches."

"Padraic Stone?" Kate leaned in. "Mom's filled me in on what's been going on at your place."

Ellie got up from the couch and began to pace. "Oh, Katie. He is amazing, so brave and strong. He takes the most amazing photos." She hugged herself. "What he sees through the lens springs to life in a picture. It reminds me of Ansel Adams."

"That is certainly high praise."

Ellie bubbled. "You should see what he did at Winifred Simpson's studio and flower gardens, well, stunning is inadequate."

"Does he feel the same way about you?"

"I think so. When he kissed me it was like the world slipped away, like it was just the two of us."

"Wait, he kissed you when? Tell all!" Kate sat at attention.

Ellie snickered. "The night of the fire. Since I've gone this far I might as well tell you everything."

Ellie plopped on the couch and leaned back into the cushions. Closing her eyes, she said, "We had gone out to dinner and afterwards we took a drive out to the lake. We had decided this was an official date and as such he needed to walk me to the front door."

"How gallant, and…"

"He ran his fingers down my face, tilted my chin upwards and leaned in, hovering over my lips for what seemed like forever, and then he kissed me."

"That's it? A nice sweet gentle kiss?"

Ellie blushed. "Katie, this is a bit awkward, but if you must know all the details it was sweet and tender at first, then I got that feeling inside, you know the one deep down when your blood starts to hum and it floods your veins in a thundering rush, like you can hear it in your head?"

"I know exactly what you mean. It feels like the kiss should never end."

"I guess it's a good thing we heard the crash inside, as much as I didn't want it to end, I'm not ready for anything more than kissing."

"You don't have to do anything until you're ready, and don't let Pad push you either!"

"Sis, he isn't like that, not at all. He's sweet and kind and patient."

"That sweet man has hormones, just like every other red-blooded male. Trust me I live with one." Kate's laughter caused the baby to stir.

Ellie checked the baby before perching on the arm of Kate's chair. "What should I do? He's going back to globe-trotting and I'll be in Loudon, running my little gallery, and he'll find someone new to stir his blood."

"Ellie, it doesn't have to end. There is such a thing as a long-distance romance, and it might be just the ticket for you and Pad since relationships are new to you. There would be no pressure."

Ellie gave a half-hearted shrug. "You have a point." She brightened. "Maybe you're right."

"Big sisters are always right."

The two sat quietly and watched the baby before Kate broached a sensitive subject. "I get the feeling you've seen Dad more than once?"

Ellie hesitated. "Three times."

"Do you want to talk about it? I talked to Mom when it happened to me, well after I got done freaking out."

"You know the night of the first break-in, I got hit over the head and locked in the closet."

"And?"

"What nobody knows, except for Mom, is Dad came to me. I heard a voice talking, urging me to wake up. At first, I was really scared. I thought whoever had hit me was in the closet and wanted to hurt me again. Then I saw him, very faint, like an old faded photo. I didn't really recognize him at first. I think it was because I was only five when he died."

"I get that."

"But I felt safe. I guess on some level I remembered what it was like when I got a bump and would climb onto his lap. He'd always take the time to hear exactly how I got hurt, examine the spot and kiss it. Then Daddy would kiss the top of my head and tell me it was a magical kiss and I was all better. The bruise or cut was just a way to remind me to be careful."

"I always thought they should disappear once we got the magical kiss from Dad or Mom." Kate grew thoughtful. "Young children believe their parents can do anything, cure anything, take away the pain all with a simple kiss."

"Too bad it doesn't work that way in real-life."

"Who says a kiss doesn't hold magic? Look at how it felt when Pad kissed you. Something wonderful happened."

"I never thought of it that way. His kiss was like nothing I had ever experienced before."

"Well let's face it, you haven't had a lot of experience in that department."

"I have been kissed before, it just never did anything for me. It was like kissing our brother."

Kate laughed. "Guess it wasn't the right guy. It should never seem like you're kissing your brother."

Ellie spoke in a hush. "Kate, what do I do about Pad?"

"When you get home kiss him hello and see how he reacts. If he seems really happy to see you and kisses you back, you'll know he's interested. Has he called you here?"

"No, but I told him not to call unless there was a break in the case."

"Why would you say that?"

"He kissed me goodbye when I left and I wasn't thinking clearly. My brain was a mush pile."

"Not too clever on your part."

"Well if you remember correctly, my sister was in labor, in case you need reminding," Ellie teased.

Kate glanced at the baby, her eyes glistening with tears. "I don't need a reminder. He was worth every minute too. Can you believe that is my son?"

"Don't cry, Kate." Mom had filled Ellie in on the hormone shift Kate would be going through, so Ellie hoped this was just one of those moments.

"I can't help it. Sometimes I get the feeling of over-whelming love for this little guy and worry I won't be a good mom."

"Oh Katie, you had a great role model. Mom is the best ever and if you're half as good with little Ben, he's a lucky kid."

"Do you really think so?" Kate sniffed.

"Of course, I do, or I wouldn't have said it."

Ellie looked at the time. "How about I fix us some lunch and then you can feed the little guy. Since this is my last day, I'm at your service. I can do laundry or clean something, whatever you need."

"That's sweet of you, El. Lunch would be nice." Kate gingerly walked over to the cradle and wrinkled her nose. "Someone's a little stinky. I wonder how long it will take before I get used to this part of motherhood."

Kate snuggled him close. "I don't care how you smell, little man."

Ellie watched her sister float down the hallway with her nephew. Thinking back, Kate and Don's marriage was put to the test when he took over the winery. The next hurdle to overcome was when Kate thought Don was the father of another woman's child. It had been a long and difficult year but love conquered everything and Kate got her happily ever after with her handsome prince and son. Maybe Dad had helped after all. It gave Ellie hope that she would find happiness too.

Don bounced through the back door. "Hey Ellie, it's nice to see you, but I was expecting to find Kate puttering in the kitchen." He grabbed a chunk of cucumber out of the salad bowl. "Is there enough for your favorite brother-in-law?"

"Absolutely. Kate's changing the baby."

Don grinned. "I'll be back."

"I'll just finish up here."

Ellie set the table on the deck and poured lemonade

into the glasses. While she was waiting for the new parents to appear, she decided to call Pad.

On the first ring, she heard his deep voice. "Hello?"

"Hi, Pad. It's me, Ellie."

"Hey. It's great to hear your voice. Are you still coming home tomorrow?"

"I wanted to let you know I'll be home late morning." Ellie swallowed hard. "Are there any new developments?"

"Not really. We know we're looking for a woman with hazel eyes, maybe red hair and of average height and slender. We've checked the system and no one popped up in the database."

Ellie fell silent.

Pad asked, "Are you still there?"

"Yes. I was thinking how it will be nice when this is over and I don't have to worry all the time." She stopped before saying anything about him leaving.

"It won't be long now. Showing her face on camera was a taunt and I take that personal." Pad's voice trailed off.

"My sister just came out with the baby, so I'll see you tomorrow." Ellie's chin trembled and she dropped the phone.

Kate gingerly sat on the chair cushion. Don placed Ben in a portable bassinet.

"Was that Pad?" Kate asked.

Ellie nodded.

Don looked from sister to sister. "Is everything all right at the gallery?"

"I just called Pad to check in and he said they've decided it's a woman and he would get her, soon."

"I don't get it, isn't that what you wanted to hear?"

Kate tried to prod him with her foot. She was unable to

make contact. "Ellie has been through a great deal these last few weeks, and it has taken a bit of a toll on her. We shouldn't pepper her with questions. Let's enjoy this delicious looking lunch."

"Can I ask a man's opinion?"

"Sure. What's up?"

Ellie's words tumbled out. "Pad kissed me and I really liked it, and him. He's going to leave as soon as we find out who broke in and, to be honest, I don't want him to leave. At least not now."

"I see," Don said. "Any idea how he feels about you?"

"How should I know?"

"Has he said anything about staying around, spending more time in Loudon?"

"No." Ellie picked at her salad. "All he said was, he'll get the person responsible. But he's never indicated he wanted to stay. Although," she brightened, "we went to dinner."

"And?" Don prodded.

"He held all the doors, paid the check, and kissed me goodnight on the front porch." Ellie searched Don's face. "What does that mean?"

"Well, I'm a guy and if I had said we were on a date that would indicate I was interested in the woman I was with and, if I kissed her goodnight on the front porch…"

"Which he suggested we do to make it an official good night," Ellie divulged.

"So, he wanted to do it right. I'm liking this Pad Stone." Don patted Ellie's hand. "I would say that he's attracted to you. Otherwise he wouldn't have gone to the trouble of the front porch kiss. If it was just to suck face he could have done that anywhere."

Kate interjected, "I think it was very chivalrous espe-

LUCINDA RACE

cially when he broke down the front door and put the fire out."

"He didn't break the door down, it was unlocked," Ellie reminded her.

Kate waved her hand. "You know what I meant, it was very courageous."

"More like his training kicked in to protect and serve," Ellie muttered.

"I know Mom and Ray think he's a good man but what did he do before photography?"

"I'm not sure, some kind of police work but he got burnt out so he took an early retirement."

"He's pretty young to have retired," Don spoke up. "Are you sure he left the force voluntarily?"

"Don." Kate patted his hand.

"Do you really think our mother would allow anyone to watch over her baby if he hadn't been thoroughly checked out by Hank Booth?"

"I guess you're right, lost my head for a minute." Don scraped his plate. "Anyone mind if I take seconds?"

"Go for it," Ellie said.

"Maybe I should stop by and see Hank on my way home tomorrow."

"Don't go poking, Ellie. Ask the man directly," Don warned.

"Don's right. Wouldn't it be better to ask Pad about his past?"

"Maybe Hank would give me more details," Ellie mused.

"Do what you want Ellie, but in my opinion being direct is better than going behind the man's back." Kate's voice held a gentle rebuke. "No one wants to feel like their privacy has been invaded."

"I'll think about it."

The baby squeaked and Ellie jumped up. She eased him out of the bassinet. Without looking at her sister, she asked, "Is it okay if I take him out for a short walk?"

Worry furrowed Kate's brow and she looked at Don. "Do you think it's too warm?"

*

*D*on patted his wife's arm. "Not at all, keep the carriage top up and he'll be fine." Don wrapped an arm around his wife as the new mother watched Ellie leave with the baby.

"Honey, relax, Ellie needs a few minutes alone and the baby getting a little air would be good for you too."

"Is that your way of telling me I'm already an overprotective mother?"

"I would never say that, specifically, well maybe just a little." Don held up two fingers pinched together and beamed. "And I'm sure we'll both have our moments as the years go by."

Kate smiled. "You may have to remind me to chill from time to time. For now, our son is with his auntie and that means we have a few precious minutes alone. Care to give your son's mother a proper kiss?"

Don pulled Kate into his arms. "Things have been hectic for the last week and in case I haven't told you lately, I love you with all my heart and seeing you hold our son, my heart has grown ten times its original size." Don traced his finger lightly over her lips. He held up his hand. "I'll be right back."

Kate's eyebrows were raised when Don returned. He handed her a long, slim box.

"What's this?"

"Open it."

Kate pulled off the top and sucked in a breath. "Oh, Don. It's beautiful!" She undid the clasp. "Will you put it on me?"

Don nuzzled her neck while securing the necklace. "I bought it the night of Ellie's opening."

"I'll treasure it always." Kate laid her hand over the stone.

Kate pulled Don close, sinking into his kiss.

21

*E*llie's hands gripped the steering wheel, her knuckles white, as she stared at the police station wondering if Kate was right. Should she talk to Pad?

"Ellie," a whisper broke her concentration.

"Daddy is that you?" She glanced in the front and back seats before seeing her father take his translucent form in the passenger seat.

"Do you know another ghost?" he teased.

"I'm sure you'll be the one and only ghost I talk to in my lifetime. It's a little unnerving how you pop in and out."

"I'm sure it's weird. I was accustomed to your mom almost expecting me over the years."

"I think she looked forward to your visits, just like Kate did."

"Has she told you about the first time we talked? Kate was going to hit me with something. I don't remember exactly what she grabbed." The soft form of her father smiled.

"If I hadn't been dealing with a head injury I might have had the same reaction. After the initial shock, it was comforting to have you near."

"I've watched over you for all these years. Your vulnerability made it possible for you to hear me."

"For the first time in my life, I was really scared. I've always been able to control all situations and as you know being locked in a closet isn't conducive to being self-sufficient."

Her dad chuckled. "No, it's not." He turned and looked at the large concrete building. "Why don't you tell me why you're here?"

"Mom asked Hank to check out Pad." Ellie stared straight ahead.

"If Mom trusts him why don't you?"

"It's not that I don't trust him, but I want to know what he's hiding and Hank has the answers, I'm sure of it."

"In my experience, especially when I was alive, the most direct way to get an answer to your questions is to talk to the people involved."

"That's what Kate and Don said too, but what if he lies to me?"

"What if he doesn't? You're not giving Pad much benefit of a doubt, are you?"

"I guess not." Ellie sulked. She hated that everyone agreed about the Pad situation.

"Are you going inside?" her Dad gently prodded.

Ellie turned the key in the ignition. "Nope, I'm going home to ask my bodyguard some questions. Care to tag along?"

"I don't think you need me for this." He began to fade. "But I'll be back when you do."

Ellie wiped away a tear. Each time he left, the chasm in her heart grew deeper. "Daddy, I need you all the time, don't leave me."

Silence hung heavy in the air. In a daze, Ellie drove back to her place, focused only on obtaining the answers she needed, one way or the other.

Winnie's van was parked on the street in front of the house. Ellie shut the car off and ran to the back door. Loud voices stopped her in her tracks.

"Pad, when are you going to tell Eleanor the truth."

"I don't know how to tell her, it's been too long and so much has happened for me to come clean now."

"It's never too late for honesty, especially now that you say you have deep feelings for her. It is imperative that you tell Eleanor everything." Winnie stamped her foot. "You know how I feel about deception."

Ellie was caught between barging in and demanding to know what the pair was talking about or continue eavesdropping.

"How can I tell her I'm a former detective from Chicago and an undercover agent, trained to-do awful things she should never have to know about? I left because I couldn't handle how it was starting to change me. You understand I got out before it was too late. If I told Ellie, she'd never be able to look at me the same way again. If that wasn't enough, don't forget our connection."

"I don't think our relationship will be a detriment."

"It's not Auntie, but…"

Ellie stormed through the door. "Auntie? Winifred Simpson is your aunt!" Ellie's anger exploded. "You're a former detective and undercover agent? Are there any other tidbits you've neglected to tell me?"

Winnie's face was ashen. "Eleanor. When did you get home?"

"Obviously not soon enough to hear more of this fascinating story." Ellie's voice was frosty. "I don't think that's really important at this moment, and if you would excuse me I need to clear my head."

Ellie stormed up the stairs and flung her bag on the bed, changed into running clothes, and ran down the wide staircase, jumping the last two. Low voices emanated from the kitchen.

Ellie burst through the swinging door unable to contain her fury. "Are you comparing stories to make sure I know just enough truth to pacify me?"

"It's not what you think, Ellie, let me explain," Pad implored.

Ellie glared at the pair. "Please let's start at the beginning. First Mrs. Simpson, why did you want to have your work in my humble little gallery?"

Winnie stammered and then drew herself up, standing tall. She spoke in a clear, authoritative voice. "I knew of you when you worked for Karlene. She had been trying to convince me to hold an exhibit in her gallery for years. At one such meeting, I watched you deal with a very temperamental young artist after Karlene hadn't been very kind about his work. I remember what you said and how kind you were. 'Art should make you feel something and not everyone likes how art makes them feel.' You lifted up that artist to new heights with your words and I admired you for that."

Ellie averted her eyes. "I remember him. Karlene wanted something more abstract, but at that time he was painting what moved him and it wasn't her vision for the show."

"Exactly. You understand the artist and you value all work, not just something that will earn you an almighty dollar. Whereas all Karlene could see was green. I knew you were going places and vowed that when you opened a place I would support you."

"How did you know I would strike out on my own?"

"It's simple. You care about the people first and the work second."

"That doesn't explain how Pad came into the picture."

"I told him he must have an exhibit here."

"No. I mean that you're his aunt. Why the secret?"

Winnie looked at the floor and twirled her finger around the charm dangling from her necklace. "We don't tell people about our connection. Over the years, we've discovered it can be exploited for other's personal agendas."

"Such as?"

"When I was younger, people wanted to meet the great Winifred Simpson," Pad spoke, his voice filled with regret. "I couldn't bring friends here for the summer as their parents tried to get Aunt Winnie to bestow artwork on charitable ventures, that weren't really for charity. Some people wanted to say they were her friend, thinking it would improve their personal status."

Winnie nodded. "As the years went by, we closed ranks and our world shrank. When Pad got involved in law enforcement, he didn't want that part of his life to intrude on my world. Our connection became a secret. I never talk about family to the press and now, neither does he. When Pad left that world behind for photography, he wanted to make it because of his talent and not because of who he happens to be related to." Winnie thrust her chin up. "So here we are today, with one big fat secret life."

"I don't understand why you couldn't tell me?" Ellie addressed Pad directly. Winnie discreetly left the room.

"Ellie, I'm sorry. At first it was just our way and then I didn't know how to tell you. I figured what difference would it make. I'd go back to my life and you go back to yours and you'd never need to know."

"What's changed now?" Ellie's sapphire eyes shimmered with tears.

"I didn't anticipate that I'd have feelings for you."

"That you didn't anticipate, you make it sound like something distasteful."

"It's not like that at all. Ellie, I'm someone who is best living alone, drifting in and out of Aunt Winnie's house for holidays, but my past isn't pretty and I had to do some things I could never tell anyone."

"Did I ask you to divulge any deep dark secrets? After all these weeks you should know me better than that, but I do value honesty above all else. If you had said you needed to keep something private, I wouldn't have pushed. But you never gave me a chance. How would that make you feel if the shoe was on the other foot?"

Pad shook his head. "I don't disagree and I wish I could change how I handled this. Can you forgive me?"

Pad grasped Ellie's hands and she pulled them away. "I'm sorry, Pad. I don't know how I feel right now. I am going to go for a run. Alone."

⚮

*E*llie ran hard, with only the beating of her bleeding heart for companionship. She felt like such a fool. To think she had wanted to tell Pad she was falling in love with him. But how could she love a man who was secretive and unwilling to share even basic information with her about his family and past? What else was he hiding? Ellie took the final turn toward the house when she noticed Karlene going into What's Perkin'. Taking a quick detour, Ellie followed her.

"Hey, Karlene. I didn't expect to see you so soon?"

Still breathless, Ellie waved thanks as Luke handed her a glass of water.

"I'm going to see Winifred Simpson, again. I'm doing my best to secure a show for her. I think she's this close to signing." Karlene held up her fingers with a small space between them.

"I hope it goes well for you." Ellie was puzzled based on the conversation she had with Winnie less than two hours ago. It didn't sound like she cared for Karlene's approach to business.

"Thank you." Karlene leaned in close. "Now tell me about the handsome man taking up space at your place. Any news there?"

After a shake of her head, Ellie drained the glass. "As a matter of fact, he'll be moving out very soon. Things have changed and he needs to get back to his own life."

"Really, I thought he had taken quite a shine to you and you felt the same."

"A shooting star Karlene, you know they're fleeting." Ellie set the glass on the counter and smiled at Luke. "Tell Mom I'll call her."

Luke gave her a quick salute and handed her a white paper box. "Something for later."

Karlene put a hand on Ellie's arm stopping her. "Does this mean Pad is on the market?"

"That's not for me to say, but I don't think he'll be staying in town." Ellie's cheeks flushed red. She closed the door quickly. Before Karlene could see the tears begin to flow freely.

Karlene smoothed her hair. "I'd like to order two black coffees to go please."

---

*E*llie walked up the drive and discovered Pad packing his rental car with bags of camera equipment.

Pausing next to the open trunk, she asked, "You're leaving?"

"I'm going to stay with Winnie for the time being. I'll find out who broke into the gallery and afterwards, I'll head to Europe."

"Are you going tonight?"

"If you'd like I can, but I was going to take over this carload and come back, sleep here, pack up the rest of my stuff and get out of your hair."

"Sure, fine with me." She longed to say they should talk but didn't know how to start, and in a split second decided it was better this way. She never wanted to fall for any guy, especially one that caused her knees to knock each time she looked at him.

"A shower is just what I need, then a hot dinner and I'll pull out that mystery book I started a few weeks ago."

With a straight back and cheeks flushed, Ellie marched inside and up the stairs.

*

*P*ad gazed up in the direction of Ellie's window. His heart was heavy, and he regretted how she learned at least some of the truth. Opening the driver's door, he noticed a small black coupe pull up, blocking his departure.

He watched Karlene stepped from the convertible, wearing high-heeled sandals, a deep blue dress, and a scarf fashionably tied around her hair. She sashayed over to where Pad stood, slid off her sunglasses, and batted her baby blues at him. "I hear you're leaving our mutual friend. Does this mean you might agree to share a coffee with me?" Karlene produced a to-go cup complete with the What's Perkin' logo.

"I'm on my way out, Ellie's in the house. Maybe she'd like to have coffee."

"I just ran into her at the café. I was going to drop in on Winifred Simpson, but when she told me your news I wanted to take a chance and swing by first." She laid a perfectly manicured hand on his arm. "Are you free for dinner? I can run my errand and then we could meet someplace and get to know each other better."

"Karlene, I don't think that's a good idea." Out of the corner of his eye, Pad noticed the curtain flutter from Ellie's bedroom window. "Do you want me to tell Ellie you're here?"

"No. I really must be going. But mark my words I'm going to wrangle a dinner invitation out of you and soon." Karlene strolled back to her car, flipping her hair. She slipped behind the wheel. Gunning the engine, she pulled away from the curb, tires screeching.

Pad shook his head and rushed into the house, calling for Ellie. He stood at the bottom of the stairs waiting for her to emerge from behind the closed door.

Pad's patience was rewarded. Ellie came down, fresh from the shower, her blonde hair damp and hanging loose to dry.

"Hey," Pad stated.

"I see Karlene was here. What did she want?"

"She brought me a coffee and asked me to dinner. But I'm not attracted to her." Pad tried in vain to catch Ellie's eye.

"I thought that would be her next step. She's always on the hunt for a handsome man to grace her arm."

"Ah, you think I'm handsome," Pad teased.

"Well, I'm sure some women might think so. It's not for me to say one way or the other. I thought you were going to Winnie's."

"I was but Karlene's going to attempt, one more time, to convince her to have a show. I wish she'd just give up. Winnie will never let Karlene host an exhibit featuring Winifred Simpson originals."

"You know I don't remember Winnie ever being at the gallery, and I was there every day it was open. I would have remembered her."

"Clearly Aunt Winnie saw you and was impressed. When she called me, after she heard about The Looking Glass opening, she felt for the first time we had an opportunity for our work to be displayed together. To say that she was thrilled was an understatement. We wouldn't have told anyone about our connection but we would have known and that's what would have mattered the most."

"I don't know what to say. I'd be thrilled to keep your photos on display if you really want to have them in my gallery."

Pad bowed his head and smiled. "I'd like that, Ellie. You have something very special here and I want you to succeed. I know Aunt Winnie has no intention of removing her paintings either. In fact, she's talking about dabbling in a new medium and wanted to talk to you about a show featuring her new work next spring."

"I'll talk with Winnie whenever she's ready. Please tell her for me?"

Pad bobbed his head. "I will." He glanced at his watch. "I think I'll get going. Maybe I can take a few pictures of the countryside on my way out to the house. I should be back before dark."

Ellie spoke quietly. "Do you have your key?"

"Yeah, make sure both front and back doors are locked. We still have the business of your intruder to deal with."

"Right." Ellie tapped her forehead with a mock salute.

Pad hesitated. He wanted to pull her into his arms and never let go. Instead, he left without a backward glance.

Ellie walked around the shop, straightening and using a feather duster to get the place ready to open tomorrow. It would be business as usual. She was tired of letting whoever the redheaded woman was derail her future one minute longer.

Ellie touched her head, where the staples had once held her scalp together, and the spot was still tender. The hair was longer now where it had been shaved. "At least I won't have to deal with a bare spot much longer. Maybe I'll bob my hair and get this to blend in better." She studied her reflection. A sharp rap on the front door drew her attention. "Who could that be? Clearly I'm not open."

Ellie glanced through the side pane of glass and pulled the door wide. "Karlene, twice in one day," she exclaimed.

Karlene's face was drawn taught. "Do you mind if I come in?"

Ellie stepped to one side and allowed her to enter. "Shall we go out back and have a glass of wine or maybe a beer?"

"Wine please." Karlene stalked through the house and out the sliding screen door.

Ellie grabbed a bottle of Chardonnay from the refrigerator, two glasses, a corkscrew, and a basket of wheat crackers and sliced, sharp cheddar before stepping onto the deck. "I hope you don't mind white. Don brought this from Crescent Lake Winery for my grand opening."

Karlene carefully sat down in the cushioned chair and artfully arranged and then rearranged her dress.

Ellie showed Karlene the label, who gave an appreciative nod. She passed a glass to Karlene before sitting down. She wondered what Karlene's problem was this time. Whenever something didn't turn out the way Karlene wanted, she got pouty, sulked, and then vented to Ellie. It was just a matter of waiting until Karlene was ready and then the floodgates would open.

"I'm furious! I went out to Winifred Simpson's. I thought it might be better to catch her off guard and she would agree to work with me."

"I gather it didn't go as you planned?"

"No, it certainly did not. I don't know how you can work with that woman. She is vile. The things she said to me, well I just don't understand how she could speak to me that way, very unprofessional."

"All of my dealings with her have been extremely pleasant. Did you catch her while she was working?"

"I don't think so. She was sitting on her porch. It was like she was expecting me as I drove up the driveway." Karlene's gaze burned. "Did you warn her I was coming?"

"How could you think something like that? I have too much respect for you to try and undermine your efforts to secure a new show."

"Well I just don't believe it was coincidence that she was outside. Other than you I didn't tell anyone but Pad where I was going and he doesn't even know the woman." Karlene took a gulp of wine. "Anyway, she informed me she wouldn't allow me to have an exhibition of her work, not now and not ever. Something about the way I treat artists, like they're dollar signs and not people." Karlene finished the wine in one gulp and held the glass out for more. "I treat everyone the same regardless of who they are to me, friend, family, employee or an artist."

"I'm sorry to hear your meeting was so, well, it didn't go as you had hoped."

"How did you get her? Did you have to sweeten the deal and give her a bigger slice of the pie?"

"No, it's the standard commission and she came to me. Actually, you could have knocked me over with a feather the day she came in and announced she was going to give me several paintings to hang, including the famed 'Waterfall,' on loan of course. You know the rumors. It was magnificent and I think it holds a special meaning for Mrs. Simpson. Well it did until the intruder destroyed it."

A smirk flashed over Karlene's face. "I guess what goes around does come around."

"Karlene, art should never be destroyed especially by someone being malicious."

Solemnly, Karlene nodded. "You're right of course. It was irreplaceable."

She picked up a slice of cheese and nibbled. "I'm surprised she left the rest of her paintings with you."

"It's not like I shredded the canvas, and she understands. Besides the police are sure they're closing in on the responsible person."

"Really, I didn't think there were any solid clues."

"We know it's a woman and she has hazel eyes," Ellie stated. "We caught her on camera the night she started the fire."

"How careless of her."

"Pad thinks it was deliberate."

"That is an interesting notion." Karlene set her glass on the table. "Two glasses are my limit as I've got a long drive. As always you've helped give me some perspective." Karlene air kissed Ellie's cheeks. "I'll see myself out, just sit and relax."

"I'll talk to you in a few days," Ellie called after her.

Ellie heard Karlene's car roar down the street. She leaned back into the chair and propped her feet up. "This is nice." Solitude had never bothered Ellie, even as a child. She'd tried to catch up to her sister and brother but sometimes the five-year age difference was too much and Ellie ended up alone, playing with her imaginary friends. As she got older, it had given her time to plan several steps ahead of her classmates, excelling in school, starting college while in high school, and preparing to open her business. Ellie never had much time for parties and other things her friends did; she was going places.

Ellie's heart pounded in her chest. What was that noise? Silently admonishing herself for dozing, she slipped off the chair and tiptoed barefoot into the house. Keeping the lights off, she wove her way through the first floor until she was able to peer out to the street. Sitting in front of the house was that same sedan with darkened windows. She patted her pockets—no cell. "Damn it," she whispered.

Stealthily, she crept into the kitchen, locating her handbag on the counter. Feeling the hair stand up on her arms, she became a statue, daring not to make a sound, wishing Pad was home.

The sound of someone walking softly reached her ears. She moved quickly now, punching in 911. Whispering, she gave her address and requested help before slipping the phone into her pocket and moving to investigate from behind locked doors.

Her heartbeat raced, the glass door was open. She ran through the house, slamming her shin into an unseen box, slid the door shut, and flipped the lock. A person in the perimeter of the yard hovered in the shadows. Ellie saw the blue strobe lights in the driveway and took what seemed to be her first breath in several long minutes. She hastened to the door and ran into Officer Greene.

"The black car was sitting in front again."

"Did you see anyone get out?" Greene demanded.

Ellie shook her head. "No. I must have fallen asleep on the back deck. I'm not sure what woke me, but I went into the house and there it was. I called you right away."

Pad ran up from the backyard. "I didn't get him. He's fast on his feet."

"Don't you mean she?" Ellie stammered.

"The person I saw tonight was built like a man, if you catch my drift. We might be dealing with two people," Pad stated.

Judy pounded up the steps. "We might have caught a break since they weren't able to take the car. We can run the plates and get the owner."

Pad gave a curt nod. "If I placed a bet, my guess, rental and untraceable."

He turned to Ellie. "Did you see anything at all, or even hear something?"

"Karlene stopped over after she saw Winnie. I stayed on the deck and drifted off. Something woke me up but I didn't see anything. I called the police and here you are. By the way when did you arrive?"

"A few minutes before the police. I was coming down the street and saw the car. I drove by, parked at the end and came up through the back."

"Was that you skulking around?"

"It was."

"Whose footsteps did I hear?"

"Where was the sound coming from?"

"Out front," Ellie stated, looking at the three faces that studied her.

Pad nodded to Greene. "Let's go."

He grabbed Ellie's arm. "Stay here," he commanded.

"Not on your life." Ellie pushed him aside and did her best to reach the front door first.

"If you insist on coming at least let me go first."

"Fine." Ellie struggled to contain her temper. It was just like when she was little and Shane was always making her stay one step behind him. "But I don't have to like it."

Pad grunted and stopped short of the front porch. "Paul, call for reinforcements."

Ellie stepped to one side and saw a box sitting on the step, wrapped like a birthday present. "What do you think it is?" Fear wrapped icy fingers around her throat.

"I don't know what to expect anymore but I can say things continue to escalate, and I don't think we should take a chance."

Pad tugged on Ellie's arm. "Let's wait over here."

"I need to call my parents before they hear about this some other way." Ellie was dialing the phone when Pad took it from her.

"Let me do the talking." Not waiting for an argument, Pad walked to the street.

"Hello, Cari. It's Pad."

"It's good to hear from you."

"I don't want to alarm you but our 'friend' left a wrapped box on Ellie's porch."

Before Cari could pepper Pad with questions, he plowed forward. "We have some experts coming and Ellie is safe. She's standing next to me. Would you like to speak with her?"

Pad handed the phone to Ellie.

"Mom, I'm fine. Pad's being careful that's all."

"Ray and I are on our way."

"Mom! Stay where you are. There is nothing you can do. I'll call you when it's over." Ellie caught sight of a familiar form across the street. "I have to go."

Ellie jogged across the street to where Dad was tucked into the shadows.

"Daddy, what are you doing here?"

"Something's wrong, I had to come. Did you tell your mother to stay away?"

If a ghost could show emotions, Ellie thought her father's ghost was spooked.

"I did, but you know Mom, she'll come anyway."

"Pixie, you need to be more careful. Falling asleep sitting on the back deck and leaving a door unlocked."

"How did you know? Oh, I forgot you can see me all the time." Ellie noticed Pad deep in conversation with Bell and Greene. "What do I need to do, Daddy, close down the gallery and let this person win? I don't know why they're targeting me."

"No but you need to tell Pad to dig deeper. This isn't really about you. You're just a convenient target to make a point."

"Do you know who is doing this and why?"

"I don't know for sure. If I did I would find a way to warn you but suffice it to say he's getting closer and you have to be vigilant. The end is near."

Pad yelled, "Ellie?"

Ellie held up a hand, acknowledging Pad. She turned to ask her father another question but he was gone.

Ellie stalked across the street.

"Who were you talking to over there?" Pad looked around. "I saw a man. Was it someone we should question?"

"It isn't anyone that can help." Ellie's voice was barely audible. "We have to keep going. We're getting close."

Pad pulled her into a one-arm hug. "We will." Sirens cut him short. "Ready?"

Greene and Bell crossed to where they were standing, indicating they needed to move further away from the house.

Activity buzzed while other officers suited up for the task. Mom and Ray burst through the security line calling out to Ellie.

"Over here, Mom."

Cari grabbed her daughter, holding her tight while Ray shielded his wife and stepdaughter. "Pad, what is going on?" he growled.

"Someone was here and left something on the front step. However, we were able to secure the car. I'm assuming we'll gather some important intel."

"I don't care about clues, Pad, you said you'd catch this person." Her mom was near hysteria. "This has been weeks with Ellie being used as bait. How much more can we take and what if next time you're too late?"

"We're doing our best. Once we see what's in the box and get the car processed we'll have more to go on." Pad spoke with a practiced soothing voice.

"Stone." Officer Greene waved him to the porch.

Ellie started to follow.

"Ray, keep her here." He hurried away.

"Ellie, please. You don't need to worry your mother any more than she is already." Ray spoke with quiet authority.

Ellie did as requested but kept an eagle eye on what was happening. The box was opened and Pad was examining the contents. After consulting with the police, he beckoned to Ellie.

She ran to his side with Mom and Ray close behind. "What is it?"

Pad grabbed her hand and walked her closer, shining a light in the box. Ellie could see it contained what looked like a smashed dollhouse.

"A broken toy?" Ellie stuttered.

"Look closer. It's a replica of The Looking Glass."

23

*E*llie's hand flew to her mouth. "Is this what I can look forward to, someone destroying my shop and Abby's childhood home? I can't stand this anymore. I'm done."

"Let's go inside and talk." Cari drew Ellie toward the house. "Pad are you coming?"

"I'll be there in a few."

Pad said, "Judy, have you found anything yet?"

"No, it's pretty clean. We're going to have someone go over it with a fine-tooth comb. Hopefully, we'll get lucky.

"We need to catch a break. I'm running out of ideas, and this person is obviously unbalanced, and doing their best to scare Ellie."

Greene walked up. "Stone, I agree with your assessment, he or she is getting bolder. To sit and wait, leave the package, and then take off."

"It's possible we're working with a team. The force used to knock Ellie out wasn't indicative of a male, but we saw the surveillance footage and that was definitely female and the person I saw tonight had a male physique."

"Pad, what's your next step?" Judy waited.

"I was going to stay on the outskirts of town, starting tomorrow night, but now I'm not sure that's a good idea." Pad rubbed his hand across his eyes. "My instincts are screaming I stay put."

"For what it's worth, I think you need to be right here." Greene jerked his thumb toward Ellie. "For her."

"Yeah, but it's complicated."

Greene snorted. "Isn't it always?"

Pad slowly walked toward the house and stopped, wondering how he could convince Ellie, when something on the ground caught his eye. Bending over he unfolded a receipt from What's Perkin'. Tucking it in his pocket, he went into the kitchen.

Cari had tea steeping, and the family was sitting around the kitchen table. A fourth mug was waiting for him.

"Any news?" Ellie jumped up.

"Nothing yet. They're going to take the box and car to the station and give them a thorough once over. With luck something will pop that will lead up to his identity."

"And, if they don't find anything?" Ray asked.

"We will, trust me. I promised all of you we would put this person behind bars and as the weeks have gone by, the charges have mounted up."

"Where do we go from here? Wait for this person to light a match? You saw the dollhouse." Ellie toyed with her mug. "I'm going to start contacting every artist and tell them I'm closing the gallery. Maybe Karlene will take me back."

"Cari, Ray, would you give us a few minutes alone?"

*T*he couple went through the arch, giving Pad his requested space.

"Ellie."

Dazed, Ellie looked deeply into his eyes. The clouds that filled hers caused him physical pain. "I said I was moving to Winnie's but under the circumstances I need to stay here."

"I am perfectly capable of taking care of myself, and I have my family."

Pad switched tactics. "That's not the point. Another set of ears and eyes can keep Abby's home intact."

"I need to think." Ellie got up and paced. "If you're staying, I think you should keep a low profile. Keep your car at your aunt's house so it appears I'm alone and vulnerable."

"I see where you're going and it might make sense. This last time the person hung around. It was only when I showed up that he took off. We might be able to catch him…"

"Or her, in the act." Ellie finished his sentence.

"So, we agree?"

Ellie stuck her hand out. "Let's shake on it."

Pad grasped her hand, feeling her pulse quicken under his touch. Inwardly, he groaned. It was going to be hard being close and not being able to hold her in his arms.

"Mom?" Ellie called out. "Can you and Ray come in here, please?"

Upon entering the room, her mom said, "I assume you've got a plan?"

"We're going to let people believe Pad isn't living here anymore. It should make it easier to surprise whoever this is."

"But you'll be here, Pad?"

"Yes. I'm going leave my car at my aunt's."

Cari's brow wrinkled and she looked from Ellie to Pad.

Ellie said, "I'll explain later."

"If you and Ray don't mind, I'd like to create a scene out front and have Ellie and I drive off in separate cars. Do you think you can stay here until we get back?"

"Sure." Her mom looked around the room. "I think we should turn on a lot of lights to make a statement." She walked from room to room, flicking on every light that had electricity.

Pad's gaze was intense. "Whatever I'm about to say isn't how I really feel but if we're being watched it has to look real." He grasped Ellie's hand and squeezed.

Ellie glanced at the clock. "Let's get this over with. I'll drive the opposite way to Winnie's and meet you there in forty-five minutes."

Pad dropped her hand and walked out to the front porch. Ellie was close on his heels. The pain in her heart showed raw on her face.

"Pad, it's over between us. With the exception of our professional relationship we won't be seeing each other anymore." Ellie's voice rose with each word. "I'll be in touch as needed via email."

"Eleanor, you need to realize there is more to life than just business."

"It's time for you to leave, Mr. Stone." Ellie turned her back to him and stormed into the house, slamming the door behind her. Pad's words stung. There was more truth in his statement than she was willing to face.

"Mom, I'm going for a drive." Ellie tore her keys from the hook.

Cari demanded, "What's been going on here? That fight sounded a little too realistic."

Ray grasped her hand. "Honey, it's not for us to intervene. They have to figure this out for themselves."

On the drive to Winnie's, Ellie's thoughts were focused on how she would deal with Pad living with her while hiding her true feelings.

Winnie's house was lit up like a Christmas tree, and Pad's car was parked at the front entrance. "Here goes nothing," Ellie muttered. Her steps slowed as she walked towards the house.

The door swung open before she could knock. Relief flooded Pad's eyes. "What took you so long? I was worried. I almost called Cari."

"I didn't realize I was on a schedule." Ellie's sharp retort was like a hot knife in his gut. "I thought we were trying to make it look like we've gone our separate ways."

"You're right and I'm sorry." Contrite, Pad glanced around the exterior shadows before closing the door. "Were you followed?"

"Pad, really? This isn't high-powered business. I own a little gallery, which I'm shocked would be of any interest to anyone besides a few people. It's more likely someone thinks there's buried treasure in the basement leftover from a couple hundred years ago."

Winnie came bustling in. "Pad, where are your manners," she scolded and took Ellie by the hand. "Please come in and we'll have something cool to drink before you abscond with my nephew."

Ellie couldn't contain her laughter. "All we're trying to do is track down some idiot who hit me over the head. Winnie, if I didn't know better I'd think you were enjoying all the cloak and dagger stuff."

"As a painter I don't get much excitement so I'm living vicariously." Her hand flew to her mouth. "Oh, my dear, I didn't mean your injury was something to make light of, I was terribly distressed to learn you were injured."

"No worries, I have a hard head."

Pad followed the two women into the depths of the house, his step light, as they seemed to genuinely like each other. "Ladies, I'll get something for us to drink, you should sit and relax."

Winnie winked at Pad and steered Ellie toward a comfy wicker chair.

"Pad's right he should be waiting on us."

"Well if you say so, but we should be leaving. After all Mom and Ray are waiting for us."

"Eleanor, I've been thinking about an idea, and I've told Pad. I'd like for you to give it careful consideration before you say no."

Ellie looked at Pad and smiled sweetly. "I'm listening."

"As I'm sure you can imagine, I've been kept up-to-date on the details. Also, I have been hounded to death by your former employer about a new exhibit. That got me to thinking. I want to announce that we'll be working together on a new exhibit of select paintings, never before seen by the public."

"And, what do you think this will do exactly?"

"Why flush out this lunatic of course." Winnie's eyes twinkled, her cheeks pink with excitement.

"All it might do is make our 'friend' angrier than he is and do heaven knows what next. I don't think we should take the risk. Besides, why do you think your exhibit will draw him out into the open?" Ellie was quick to add, "No offense Winnie."

"None taken, my dear, but when Pad told me the only

thing in your establishment that was deliberately destroyed was my painting, it got me to thinking, this is personal and directed toward me." Winnie's head bobbed. "Logically, something like this will most assuredly make them surface."

"I can't let you do this. Your paintings are in jeopardy of being ruined. It's better to close down than let that happen again."

Pad dropped into a chair, resting his hand on her knee. "El, this might be the best idea we've had. Winnie is going to contact John Barton. He's been completely supportive of her exhibiting in The Looking Glass. If it is about Winnie, we'll find out pretty quick."

"I don't know." Ellie hesitated. "It sounds like you're convinced. When do you want to do this show?"

"We should announce it tomorrow," Winnie proclaimed. "The sooner the better I say."

Pad nodded in agreement. "Do you think you could write a press release and get it out?"

"Well of course, but I still don't know if this will work. Maybe we should wait a few weeks."

"This is exactly what we need, now."

Winnie handed Ellie a sheet of paper. "Here are a few points you should cover. I've given a brief description of a few paintings, just enough to tease. Then in a couple of days, I'll come over and if we're being watched whoever will pick up on the immediacy of our plan."

Ellie frowned. "It seems that I don't have a vote in this little scheme."

Winnie stood up. "No, you don't. Now you need to get back to town, and I need to pick out my outfit for our meeting." Winnie affectionately kissed Pad and Ellie and shooed them out the door.

"I never would have thought Winifred Simpson would enjoy something fraught with danger so much."

Pad laughed. "She's just getting started."

The drive back into town was silent and uneventful. Pad had Ellie pull over in a vacant lot so he could lie down in the backseat. "When you get to the house, pull up as close to the back door as you can and I'll sneak in."

"Sounds like you've had some practice sneaking into a girl's house before." Ellie smirked.

"Maybe a time or two, but never tell my aunt. She'd kill me."

Ellie slowly drove down Main Street. "We're almost there."

Ellie looked right and then left to see if anything was amiss. "Looks quiet out there," she whispered.

The backlight came on automatically and Pad hissed. "Turn that off when you get inside."

Ellie didn't respond. She walked into the house and within minutes, darkness blanketed the driveway.

Pad switched off the interior dome light and slipped out of a narrow opening in the door, softly closing it. He stayed hidden in the shadows and pushed open the back entrance, grateful Ellie had thought to leave it ajar.

Ray and Mom were pretending to watch the news as if they didn't have a care in the world. They had deliberately left most of the interior lights on low to minimize the possibility of someone noticing a fourth person had joined them.

"I guess we had better get used to dim lighting," Ellie joked half-heartedly.

Her mom rose from the couch. "We're going to head home."

Ray tweaked Ellie's nose. "Call if you need anything at all."

"I will, thanks for coming over and hanging out for a while." Ellie kissed her mom. "I'll call you tomorrow."

Ellie locked the door and pretended to watch them leave, but in reality, she was doing her best to steady her racing heart. To be this close to Pad but feel like they were a million miles apart was impossible when all she wanted to do was confess her true feelings.

"Um, El?" Pad hung in the shadows. "I think we should talk about what tomorrow will bring."

"Yeah, right." Ellie carefully crossed the semi-darkened room.

Pad wanted to grab her and hold tight and promise her tomorrow and all that followed. However, this wasn't the time to start something he couldn't finish.

"Tomorrow you need to go about your normal day. Go for a run, stay on a well-traveled path and make sure your phone is fully charged and on. Come back and open up the gallery and issue the press release announcing Winnie's very special, one-woman, event. If anyone asks, I've moved on to a new assignment and you're not sure if I'm coming back. That goes for your family too."

In a monotone voice, Ellie said, "My family would never say anything."

"I'm sure they wouldn't say anything but be reasonable, the fewer people that know I'm here the better chance we have of finishing this and we can both move on with our lives."

Ellie scowled. "I didn't know you were so eager to leave."

Pad refused to accept the bait dangling in front of him.

"I'm going upstairs. I'll leave my door open so if you hear anything, shout. I'm a light sleeper."

"You couldn't even say goodnight." Ellie stalked into the kitchen. She rummaged in the fridge for something. Surely, Mom had left a snack for her.

Peering at the shelves, Ellie wondered if she'd ever get the chance to talk to her father again. There was so much she wanted to tell him about Kate's baby and maybe get one last chance to tell him how much he was missed every single day.

24

"*E*llie. I'm here."

"Daddy?" Ellie gasped. "How did you know I needed you?"

"That is how I was pulled back to you, sometimes it just works this way." Her dad perched on a kitchen chair.

Ellie settled onto a stool. "I don't know what to do anymore."

"Talking can bring clarity." He searched her face. "What's troubling you to cause that frown?"

"It's everything, it's all messed up," Ellie wailed.

"Start at the beginning," he gently suggested.

"Well that would take hours, and I don't think you have that much time." Ellie wiped the tears from her face with a tea-towel. "For as long as I can remember, I've had my life planned out. Work hard in school, graduate, get a job and then open my own business."

"And you've done all that, Ellie, so what is the issue?"

"Daddy, I've never wanted to fall in love or be in a relationship."

"Why ever not? Love is a wonderful and amazing blessing that should be savored."

"There's a flip side too. It's complicated, messy, and heartbreaking when one person leaves. Why on earth would I want to have my heart broken, over and over?"

"Are you talking about boyfriends as you were growing up or something more, well shall we say, permanent?"

"We need to face facts, Daddy. When you died the four of us, Mom, Kate, Shane, and me, built huge walls, more like a fortress. It was devastating losing you, none of us wanted to ever feel that again."

"But look at your mother, Kate, and Shane. They all put themselves out there and found, that despite any hurdle, love was worthwhile."

Ignoring her father's ghost, Ellie kept talking, "And here I sit, I've just fulfilled my dream of opening the gallery and someone comes along trying to destroy it."

"Eleanor that is not the real issue and you know it."

Struggling to contain her emotions, she continued, "I didn't ask for him to come along and find the soft part of my heart that I've so carefully protected."

"Who?" Dad prodded.

"You know who. Padraic Stone."

"He's a good man."

"He is a liar. He didn't bother to tell me about his connection to Winnie and what he did in his past. It's all been a big secret."

"Don't you keep secrets too, El?"

"Not like that."

"Are you sure? You have strong feelings for this man and yet you haven't told him or given him any indication you'd like him to stay."

"I'd rather have him leave now than stay for a while and make it harder on both of us."

"Who are you protecting, Pad or you?"

"Whose side are you on? It sounds like you want me to jump into his arms and declare my undying love!"

Her dad chuckled. "Is that what you want to do, Pixie?"

"Of course not." Ellie's eyes sparked.

"I remember that look, even as a small child your eyes betrayed you every time."

"Well if you want to stay and talk we should change the subject. Pad is leaving soon and not by my choice."

"What about the gallery? Do you intend to stay open?"

"Well there is another hair brained scheme to catch this person. But truthfully, I don't want to cave in to this pressure and close. I want Mom to be proud of me and to show her I learned so much by watching her."

"What do you think your mother would do?"

"She'd stay open and be very successful in spite of these setbacks."

"Then I guess you have your answer. Follow in your mother's footsteps and fight."

Ellie set her jaw. "I will, you'll see."

"I've been honored to be your father since the moment you were born and you gazed up at me with those enormous blue eyes. You're going to do great things, Ellie."

"Speaking of great, Kate wanted you to know she named your grandson Benjamin Samuel Price. She told me you were there to guide her toward happiness."

"I was simply being her father, just as I'm trying to do with you."

"You are. I am going to stay open and grow my business in spite of this mess. I'll overcome all obstacles and challenges in my way."

"What about love?"

"Maybe someday I'll be brave and fall in love with an amazing man. But for now, I'm okay on my own."

"Life isn't filled with endless chances. Look at your mom and Ray, they almost lost their chance. Don't squander what is right in front of you."

Ellie wiped her tear-filled eyes. "Oh Daddy, I wish you were here all the time." But he was gone. Ellie hung her head and wept until she was spent. She flicked off the lights and dragged herself upstairs.

When all was quiet, Pad returned to his bed. He knew leaving was the hardest decision he had to make but after listening to Ellie weep, he was certain it was the right one.

When Ellie opened her eyes, the sun streamed into the windows. She bolted out of bed and ran through the shower, pulling her wet hair into a bun on the top of her head. "Thank heavens I remembered to set the coffeepot." Ellie started down the stairs and discovered Pad was sitting at the kitchen table, reading the paper.

"Good morning, did you sleep well?" Pad noticed her red-rimmed eyes.

"Yes, thank you, and you?" Ellie's voice was clipped.

"Like a rock."

"Did you go out this morning to get the paper?"

"This is yesterdays. I was up early. I decided to work on the crossword puzzle. I'm sort of under house arrest remember?" Pad's lazy grin caused Ellie's stomach to flip over.

She left the room and came back, handing him a folded newspaper. "Here you go. Two puzzles should keep you entertained."

"Someone got up on the wrong side of the bed," Pad teased.

"I did not." Ellie's voice was far too sharp for a pleasant conversation. She took her coffee into the other room stating, "I have work to do."

Pad returned to his puzzle, keeping one eye and ear open.

The day dragged as Ellie slogged through the paperwork that needed to be done announcing the one-woman show. After hitting send, the release was out and she had called in a favor to get it in print for the next day. Stretching the kinks out from her back and arms, Ellie got up from her desk and wandered into the kitchen only to discover Pad was in the same spot.

"Have you moved since breakfast?" Ellie grabbed a snack.

"I've been doing some research online and light reading." Pad followed her out back.

"Do you think it's a good idea, being exposed?" Ellie squinted against the bright sun. "After all, if someone sees you, our plan is shot."

"I don't think we'll get any movement until tomorrow," Pad stated matter of fact. "You're expected to be in shock today. The broken model and our fight."

"Who are you? A profiler or something?"

"I've been around long enough to know this is how the mind works."

"Good to know. Well I've done my part; the release is out and it's business as usual." Ellie was interrupted by the buzzer Pad had installed on the front door. "I'll be right back."

Pad sat back in the chair as he eves-dropped on the conversation with a customer. Reminders of Ellie in his arms played in his head. How can I convince her that my feelings are strong, honest, and I'm a true-blue kind of guy and that we should try long distance?

"Tell her."

Pad sat up straight. "Who's there?"

Silence answered him. He leaned back in the deck chair and closed his eyes.

"Tell her you've never loved another. Bare your soul."

"Show yourself. NOW!" At this point, Pad was on alert, all his senses in overdrive.

"Pad?" Ellie rushed out. "I can hear you inside. Who are you shouting at?"

Pad felt foolish telling Ellie he was hearing voices. "I must have been dozing. Sorry if I startled you."

Pad ushered Ellie back inside while glancing behind them. He flipped the lock on the door.

"Why did you lock it?"

"I have to go upstairs and we need to be careful."

Ellie shrugged her shoulders. "You're the boss."

She returned to her customer, Pad quickly forgotten as she got down to the business of closing a sale.

"Day three," Ellie muttered as she studied her reflection in the mirror. "Maybe today is the day our bad guy shows up. Well at least Winnie will do her best to flush them out."

Pad stood in the stairwell observing her. Ellie rested her head in one hand when Pad called out, "Good morning, Ellie."

"Aren't you cheery this morning."

"Why shouldn't I be in a good mood? We had a quiet

night which means we're getting really close to something happening. I have a sixth sense with these things."

"I'm glad you think so. I find this infuriating. I've had zero customers for two days, which I guess is fine but I haven't had any distractions. All I've done is jump at every noise and worry."

Pad's fingers ached to follow the delicate curve of her arm. "You look great today, business-like and distinctly feminine at the same time."

Color rose to her cheeks and she glanced toward the door.

Pad continued without waiting for a response. "What time is Winnie due to arrive?"

"She's making her grand entrance at eleven."

Pad chuckled. "That is an accurate statement." He grabbed a water bottle. "I'm dying to go for a run."

Ellie smirked. "It was great earlier; the temperature was perfect."

"Ah, now you're just torturing me. You could have said it was too hot or something."

"My mother always said, honesty is the best policy." Ellie took her empty plate and put it into the dishwasher. "Well I'm off to work."

Pad called after her, "Good to see your sense of humor's intact." He paused to enjoy the view of her skirt swaying as she walked. He prayed this would be behind both of them soon. He wasn't sure how much longer he could hold out before throwing caution to the wind.

Pad hung out in the upstairs hallway so he could keep watch out the window and be able to fly down the stairs if needed. He glanced at his watch. It wasn't like Winnie to run late.

Before he could hit send on a text message, Winnie's

van pulled up next to the sidewalk and a man strolled up the path. After a brief exchange, the pair walked up the slate walkway.

"Eleanor," Winnie called out as she pushed open the door. "I'm here with paintings and my long-time friend and gallery owner, John Barton. He's come in from New York to see what we're up to and spread the word."

Ellie stepped from the behind the counter.

She extended her hand. "Hello, welcome to The Looking Glass." She paused in mid handshake. "Have we met before?"

"I don't believe I've had the pleasure."

Winnie watched the exchange between the two gallery owners. "Eleanor, this is John. I've worked with him for years."

"It's very nice to meet you, Mr. Barton."

He gave a courtly little bow. "Very nice to meet you as well. Your space is quite charming."

Bells went off in Ellie's head. "Would you excuse me for a moment?" Ellie smiled at Winnie and the newcomer and casually walked up the front staircase.

"Pad!" She hissed.

He stepped out of the alcove. "What's up?"

"The man with Winnie, is John Barton." She peeked down the stairs. "Remember the man who was in here with the suit and fuchsia handkerchief?"

"I do, why?"

"That's Winnie's gallery guy. He just introduced himself and when I mentioned he looked familiar, he said we had never met. He has hazel eyes, maybe he's our guy."

"Okay, here's what you're going to do. Play along with everything and I'm going down the back stairs, but keep him away from the kitchen door. This way I can overhear the conversation but don't let on that you know he was here before."

"All right, but we're going to have to tell Winnie."

"We will, but not until he's gone. Now get back down there and see what he says."

Without another word, Ellie sailed down the stairs, smiling as if she didn't have a care in the world. "I'm sorry about that."

"Eleanor, we understand there is much that needs your attention." Casually she glanced around searching for her nephew. "The gallery is quiet this morning."

Ellie picked up on Winnie's unspoken question. "I've had one customer in so far."

"Excellent." Winnie smiled. "I think we should bring in the paintings and decide how best to display them."

"If you'd like to stay here I'll bring them in."

"We'll help Eleanor, won't we John?"

"Of course, Winifred, I'm happy to help." John followed Ellie outside, and she wondered if a strong wind could blow him over. "Ms. McKenna?"

"Please call me Ellie."

"You're very gracious, Ellie. Winnie has shared with me the unpleasantness you've had to deal with. Has that affected your business?"

"Truthfully, all the artists have remained steadfast in their support and my clientele is continuing to grow."

"That's certainly good to hear. I'm sure you understand I must look out for Winnie's best interest and these paintings she wants to exhibit here should be heavily promoted."

"I completely understand what needs to be done."

"Now John, stop being so hard on Eleanor. I have all

the confidence in the world she has the necessary skills to draw attention to my work." Winnie opened the side door to the van and inside the paintings were secured in specially designed racks for transportation.

"Here they are."

Ellie painstakingly released the woven straps and carefully picked up the first framed canvas. She drew in a sharp breath as the protective covering pulled back from one canvas.

"Winnie, these are the watercolors of your gardens." Tears welled up in her eyes, knowing the sacrifice Winnie was willing to make. The words threatened to stick in her throat. "You shouldn't have done this."

With a wave of her hand, Winnie announced, "I have always done what I wanted to do, this isn't any different."

Ellie set down the painting and threw her arms around the older woman. Whispering in her ear, Ellie said, "Thank you, Winnie."

Winnie extracted herself from the embrace, but not before pecking Ellie's cheek.

For John's benefit, she announced, "Eleanor, please remember this is a business arrangement."

Ellie dropped her gaze and hid her grin when Winnie admonished her. "Of course. I'll bring them in and you can arrange them."

John relegated the work to the young woman, tucking Winnie's hand in the crook of his arm as the two meandered to the front porch.

*U*nable to help, Pad watched as Ellie made trip after trip. He wished Winnie had called him to pick some of them up yesterday or even tomorrow.

From the kitchen door, Pad's attention was drawn to John Barton. He watched the odd little man flit from one exhibit to another, jotting notes that Pad surmised were artist names and the type of art they produced.

Pad shot a text to Greene requesting a background check on Barton, but he doubted anything would turn up.

"Take all the notes you want, Mr. Barton," Pad muttered under his breath.

25

*W*innie and John stepped out to pick up lunch for them before starting the process of planning the show. Pad was lurking out of view when the bell on the front door jingled. Ellie glanced up to see Karlene gliding into the shop, looking perfectly pressed, as usual, despite the summer heat.

"Well this is a surprise." Ellie greeted her at the door. "I didn't expect to see you today. I thought you were up to your elbows in the new exhibit with your novice."

"I just couldn't stay away after I read the news. Winifred Simpson is going to allow you to display never before seen watercolors? That is quite a coup, and in spite of everything that has gone on as of late in your little gallery."

Ellie could hear a touch of something in Karlene's voice but quickly dismissed it, reminding herself Karlene had always been very supportive.

"Actually, this was Winnie's idea. I thought after the last incident she would pull everything but instead we're moving forward with the new collection." Ellie glanced around the room and dropped her voice to a hush. "They're just breath-taking. I've never seen anything like them in person, let alone hold one in my hands."

"Is she here?"

"Yes, as a matter of fact she and John Barton, you know from The Barton Gallery, went to pick up lunch. You're welcome to join us."

"I'd love to stay and meet John. I've heard so much about him." Karlene dropped her handbag on the desk and wandered about the room. "I see your walls and shelves are still full. It's a wonderful testament to the faith people have in you. If I were an artist I'm not sure I would have remained." Glancing over her shoulder, Karlene said, "At least I am assuming you still have all your artists intact."

"I do. I'm very lucky they've stuck by me throughout all the troubles."

The rustling sound from the front door interrupted Ellie.

Winnie and John burst through the door arms laden with bags. "We're back," she sang out. As soon as Winnie saw Karlene, her cheek-splitting grin faded, replaced with a tight smile.

"Hello, Karlene, this is an unexpected surprise." Winnie set the bags on the table. "Allow me to introduce you to John Barton…"

"Mr. Barton," Karlene gushed. "I've been to your gallery and it is truly amazing."

John looked from the young woman to Winnie. Shaking her hand, he said, "The pleasure is mine."

"John," Ellie interjected. "I worked for Karlene prior to opening this gallery. She taught me everything I know."

"Oh stop, Ellie, you'll make me blush. In all honesty,

she has an innate sense when it comes to art and how to get a customer to part with their hard-earned money." Winking, Karlene prattled on. "After all isn't that what we want most from a visitor to our galleries?"

Winnie ignored Karlene's comment. "Eleanor, where shall we have lunch? On the back deck?"

"I think the front porch would be lovely, Winnie, there is more shade this time of day." Ellie picked up the bags and ushered her company outside. Making sure she spoke loudly enough so Pad would go into her room where he'd be able to hear every word.

"John, don't you just love how Eleanor took this historic old home and enhanced all its finest features?"

"Indeed. Do you own the house, Ellie?"

"No, my sister-in-law does. She grew up here and I'm renting for now, longer term I'd like to buy a building." Ellie set the containers on the wrought iron table. "If you would excuse me for a minute I'll just run inside to get some napkins."

Ellie stopped just inside the door and listened to Karlene pounce.

"Winnie." Her gaze locked on the older woman. "Ellie told me you're going to preview a collection of watercolors for your upcoming show. When I arrived, Ellie wouldn't show them to me. Would you mind if I stayed?"

John leaned forward. "You know this is why I came down too. Once Winnie told me of the plan for Eleanor to host this show I just couldn't resist."

"You've never seen them either, John?"

"No, I've never been permitted to display them and Winnie has such talent, her oils are big business on their own."

"This must be frustrating for you, to know that Winnie

is giving away such a glorious opportunity to a newbie, so to speak."

"Not at all. When I was just starting out, I too had a patron in the art world. I actually commend Winnie for taking an interest in The Looking Glass. It's good to cultivate the next generation and besides it's good business for all galleries to have something like The Looking Glass. Don't you agree?"

Karlene ran a hand over her perfectly coiffed hair. "Of course, and Ellie isn't just anyone. After all she's my protégé, so I know what she is capable of accomplishing."

Ellie pushed the door open. "Sorry that took a little longer. I wasn't sure how many serving spoons we needed."

"I thought you were getting napkins, Ellie." Karlene pointed out her mistake.

"I got those too." Ellie held up a stack of white napkins. "Let's eat before it gets warm."

Winnie swooped in for the rescue. "Eleanor, please sit down and allow me to serve lunch. After all this is an exciting day for us all."

"No, really it's fine and it has turned out perfectly as Karlene wants to see the paintings too, her timing is impeccable."

Karlene murmured, "Yes, timing is everything."

Winnie passed out small containers of a cold corn and shrimp soup with tender buttermilk biscuits and a small selection of fresh cut fruit.

"I see you stopped in at What's Perkin'. This was one of my mom's first summertime lunch specials."

"I did and she said it was perfect with the biscuits and fruit. But as an added bonus, I picked up some of the most delicious looking cupcakes. I think Cari said Dani had created the recipe a few years ago, a peach cake with buttercream frosting or something. They sounded too good to pass up."

"They are delicious but plan on doing an extra lap on your walk tomorrow, they're not low calorie or fat free."

Ellie smiled and passed Karlene a biscuit.

Karlene held up her hand. "I'll just have a little soup and fruit, thank you."

Ellie could see Winnie was taken aback by Karlene's rude tone.

Ellie said, "I'll save it for later then. They're as light as air."

John groaned, "I'll take the extra biscuit, they're so tender." He dipped a piece in the soup and closed his eyes. "I don't care how many calories I've ingested, I've died and gone to heaven. I haven't had biscuits this good since my mother, rest her soul, baked them."

When the foursome returned to the gallery the excitement was palpable; it was time for the grand unveiling.

One by one, Winnie unwrapped ten paintings. When finished, she looked from one face to the next.

"Would someone say something, you're making me a nervous wreck." Winnie's voice trembled. Rapidly, she began talking. "It's always like baring my soul, warts and all."

John appeared awestruck. "Winifred, I must say these are your finest pieces to date. The colors and brush strokes are bold and vibrant. I feel like I'm in the midst of Eden."

"John, I'm so glad you like them. I played around a bit to get just the right depth of pigment. I hope you're a tad envious that Ellie will have these on display."

John proclaimed, "Don't give that another thought. They will be perfect in this setting."

Ellie stood back and studied the wall. "Winnie it's like your garden has been transplanted into my gallery." She clasped and unclasped her hands. "Winnie these are exquisite and belong in a high-profile gallery where you would receive suitable exposure and accolades."

"Winnie," Karlene ran a hand down the front of her dress. "If I could be so bold, I think what Ellie is trying to say is her little gallery doesn't have the pull yet. I'd be happy to host the show for you." She quickly pointed out, "It's still out of the hustle and bustle of the city and relatively close to your home, so we can bill it as a hometown show just as you intended."

Ellie's jaw dropped. "Karlene, that isn't what I said. Please, don't put words in my mouth."

"I'm just trying to help, Ellie. After all this would be an enormous opportunity for you but you're not on the map yet." Karlene rolled her eyes. "If you know what I mean."

"I believe I know exactly what you mean."

A customer entering the gallery interrupted Ellie's retort. She excused herself from the group and saw Pad waving at her. After helping the customer, she slipped unnoticed into the other room.

"What?" Ellie peeked out of the doorway. "Someone is going to catch us."

"I need for you to get something that each person touched at lunch and make sure you know whose is whose."

"Have you lost your mind? How am I going to do that without raising suspicion?" she hissed.

"Say you're going to take a few minutes to clear the leftovers. But again, make sure you take care to know who handled what. I'm positive the intruder is either John or Karlene."

Shock didn't begin to describe how Ellie felt as Pad put Karlene in that category. "I'll do as you ask but I'm sure it's John."

Ellie studied the table, trying to carefully segregate each person's place setting and glass. Thank heavens she used real dishes and silverware.

Winnie came out to the front porch. "Eleanor, can I help you?"

Whipping around, Ellie forced a smile. "Thank you, Winnie but I'm all set. Why don't you go back inside and keep John and Karlene company? I'll just be a few minutes." Trying to act casual, she said, "You know how I like to keep everything tidy."

Ellie watched Winnie scoot the others away from the door.

"Pad," Ellie whispered, entering the kitchen. "Are you here?"

Pad appeared and took the tray.

"Good job."

He pulled out a few clear plastic bags and held one open. Ellie dropped silverware and the glass in the first bag.

"John's."

They repeated the procedure two more times, marking the outside of the bag with a black marker. Pad slipped the bags into a small tote bag.

"As soon as everyone leaves, I'll take these down to the station." Pad cocked his head "You should get back out there, it sounds like Winnie is going to run out of small talk soon."

Ellie slipped into the main area. "Well that's all cleaned up so let's get back to the matter at hand."

"As I was saying, Ellie, this work should be displayed

in a larger gallery but Winnie is convinced this is the best location so, reluctantly, I'll defer to her judgment," Karlene stated.

"I firmly believe The Looking Glass is the only place to unveil my watercolors." Winnie glanced at Karlene. "I do hope you'll join us for the grand opening and reception."

Cutting the tension, John said, "Winnie I haven't missed an opening of yours in too many years to count so I will be here."

Ellie was astonished how easily Winnie got Karlene to drop the subject of moving the exhibit. "All we have left to do is pick the actual date."

Winnie picked up her handbag. "Eleanor, I'll call you later."

She turned. "John, Karlene will you walk out with me? Eleanor has much to do to get ready for our big event."

"I think I'll stay and visit with Ellie," Karlene announced.

"I thought we could stop for a coffee and get to know each other a little better." Winnie cracked open the door and dangled just enough bait for Karlene to bite.

"Oh, of course I would love to join you both." She turned. "You don't mind if we catch up later, do you Ellie? I would enjoy spending time with Winnie."

"Not at all. I'll call you in a few days when the details have been ironed out."

As soon as the door closed, Ellie sagged to the bottom stair.

Pad appeared next to her. "Are you all right?"

"It's hard to wrap my head around the notion that one of those gallery owners hit me over the head and locked me in a closet. I don't understand why either of them would do something like that. I've never done anything to them."

Pad slipped his arm around her shoulders and pulled her close. "I can assure you it's about Aunt Winnie's paintings and you're the obstacle. To get you to give up your business would give them what they wanted most. Now it's my job to find out for sure who it is, and believe me we'll know within a week or two."

"Why will it take that long if we have prints from the break-in and we have both sets from today? Won't it be easy to compare?"

"Ellie, I'm sorry to say but it takes time. It's not like on television where they are scanned in and moments later the match pops up with a picture of someone. The process depends on the original set of prints and how good the prints are we got today, are they a full or partial print, are they smeared. You get the picture?"

In a high-pitched laugh, Ellie said, "I like the TV version better."

Pad chuckled. "The police wish that were true too. It certainly would make their jobs easier. The good news is we don't have to compare a lot of prints to the originals, we're doing a side by side comparison but we want to get all five markers to match. It will give us the best chance for a conviction and that is our ultimate goal."

"We get the bags to the police and wait?"

"That's part of the plan. You need to move forward with the new exhibit. Promote the heck out of it and we wait."

"Do you think they'll be back?"

Pad understood Ellie's concern. "I think at the moment things will remain calm, but my bet will be on the opening. Something will either happen right before or the night of the event."

"That's not comforting. How am I supposed to plan a spectacular party with this hanging over my head?"

"Try not to worry about anything, leave that to me." Pad caressed her hand.

Ellie pulled her hand away and sat up straight. "I think you should try to remember who you're living with. I'm stronger than I look."

"I haven't forgotten you're a dynamo, but you need to concentrate on what you do best and let me do what I do best."

A glint appeared in Ellie's eye. "And what is that exactly?"

Pad knew there was no way of avoiding this conversation. He had to come clean. "Ellie, I was undercover for a federal agency. I started out as a cop and after a big bust, I was recruited for a specific assignment. That lasted a couple of years until we solved the case and put the bad guys behind bars."

"It sounds like you were some hot shot. Why did you leave?"

"I was like a soldier going into a war zone, and like them, I came home reliving things I can never forget. I was damn good at my job, but over time it was changing me into someone I didn't want to become. I walked away to preserve my soul."

Ellie leaned in. "Do you miss it? The job?"

Pad was quiet for what seemed like forever.

"There are some things I miss, and since I've been helping you I've been reminded of why I became a cop. I love the life I have and the travel, but someday I want a place to call home."

Ellie held her breath, praying Pad would say he wanted to stay in Loudon.

Abruptly he dropped her hand and stood up. "I need to get these to the lab. Can I take your car?"

Ellie nodded and pointed to the keys on the desk.

He rushed out the back door.

"I guess I have my answer." Ellie sat on the stair and wondered how she would forget this man who had stolen her heart.

26

*P*ad drove aimlessly. Why didn't he speak up and say he wanted to stay in Loudon, and that he would give anything to stay by Ellie's side for as long as she'd allow?

"Stone, you're an idiot. She gave you an opening and you blew it." Grabbing his cell, Pad hit a well-worn button.

"Hi Auntie, any chance I can swing by?"

"Of course, Pad, I'm always here for you. Are you coming out now?"

"Yeah."

"This is certainly a surprise." Winnie drew Pad inside. "Is something wrong? I thought everything was going as planned."

"No issue there. I had Ellie grab all the utensils and glasses and I've dropped them off for processing. We'll know soon enough if it's John or Karlene." Pad strode down the hallway. "Do you have anything to eat? I'm starving."

"Help yourself."

Pad made a thick roast beef sandwich.

"Can I make you one?" Pad paused, holding a knife mid-air.

"I'm fine. You go ahead." Winnie suppressed a giggle.

"You're pretty sharp narrowing this down the way you did. You're a regular Miss Marple."

"Don't give me all the credit. You kept me in the loop so it was easy to see someone wanted to discredit Eleanor and gain my business. My money is on Karlene by the way. I just can't believe John would ever be motivated by greed. But that woman? Absolutely."

"I think you put too much trust in John Barton but time will tell." Pad dropped the knife in the sink and plopped down next to Winnie.

"I'm not here to talk about the case."

"I thought as much. You're here to confess you've fallen in love with Eleanor McKenna." Winnie stated his news with such a matter-of-fact tone that Pad wondered if she was a mind reader.

"What makes you think I've fallen for that stubborn girl?"

"For one thing, you've stayed put much longer than I expected. You called her stubborn, which is a good match for you, and I see how you look at her. Your uncle has been gone a long time but I'll never forget how he looked at me and there are so many times you remind me of him." Pad wiped away a tear from her cheek. "What I don't understand is what are you both waiting for?"

Pad's head snapped up. "What do you mean both?"

"She has feelings for you. It's plain as the sun drifting through the cloudless sky. For some reason, you're both tap dancing around the subject of love."

"I'm passing through. After what I've been through,

living under cover, I'm not relationship material. I'm better off alone."

"That's hogwash Padraic Stone and you know it. You don't want to be vulnerable."

"You know what it is like to have the person you love most in this world to be ripped away from you. Ellie's already been through that and so have I. We both lost parents when we were young."

"That doesn't hold water with me, young man. I wouldn't have missed being married to your uncle for one second. Even to avoid the heartache and loss that I've suffered and believe me I have. But being loved, truly loved, is a gift and it doesn't come around like ants at a picnic."

"Aunt Winnie you have such a way with words." Pad smirked. "Unfortunately, you haven't changed my mind. Once the perp is booked I'm going to Scotland and wander the highlands."

Winnie held up her hand. "I know and you've said, 'my camera is my only companion.'"

Winnie's chair scraped across the floor. "That's a great place to run. Maybe as you traipse around the hills you'll come to your senses before she's lost to you forever."

"Well since you're not helping me I'll head back to town." Pad dropped a kiss on his aunt's cheek and left.

He was lost in thought when he pulled behind Ellie's house. A place he had begun to call home. Ellie ran out to greet him.

"Hey, what do you think you're doing." Ellie hissed. "Anyone can see you."

Pad dashed into the house. "I'm sorry I wasn't thinking."

Ellie demanded. "What happened at the police station?"

"I dropped everything off and talked with Greene. He knows who we're looking at so he's going to check into a few things."

"When will we know something concrete?"

"Soon." Pad glanced around. "Was everything quiet after I left?"

Ellie nodded. "Yeah, like a church mid-week."

"Good. Have you figured out when you're going to have the opening?"

"I have to talk to Winnie but I think it will take about a month."

"The timing should work. You should be in the clear by then if my hunch pans out."

"And then what, Pad?" Ellie's voice cracked. "We're really going our separate ways?"

"Yes."

$\mathcal{E}$llie's shoulders drooped. In that moment she had never felt more lost and alone. To feel love but not have it returned was far worse than never to have felt the longing for this man.

Ellie heard a knock at the back door. She discovered Winnie standing with a picnic basket in one hand and a bottle of wine in the other.

"Hello, Eleanor, I hope you don't mind that I'm dropping by unannounced but I didn't want to have dinner alone, again." She held up the bottle. "It's CLW."

Winnie's smile was contagious and Ellie opened the door.

"Please come in. Pad's upstairs."

"Eleanor, I didn't come to have dinner with my nephew. He can find his own supper. I wanted us to get to know each other better. We have talked a great deal about me over the last weeks, but I really want to get to know you." Winnie set the basket down. "Cork screw?"

Ellie passed it to her and Winnie continued. "I want us to be friends, not just business associates. I find it is the best way to trust someone with my work."

Ellie stammered, "I'd that like too, Winnie. I just thought, well you know, since Pad's leaving I would see you for the show and then just occasionally."

"Pish pawsh, that's not how I work with dear friends." Winnie poured wine into the glasses Ellie produced. "Would it be possible to sit outside and enjoy our picnic?"

"I'm sorry, where are my manners?" Ellie let the older woman go through the slider first carrying a glass and the bottle, and Ellie followed her with the basket and her own glass of wine.

Ellie wondered if Pad could hear them through the bedroom window. What should he care if Ellie developed a friendship with his aunt. It wouldn't matter he would be gone.

Ellie spread the contents of the basket on the table. "This looks delicious, crusty bread, all the required items for a wonderful antipasto and what's this?" Ellie held up a container filled with a dark liquid.

"Fudge sauce of course," Winnie announced. "A picnic isn't complete without strawberries, and strawberries aren't complete without chocolate."

Ellie grinned. "Now you're talking!" She filled a plate and set it in front of her guest and then joined her.

Winnie said, "So are you ready for Pad to leave Loudon?"

"Jeez, you don't beat around the bush. But, I'm not sure I understand the question. I don't have a vote."

"Are you sure about that?" Winnie looked at Ellie over her glass. "I think you most assuredly do if you wanted one."

"I think you've misunderstood what our relationship has been. We're friends, I think, but he was here at my mother's request to keep me safe and find out who has been threatening me. As we're very close to the end of this situation I would assume he's ready to resume his life."

"Is that all Pad is to you, a friend?"

"I will always consider him a good friend, but I have no right to ask him to stay. There isn't anything here for him but there is an entire world waiting for Pad."

"Eleanor, I'm going to ask you one question and then I'll drop the subject."

Ellie waited.

"Are you in love with my nephew?"

"I'm not sure what being in love feels like. My answer is no." The lie rolled off Ellie's tongue.

Winnie shook her head. "You two could see what developed if only you asked him to stay."

"I thought you just said you'd drop the subject after your last question. Besides, Pad's comfortable with his decision to pack up and hit the road."

"You're right I did. But love isn't a gift to be dismissed. It should be embraced and treasured." Winnie selected an olive off her plate. "Have you tried one yet?"

Ellie had one, lingering question: Would Pad still be in town for Winnie's show?

❧

*P*ad sympathized with Winnie's and Ellie's growing impatience. With each passing day, waiting for the results of the fingerprints was torture. He had taken to running at his aunt's place—less chance to be spotted by people—when his cell phone vibrated. He stopped running long enough to look at the text message. It was from Greene.

Meet us at HQ-we have news.

Pad broke a record for the fastest shower in order to get to the station. Maybe they finally had answers. He hesitated. Should he call Ellie and let her know they had an update? Deciding against it, Pad burst through the main door and glanced around the lobby. Paul and Judy weren't waiting for him. He walked over to the desk. "I'm here to see either Officer Greene or Bell, they're expecting me."

The desk officer picked up a phone and buzzed him through security.

"Wait just a moment."

The minutes dragged. Pad shifted from one foot to another.

Paul came to the door. "Pad, come with me."

He fell in step next to the police officer. "This might be the break we've been looking for."

"Yeah, but it's not what I was expecting."

"I figured out a long time ago to expect the unexpected."

Paul nodded and stopped at his desk.

Judy was sitting at her work station. "Nice to see you again, Pad." She smiled. "I'll bet you're itching to read the report?"

"I am." Pad took the folder and started to read.

Halfway through, he stopped and looked up. "Hm, any chance I can take a copy? Ellie isn't going to believe this unless she reads it for herself."

"Treat it as confidential. But you're right she'll need to see it." Judy was one step ahead of him, already handing Pad a folder. "After you talk to her, give us a call and we can decide how we're going to move forward."

With a curt nod, Pad walked out of the station.

"Ellie, are you home?" Pad shouted, entering the kitchen.

"In here. Winnie and I are rearranging the paintings. Come see how it looks."

Pad followed Ellie's muffled voice.

He wore a stern look on his face and watched the color drain from Ellie's. "I want you to sit down and Winnie, you should join us."

Ellie wasn't sure what was going on but did as Pad asked.

"Auntie, please have a seat. I have something to tell you and then we have to make a plan."

Winnie collapsed in a chair.

"Pad, you're freaking me out. What is going on?" Ellie demanded.

"We have a match to the fingerprints, and we have proof who broke in, hit Ellie on the head, and started the fire."

"It's John Barton, isn't it?" Ellie jumped up to pace. "He's upset that Winnie has chosen to support my gallery. He has a slim build and his eyes are the right color."

"Eleanor, slow down." Ice filled Winnie's voice. "John would never be threatened by my relationship with you. We have worked together for many years, and he's gotten quite wealthy hosting my events in New York." Winnie attempted to reassure the young woman.

"Exactly, I'm taking money out of his bank account. But what I don't understand is why he would destroy a painting that was very special to you?"

"That's my point, Eleanor. John would never mutilate a painting. He values art far too much to do something like that."

Pad listened as the women debated the merits of John being a criminal, wondering how long it would take for them to realize he had all the answers to their questions.

"Pad, what do you think?" Ellie addressed him.

"Read this." He handed her the folder.

Ellie read it once and then twice and passed it to Winnie.

Winnie glanced at that page and looked up. "Is this accurate?"

"Yes. The prints matched at five points."

Ellie's face had gone stark white.

"Are you okay, Ellie?" Pad knelt next to her, rubbing her cold hands in his.

"What's our next step?" Ellie's gaze was unforgiving. "I want to put an end to this today."

"I understand your sense of urgency, but we have to move slowly and plan this out. Catching the perp in the act helps make the conviction stick."

"Then we're going to make this so enticing it will be irresistible."

Winnie saw the gleam light up Ellie's eyes.

"What can I do to help?"

"Well who do you know that would be willing to announce they'll give me an exclusive event following the close of the watercolor exhibition?"

Winnie grinned and tapped the tip of her nose. "I like the way you think."

"Auntie, do you know someone who will help us?"

"Padraic, be a dear and bring me my handbag. It's just a matter of making a phone call or two. The art world is small, and I do have a few close friends who would love to help us."

*W*innie walked up to the front door. Accompanying her was a stylishly dressed woman.

Ellie stared, star-struck and thankfully remembered to open the door. "Winnie, it's so nice to see you today."

"Good morning, Eleanor. I'd like to introduce you to Arielle Clark."

"It's a pleasure to meet you, Ms. Clark. Welcome to The Looking Glass."

"Please call me Ari." Glancing around, she said, "This is just lovely."

"Thank you and I would like to thank you for agreeing to help us. I'm sure Winnie explained what has been going on since I opened the gallery?"

"She did and I have to say I'm really looking forward to getting out of my studio and spicing things up a bit."

Winnie giggled. "Eleanor, I told you not to worry. Ari would be tickled to help us launch, 'Catch and Convict.' After all, as independent business women, we understand how hard it is to live our dream."

Ari's head bobbed. "Tell me what my part in this will be and let's get started."

"Pad and the police officers should be here any minute, and they can outline the sequence of events. Basically, we hold a mini press conference, announce your paintings will be gracing my walls, and see if the bait is seized. But first we need to stage a little play."

As if on cue, Pad and the cruiser pulled up to the front of the shop.

"Ladies, if you're ready let's go outside. Just to make sure we're observed. As we've discovered the front porch has a camera feed. If you'll follow my lead?"

"Absolutely," the two artists said in unison.

Ellie stood on the top of the stairs with her back to the hidden lens. "Hello Pad, Officers. Do you have any news?"

Officer Greene took one step forward. "I'm sorry to inform you but we don't have anything new to report. Of course, we'll keep the case open and, we'll be in touch if anything changes."

Pad's gaze was hard. "Ellie, I just came back into town to wrap up a photo shoot when I decided to check in with Greene and Bell. Stay vigilant, keep your security cameras rolling, and if anyone tries anything be sure to call them right away."

"You're really leaving, Pad, for good?"

"I am."

"Before you go, I'd like share my exciting news with you. Arielle Clark is going to have an exclusive showing here. You should stay."

Pad addressed Ari. "Forgive me, Ms. Clark. I'm sure you can understand; my muse is calling me and I must get to Scotland. In fact, I leave tonight."

Ari smiled. "Another time perhaps, Mr. Stone. I'm an admirer of your work as well."

"Ellie, I'll email you when I get settled, and you can let me know how both events were received. I wish you the best of luck." He kissed her cheek.

Ellie held back very real tears. "Safe travels, Pad." She watched him walk away with the officers.

Ellie squared her shoulders. "Well should we get started with our plans, ladies?"

"That is a lovely idea, Ellie." Ari whisked through the front door, every inch the world-famous artist. "Now let me show you what I plan to have shipped here."

Ari's voice trailed off. Ellie was sure each word was heard and hoped their performance had been convincing. She whispered, "It's just a matter of time now."

Ellie's nerves jangled. It was a beautiful Saturday afternoon, and she was ready to unveil Winnie's watercolor exhibition. All players were in place and ready for action. Winnie was playing the part of the gracious and humble artist while Pad lurked in her bedroom, able to watch people come and go. The exhibit would open with Winnie present for a couple of hours. A celebratory dinner was planned for a few close friends and family, and of course Winnie. If all went according to plan things would get interesting after the last guest departed.

Her mom and Ray insisted on finishing the last of the dirty dishes as the family went their separate ways. Concern filled Cari's eyes as Ellie hugged her.

She whispered, "Don't worry. Pad is upstairs and I have two police officers inside. I'm perfectly fine."

Her mom gave her one last fierce hug. "I'll talk to you tomorrow." Ray tucked a stray lock of blonde hair behind Ellie's ear before taking his wife's hand.

Ellie's gaze trained over the front yard, and all looked quiet. She turned, shut and locked the front door. After clicking off the outside lights, Ellie turned off the overhead lights inside the gallery, leaving a few to illuminate Winnie's display and the newest addition of Arielle Clark's well-known painting, 'Tapestry.'

Ellie tried not think about how much the single canvas was worth and prayed nothing would happen to it while on loan to her gallery.

Speaking out loud, she said, "Well those dishes aren't going to wash themselves."

Moving at a snail's pace, Ellie tidied up the kitchen before heading upstairs to read. She double-checked both the back and front doors. Everything was secured. She had no idea where Greene and Bell were hiding. The silence was unnerving. Ellie flicked on several lights in her bedroom and settled into the armchair with a book. Unable to concentrate on the page in front of her, she picked up a magazine and looked out at the landing.

From the corner, Pad winked at her and mouthed, "It won't be long now." He touched his ear as if to say, "Listen."

Ellie closed her eyes and devoted all her senses to listening to what he had heard. Ah there it was: the door-knob was being clicked very slowly. Thank goodness for old knobs. Before the door was eased open, Pad rose to his feet, tucked in the shadows, ready to leap down the stairs.

Ellie heard the door close with a soft click, a tiny flicker of light extinguished with a blink of her eye. If she hadn't been paying attention, Ellie would have missed it. Her heart pounded. It took all her will power to stay put. She waited for a sign from Pad. Ellie wanted to rush down the stairs, ready for a confrontation, and then it happened. Someone stumbled over the stool—that was the signal.

Pad held up a hand and shook his head.

Ellie scowled; she was ready even if he wasn't. Logically, Ellie knew they needed to have a smoking gun, and she had to wait for another minute or two. It wouldn't be long now.

Another crash. The chair she moved into place toppled to the floor.

Pad nodded.

Ellie got up and walked to the top of the stairs.

"Who's there?" she demanded. Silence answered her.

As planned, Ellie returned to her room and then she smelled the sulfur of a match. She ran to the top of the stairs at the same time Pad began his mad dash down the back.

Ellie flipped the switch and the overhead lights flooded the room.

Greene and Bell shouted in unison, "Hold it right there. You're under arrest."

A black clad figure stood frozen in place, holding a burning match in one hand as if trying to decide to drop it.

"I would strongly suggest you blow it out, Karlene." Pad growled in her ear as he wrapped her wrist in a vise grip.

"Take your hands off of me," she sputtered. "You have no right."

"Protest all you want. I'm a citizen protecting my friend's home. But we have two police officers here ready to read your Miranda rights and take you down to the police station, and book you on numerous charges."

"I haven't done anything wrong." Karlene's eyes

darted around the room and settled on Ellie. "Tell them, Ellie. Tell them we're friends."

Ellie planted her feet and stood with hands on her hips. "Friends don't lock friends in a closet with a head wound, try to burn down their home and business, and friends certainly don't break into another friend's house and get caught holding a burning match." Ellie's voice was frigid and Karlene visibly shrank at each word spoken.

"I have one question, Karlene. Why? Why did you want to put me out of business? I wasn't any threat to you."

With her arms secured behind her back, Karlene stood ramrod straight and snapped, "Winifred Simpson and now Arielle Clark. They should have chosen me, not you. A little nobody with zero reputation."

Ellie's expression never changed. "Please remove this person from my property."

Greene and Bell held tight as they marched Karlene out the front door, reading her rights from a card as Karlene shouted, "This isn't over, Ellie. My lawyer will get me out in no time, and you'll be out of business in three months, tops!"

Pad wrapped his arms around Ellie and held her tight. She was ice cold. "I'm going to call your mom and have her stay with you while I'm at the station."

Ellie pulled away from him. "Go ahead. I'll call her."

"Are you sure, El?"

"Yeah, we know the right person has been arrested. Just do me one favor?"

"You got it."

"Will you ask Hank Booth to let me know when she makes bail?"

Pad handed Ellie her phone. "Call your mom."

*P*ad listened as Ellie talked to her mother, asking if she and Ray could come over.

Hank Booth met Pad in the conference room. "Good job on the arrest. If you're ever looking for a job, our door is always open. We could use someone with your skills and tenacity."

"Thanks, Chief. I'd like to talk to Karlene, with your permission of course."

Pad wanted to know at what point Karlene turned against Ellie and felt he might have a good chance of ferreting out the truth.

"Sure, just keep either Greene or Bell in the room." Hank shook Pad's hand. "I understand you're leaving town? Drop a line if you get a chance." The chief disappeared into his office.

Pad rapped on the interrogation door. He stepped inside and found Bell sitting with Karlene.

Karlene snarled. "Did your little girlfriend send you?"

"No one sends me anywhere." Pad spoke in a low monotone voice. "I thought we might have a short conversation."

"Ha, like I want to say anything to you. I'm not confessing to anything, and I'm waiting for my lawyer before I say another word."

Pad admired her bravado. "I'd never expected you to confess, but I am hoping you could clear up a few things. Just because I'm a curious sort of guy."

"Suit yourself. You can ask anything, it's a free country." Karlene studied her deep purple painted nails.

"When you were being removed from Ellie's, you mentioned this was all because Winifred Simpson and

Arielle Clark decided to have an exhibit at The Looking Glass. I thought Ellie was your protégé and you encouraged her to start her own gallery?"

"I did because what she wanted to do was never a threat to my clientele. If she wanted to promote what she considered art, pottery, jewelry, wood carvings and the like and not focus on great paintings who was I to stop her? I thought she had learned more from me, but I guess I was mistaken." Karlene shrugged her shoulders. "But then out of the blue, the great Winifred Simpson befriends her and decides to exhibit in The Looking Glass? I've spent years trying to do even a small show with her, but she never seriously considered working with me."

"How was that Ellie's fault?"

"I started thinking the last time I had a meeting with Winnie, at my gallery. Ellie was working and she must have said something about opening her place." Karlene looked at Pad with startling green, cat-like eyes. "It's obvious she poached Winifred right out from under me."

"And then…"

"Oh yeah and then I hear that Arielle Clark is hanging her painting, Tapestry? That was the straw that broke this camel's back. She was not going to get away with scooping two of the biggest names in the art world."

"The first night was just to scare her into closing down? When you broke in, hit her over the head, and locked her in the closet?"

"Well I didn't mean to put her in the hospital. That was an accident. But she didn't get the message and reopened. So, I waited until you had your big romantic date and at just the right moment I started the fire."

Pad just let her talk, boasting about her methods of intimidation.

"You know I could hear everything you were saying but you sure did take your sweet time getting home that night."

"You waited for us and then struck the match?" Pad led her further down the confessional path.

"I didn't want to damage a historical home. I'm not a monster. I really thought that would do the trick. You know," she studied Pad, "I think if you hadn't been in the picture my plan would have worked."

"I have one last question, and I think I know the answer but maybe you'll humor me and fill in one final detail. Which is your real eye color, blue or green?"

Karlene laughed. "Actually, they're brown, but I adore colored contacts. They're more interesting don't you think?"

"Officer Bell did you get it all?" Pad asked.

"Yes. I did. We have enough to make it a little harder for her to get a reasonable bail."

"What are you talking about? I haven't confessed to any crime." Karlene tried to stand up when Officer Greene used that moment to walk in.

"Have a seat, Ms. Johnson. You spoke freely to Mr. Stone and if you remember we had asked to be on the record, so it's all been recorded as evidence."

"You can't do that," Karlene sputtered.

"They can and they did, Karlene. You spoke freely to a civilian, in the presence of a police officer." Pad stood up. The metal chair legs sounded like nails on a chalkboard over the cement floor. "I'll be back for your trial, and I promise I will do everything in my power to make sure you have a nice long stay in prison. As my gift to you, I'll make sure you get the newspaper daily, so you can read every detail about the success of The Looking

Glass." Pad flung open the door and left without looking back.

There was only one thing left for Pad to do. Talk to Ellie one last time.

28

*P*ad lingered on the front steps. This would be the last time he'd think of this house as home. He couldn't remember any time in his adult life where he had the instant sense of belonging he had felt here.

He squared his shoulders. It was time to rip off the Band-Aid. "Ellie, where are you?"

He heard a faint response. "On the deck."

A heaviness in the pit of his stomach weighed him down.

He found Ellie lounging in a chair, her feet propped up on the stool, soaking up the afternoon sun, toying with the necklace she wore.

Pad slid open the screen door. "Enjoying the sun?"

"I am. For the first time in a very long time I don't have a shadow obscuring the light." She squinted. "If you know what I mean."

Pad dropped into a chair facing her and sat quietly.

"I do."

"Pad, what did she say?"

"It wasn't pretty. Karlene was hostile and felt justified

by her actions. It was jealousy, pure and simple. Karlene thinks you stole a potential exhibition of Aunt Winnie's work from her. Her anger festered and turned to hate, blaming you for luring Winnie to your gallery. She wanted to scare you out of business."

"This is like a bad dream." Ellie shook her head. "I thought we were friends."

"Maybe at one time, but she's an ambitious woman and uses people to get ahead. You were talented and useful until you decided to go out on your own. In the beginning, she thought The Looking Glass wouldn't be any competition but then you announced you were exhibiting Winnie's oils, and, well, that had been her platinum trophy."

"I guess that could have pushed her over the edge. What about John Barton? I guess it was just coincidence they're built alike."

"It's a good thing for John that Winnie believed in him and knew he couldn't be involved. He truly is supportive of you or anyone starting a business." Pad looked away. "However, Karlene knew about him and used his physical features to her advantage which is why she wore contact lens and made sure the camera caught the eye color of her contacts the night of the fire."

They sat quietly, each lost in their own thoughts. Ellie broke the silence.

"It's over," she said softly.

"I'm going to get…" Pad swallowed hard. "I mean, I'm leaving early."

Ellie's head bobbed.

Pad pulled her into his arms, deepening the kiss, demanding more. His hands roamed over her slender back. With eyes closed, he committed every curve, every smile, and every expression to memory praying it would be enough to last him a lifetime.

Pad hesitated, leaning in, tilting her chin upward. He wiped away the trickle of tears. "I'm going to miss this." His head dipped, tenderly kissing her wet, salty lips.

A shiver ran down Ellie's back.

*E*llie drank Pad in, reveling in what it felt like to come alive in his arms. All too soon he released her.

Pain constricted her heart but Pad let her go before she could beg him to fall with her into the swirling vortex of emotions that threatened to engulf her.

In a hoarse whisper, Pad said, "Goodbye, Ellie." His fingertips caressed her lips one last time, and he left without looking back.

Ellie wrapped her arms tightly around her body, unable to speak, watching the man she loved walk out of her life.

*W*innie breezed in and out of Ellie's gallery every few days. It had been several months since Karlene was locked up, permanently, and Ellie was feeling like herself again. Winnie said she talked with Pad regularly and he asked about the trial, but nothing else was divulged about his where abouts.

"Winnie." Jubilant, Ellie thrust the newspaper over her head. "Look! The reviews on your water colors have been outstanding and the demand is causing a bidding war. Did you think this would happen?"

"My dear, Ellie." Winnie had stopped calling her Eleanor, which suited Ellie just fine. "You can never tell what the public wants when it comes to art. I create something that warms my soul. The rest," Winnie shrugged, "is out of my hands."

"The paper's saying Ari's next shows, in New York and Los Angeles, will have a huge buzz around them based on Karlene's shenanigans."

"Again Ellie, you never can tell what will fuel people's imagination."

Ellie returned to the paper.

"Is something wrong?" Winnie took a step toward the girl. "Ellie?"

"No, everything's fine." She dropped the newspaper in the recycle bin. "I'm going to make some tea. Would you like a cup?"

"That would be lovely. Lady Gray?"

Ellie smiled but it wasn't reflected in her eyes. "Of course. It's your favorite." Winnie made sure Ellie couldn't see her when she retrieved the paper. Unfolding it, she saw what caused her distress. The Barton Gallery had announced a new show, featuring Padraic Stone.

"She does love him." Winnie dropped the newspaper back into the bin.

"Here you go." Ellie handed Winnie a mug of steaming tea. "Did you want a cookie?"

"No thank you." Winnie took a sip. "Ellie can we be honest with each other?"

"Of course." Ellie settled into her favorite overstuffed

velour arm chair and Winnie perched on the matching sofa.

"How long are you going to keep denying your feelings?" Winnie's direct approach caught Ellie off guard.

Ellie pressed her fingers against her tightly shut eyes. "Winnie, in case you didn't notice, Pad left Loudon, and me. He has places to go and things he wants to conquer." Her gaze swept the tidy gallery. "My home is here." The feelings Ellie had been suppressing threatened to bubble back to the surface. "Maybe you should talk to Pad, he's obviously moved on."

With a crisp nod, Winnie said, "I might just do that." Winnie sipped her tea.

EPILOGUE

*P*ad sat in his rental car oblivious to the freezing cold temperature. The buildings that lined Main Street were decked out in holiday greenery but the beauty was lost on him. This was the second day of his self-imposed stakeout, trying to summon the courage to knock on her front door.

A sharp rapping on the driver's window broke Pad's concentration. "Aunt Winnie?"

"Padraic Stone, what are you doing?"

Pad stepped out of the car and pecked his beloved aunt's velvety soft cheek.

"It's good to see you, Auntie. It's been a while."

She tugged his jacket closed. "Zip up, or you'll catch your death. We will talk about your long absence later, but at this moment you need to answer my question. Why are you lurking on this particular street?"

Pad leaned against the car and sighed. "I've made a huge mistake."

Winnie couldn't help but notice his striking amber eyes

were dull. "Pad why didn't you just come home? The door is always open."

"I'm here now, and you know I can't stay away during the holidays. You're my only family." Pad's smile was weak. "I've been distracted."

"I see that." Winnie cupped his chin in her hand and gently turned his face to her. "Go. Talk to her."

He dropped his gaze. "What if I'm too late?"

"You won't know until you knock on the door." Winnie kissed his icy cheeks. "I'm going home and when you're ready I'll be waiting."

*P*ad hesitated. He grasped the old door-knocker and rapped twice. The clang of brass hitting brass echoed in the silence. It was louder than he remembered.

Ellie leaned heavily on the other side, listening to the deep resonating knock. Wiping tears from her eyes, she flipped the lock.

Pad was stunned. The woman who haunted his dreams stood before him more beautiful than he remembered. The words he had so carefully planned to say evaporated.

"Hello, Ellie."

A smile hovered on her lips, and her voice quivered.

"Welcome home, Pad."

Keep reading for a sneak peek of in the Loudon Series
Magic in Rain
Order Here

MAGIC IN THE RAIN

Prologue

Dani jiggled the knob. Satisfied the café door was secured, she paused to check her reflection in the window. Being a brunette suits me. She ran her fingers through her shoulder-length curls. I guess that's why I was born one. I'll keep this color for a while. I'm tired of not recognizing myself in the mirror.

After taking the stairs two at a time, she pushed open her apartment door. Stepping out of her clogs, she left them by the door. She flopped onto the sofa and propped her feet up onto the coffee table. Sorting through the mail, she said, "Junk, bill, junk…" She turned the square, cream-colored envelope over. There was no return address. She lifted the envelope to her nose. The distinct musk smell was faint but unmistakable. Dani's heart quickened.

"It can't be."

She dropped the envelope onto the table as if it burned her fingers, staring at it.

"I'm not going to open it. It's going in the trash."

She dropped it on top of the garbage and grabbed a bottle of water from the fridge. Taking a long drink, she watched the envelope out of the corner of her eye, as if expecting it to come to life.

Curiosity got the best of her. She retrieved it from the trash. She ripped open the envelope. A strangled laugh filled the small room. Why was she afraid of a silly puppy card? She flipped it open.

Looking forward to seeing you again. It was unsigned. But the handwriting… "Derek."

She ripped the card and envelope into tiny pieces and buried it at the bottom of the can.

CHAPTER 1

Dani surveyed the contents of the farm stand basket, thrilled to see apples and a couple of sweet pumpkins to spice up the baking case. She loved the fall season with the comforts of stews and soups simmering and a reason to bake lots of pies and cookies. Not that Dani needed an excuse to bake. Since becoming the primary cook at What's Perkin', she thought she had died and gone to career heaven. Peeling, slicing, and dicing the pumpkin and contemplating a new muffin flavor, Dani heard the front door bell ring. Wiping her hands on a towel, she peered through the window to see who had arrived.

"Morning, Luke. When you're ready, come on back and we can go over today's specials."

She really liked working with Luke Ford. He handled the front with ease while she filled all the orders he sent her way. It was a perfect working relationship.

"Give me five. I want to get the lights on and coffee brewing."

Dani glanced at the wall clock, wondering what time

Cari would be in, when the back door slammed with a bang. Cari entered, shaking off her coat.

"My gosh it's windy out there and raining buckets." She glanced at Dani. "Did you happen to hear the long-range forecast?"

"I did. Damp and rainy. It's a good day for a new beef stew and your signature buttermilk biscuits."

Cari smiled. "That's why you're perfect for this job, you read me like a book."

"The one thing I've learned since working here, comfort food is always on the menu."

Cari's smile was genuine and lit up her deep green eyes. "What's it been, almost two years since you started working for me? We need to talk about a raise."

"Cari, that isn't necessary. You've been more than generous with my pay, and the rent on the apartment upstairs isn't really the market rate. I'm perfectly content with how things are."

Cari's eyebrow arched. "I've never heard of anyone saying, don't give me a raise. You're a rare breed, Ms. Danielle Michaels."

Dani was pleased with the opportunity to take over the kitchen for Cari's daughter, Kate. It was the highest compliment Dani could have received. Then, to top it all off, when Dani asked for some ideas on where she could find a decent place to live, Cari and her husband, Ray, showed her the upstairs apartment and said it was hers if she wanted it. Dani had been bowled over.

"Right back at ya, Cari. I don't know of many people who would give a stranger a job and apartment with zero references."

"You underestimate yourself, Dani. We put you through a week-long screening process. It might not seem like it was a long time, but you stepped up and showed us your talent. You deserve to stand in front of this stove."

Luke popped his head inside the swinging door. "Dani, are you ready to fill me in? It's almost showtime."

Dani rattled off the breakfast and lunch specials with Luke taking notes. He would transfer it to the blackboard out front. She returned to the baking list, finishing the house specialty, blueberry muffins, cookies, and breads until the front cases were overflowing with tempting treats. Later, she was going to whip up a batch of pumpkin caramel cupcakes. On weekdays, with the exception of holidays, all breakfast platters were some type of sandwich combo or burrito, and then on the week-ends, Dani would whip up eggs and pancakes. The bakery portion of the café was in higher demand Monday thru Friday, as many customers were on the commuting trek.

Dani smiled when Cari wandered into the kitchen and broke off a piece of a fresh oatmeal cookie. She perched on the stool.

"Dani, I'd like to talk to you about something. If you think I'm sticking my nose into your private business, I'll drop the subject."

Dani didn't look up from the batter she was stirring, "What's up?"

"You're a hard worker, whether it's in the shop, babysitting for Jake and Sara's triplets, or lending a hand at Ellie's gallery, but I don't see you dating. You're not obligated to the McKenna-Davis clan. You can say no to us any time we infringe on your personal time."

Dani laughed. "You don't have to worry, Cari. I love feeling like I'm an honorary member of the family. As far as The Looking Glass, I never had much time to appreciate art in any form. This has opened a whole new world for me, and Ellie and I have become great friends."

"I know Ellie feels the same way. She's always had trouble letting people in, but I think Pad Stone has helped Ellie blossom."

"It certainly doesn't hurt to have a handsome man in your life." Dani slid a tray of cupcakes into the oven and avoided Cari's gaze.

"And, what about a handsome man for you, Dani?" Cari spoke softly so Luke wouldn't over hear the conversation.

"Boyfriends and me aren't a good combo. I'm better off alone." Dani dropped the bowl in the sink and was grateful when Luke announced an order and put it on the pass-through shelf.

Dani picked up the order. "I need to get this ready."

"All right." Cari stood. "Well, if you need a hand, let me know."

Dani steadied her racing heart. If Cari only knew the truth, would she want Dani working for What's Perkin'? Fearing she knew what the answer would be, she reminded herself she had to keep the past in the past. Reinventing herself was the right move at the time and keeping it a secret was her only choice.

🐜

Ellie bopped in the door of the shop. "Hey, Mom, Luke. How goes the morning?" She mopped her forehead with a napkin. "Any idea what Dani is whipping up for today's specialty cupcake? I was hoping to pick up a few. Pad's coming for dinner tonight."

"And what makes tonight different?" Luke teased. "I

thought you two were stuck like glue. He spends more time with you than at work."

Ellie grinned. "Tonight, is Pad's turn to cook, and my job is dessert."

Cari smiled at her youngest daughter, "Been for a run already?"

"Of course, can't you tell by the rain running off my face?" Ellie took the glass of water Cari handed her.

"Breakfast, Ellie?" Luke paused at the kitchen door.

"Um, yeah, I guess I could suffer with a little something."

Laughing, Luke went into the kitchen and told Dani that Ellie was out front.

Dani set a plate in front of her friend sitting at the counter. "Just the way you like it with extra cheese and hot sauce."

"A burrito." Ellie picked it up and took a huge bite, sauce dribbling down her chin. She closed her eyes. "This is so good." Ellie winked at Dani. "Don't ever tell Kate, but this is better than hers."

Dani made a cross over her heart. "Your secret is safe with me." Dani poured herself a cup of hot water and dropped a tea bag in. "Care if I sit?"

Ellie twirled on the stool to face Dani. "Sure. We haven't talked in what eight hours?"

The girls chatted and laughed, happy to have found a kindred spirit in the other. Ellie had been through some rough patches, losing her dad when she was barely five, pushing herself to get through college early, and then opening up a gallery only to have it threatened by her former boss. In the process, she allowed herself to open her heart to find love and friends. She often wondered how Dani had found her way to Loudon alone and lived out of a tent. It didn't matter, Dani had found her place at What's Perkin' and as an extended member of the family. However, nothing was ever as simple as it appeared.

Order Magic in the Rain

Thank you for reading my novel. I hope you enjoyed the story. If you did, please help other readers find this book:

This book is lendable. Send it to a friend you think might like it so she can discover me too.

Help other people find this book by writing a review.

Sign up for my newsletter at http://www.lucindarace.com/newsletter

Like my Facebook page, https://facebook.com/lucindaraceauthor

Join Lucinda's Heart Racer's Reader Group on Facebook

Twitter @lucindarace

Instagram @lucindraceauthor

OTHER BOOKS BY LUCINDA RACE:

The Crescent Lake Winery Series 2021

Blends

Breathe

Crush

Blush

Vintage

Bouquet

A Dickens Holiday Romance

Holiday Heart Wishes

Holly Berries and Hockey Pucks

Last Chance Beach

Shamrocks are a Girl's Best Friend

Orchard Brides

Apple Blossoms in Montana

The Matchmaker and The Marine

The MacLellan Sisters Trilogy

Old and New

Borrowed

Blue

The Loudon Series

The Loudon Series Box Set

Between Here and Heaven

Lost and Found

The Journey Home

The Last First Kiss

Ready to Soar

Love in the Looking Glass

Magic in the Rain

ABOUT LUCINDA

Award-winning author Lucinda Race is a lifelong fan of romantic fiction. As a young girl, she spent hours reading romance novels and getting lost in the hope they represent. While her friends dreamed of becoming doctors and engineers, her dreams were to become a writer—a romance novelist.

As life twisted and turned, she found herself writing nonfiction but longed to turn to her true passion. After developing the storyline for The Loudon Series, it was time to start living her dream. Her fingers practically fly over computer keys as she weaves stories about strong women and the men who love them. And if she's not writing romance novels, she's reading everything she can get her hands on. She has published over twenty books.